"A most unlikely feel-good fairy tale."
BBC Radio 4 — Open Book

C333618901

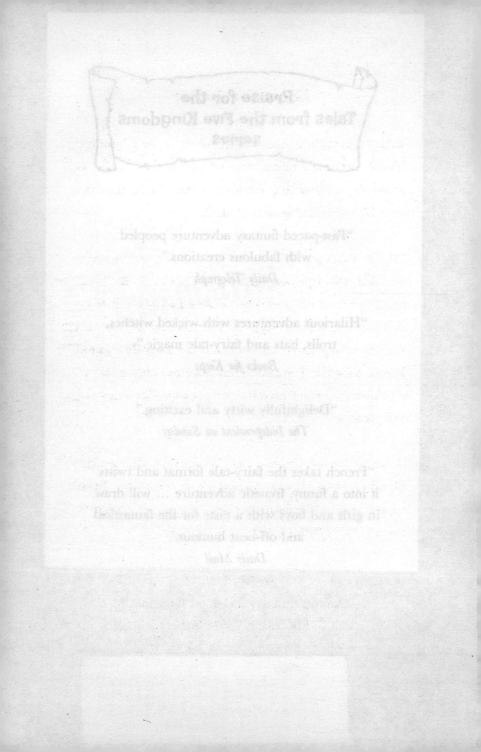

Praise for the Tales from the Five Kingdoms series

"Fast-paced fantasy adventure peopled with fabulous creations."
Daily Telegraph

"Hilarious adventures with wicked witches, trolls, bats and fairy-tale magic."
Books for Keeps

"Delightfully witty and exciting."
The Independent on Sunday

"French takes the fairy-tale format and twists it into a funny, frenetic adventure ... will draw in girls and boys with a taste for the fantastical and off-beat humour."
Daily Mail

About the Author

Vivian French is the author of over two hundred books, but she's never enjoyed writing as much as when she was writing the first of the Tales from the Five Kingdoms, *The Robe of Skulls*.

Of *The Snarling of Wolves*, she says, "I had just as much fun with this book as I did with Robe. At long last I could write about werewolves (much to Ross Collins' delight), and I could fly with Marlon and Alf over all the Five Kingdoms, and out into the Less Enchanted Forest as well. I suspect I'm turning into a bit of an Ancient Crone myself – or perhaps I'm Bluebell? Who knows.

A very special thank you to Oliver Brooks (10), Hannah Firth (11) and Isobel de la Hey (11). Their support and enthusiasm has been invaluable, and they are all WONDERFUL!"

Tales from the Five Kingdoms:

The Robe of Skulls

The Bag of Bones

The Heart of Glass

The Flight of Dragons

The Music of Zombies

The Snarling of Wolves

Vivian French

Illustrated by Ross Collins

WALKER
BOOKS

First published 2014 by Walker Books Ltd

87 Vauxhall Walk, London SE11 5HJ

2 4 6 8 10 9 7 5 3 1

Text © 2014 Vivian French

Illustrations © 2014 Ross Collins

The right of Vivian French and Ross Collins to be identified as author
and illustrator respectively of this work has been asserted by them in
accordance with the Copyright, Designs and Patents Act 1988

This book has been typeset in Baskerville

Printed and bound in Great Britain by Clays Ltd, St Ives plc

British Library Cataloguing in Publication Data:
a catalogue record for this book is available from the British Library

ISBN 978-1-4063-4128-7

www.walker.co.uk

For my dream team:
Caz, Alice, Jacky and – of course –
the ever starry Mr Ross Collins
xxx

PRINCIPAL CHARACTERS

Prince Marcus
Gracie Gillypot
Gubble
Foyce Undershaft

BATS
Marlon • Alf • Billy

KINGS, QUEENS AND DUCHESSES
Hortense............... Dowager Duchess of Cockenzie Rood
Queen Bluebell......... Queen of Wadingburn
King Frank............. King of Gorebreath
Queen Mildred......... Queen of Gorebreath
Queen Kesta........... Queen of Dreghorn
King Horace........... King of Niven's Knowe

PRINCES AND PRINCESSES
Albion • Arioso • Fedora • Loobly • Marigold
Nina-Rose • Tertius • Vincent

WEREWOLVES
Jukk • Keel • Agony Clawbone

THE ANCIENT CRONES
Edna.................... the Ancient One
Elsie.................... the Oldest
Val...................... the Youngest

Chapter One

"**W**OOOOOOOOWL!" The sound echoed over the moonlit forest. Small creatures shuddered, and ran for the darkest cracks and deepest crevices. Birds shivered on their branches, and rabbits cowered at the bottom of their burrows.

The tall thin figure of Agony Clawbone stood still, and listened. As the mournful wailing faded she heard an answering howl from further away, and she sighed as she walked on between the silver stippled trees. The moon was nearly full, and it was the time of howling, but she dared not join in. The company of werewolves was not for her, even though she was werewolf by birth. She had been cast out ... cast out for ever, because many years before she had made a terrible mistake. Soft words and false promises had persuaded her to marry a man, an ordinary human.

She had soon discovered that humans could be cruel. Not only cruel, but evil. And when she finally made her way back to the forest, there was no sympathy for her. She had betrayed her kind, and was no longer welcome.

On she strode, her cloak wrapped tightly round her bony shoulders.

"Wh-wh-who's that, Mr Alf?" The very small bat circling high above was staring down, his eyes wide. "She looks WEIRD!"

His companion looped a speedy loop. "That, Billy my lad, is a typical inhabitant of the Less Enchanted Forest. Zombies, werewolves, trolls, dwarves, goblins – you get all types around here. She's a werewolf. Bit of an odd one, Unc says, but that's what she is."

"A werewolf, Mr Alf?" Billy squeaked. "A real werewolf?"

"Ssh…" Alf warned. "Keep cool, Billy – keep cool."

The very small bat landed on the top twig of a tall pine tree in order to give this idea proper consideration. He found it difficult to fly and think at the same time.

"So has she got sharp teeth, Mr Alf? Does she go all bristly when it's full moon? Does she eat people?"

Alf waved a dismissive wing as he flew down to join Billy. "Don't ask so many questions, young 'un. Watch and listen, that's the thing. Watch and listen, and one day Unc might let you be One Of Us."

"Yes, Mr Alf. Billy fluttered in apologetic agitation. "I mean, sorry, Mr Alf. Erm ... might you be meaning –" he took a reverential breath – "your Uncle Marlon?"

"The very same." Alf's small chest puffed up with pride. "Taught me all I know. Made me a fully paid-up member of the Batster Super Spotters last week. And –" he gave a modest cough – "AND he gave me my training certificate. First one ever, he said. So you pay attention to what I tell you, Billy my lad."

"Oh, I will, Mr Alf. I will!" The little bat quivered with enthusiasm. "Just you wait and see! I'll be the best Super Spotter there's ever been! I'll remember everything! I'll—"

Alf held up a claw. "What did I say, Billy? Cut the cackle. Watch and listen!" Then, as Billy subsided, he went on, "Unc said we should start with a tour of the Five Kingdoms." He pointed towards the moonlit horizon. "See those tall trees? That's the end of the Less Enchanted Forest, that is, and the beginning of what we Super Spotters call the civilized lands. Gorebreath, Niven's Knowe, Wadingburn, Cockenzie Rood and Dreghorn." He paused, so his next statement would have maximum effect. "Know them all like the back of my toes, I do, even though I say it myself."

"Woweee!" Billy whistled his admiration in a highly satisfactory fashion. "You're ever so clever, Mr Alf! And –" his voice dropped to a hushed whisper – "my cousin told me you've actually met Royalty."

Alf nodded. "Some of my best mates," he said casually. "Now, save your breath for speedy flying. And I've thought of something else. We'll call in on the Ancient Crones on the way 'cos we'll be practically passing the House."

Billy all but fell off his twig. "But…" he stuttered. "But … Mr Alf! My ma says they're witches! That's worse than werewolves, Mr Alf! We can't go there!"

"Witches?" The disapproval in Alf's voice made Billy flinch. "The Ancient Crones? You'd better thank your lucky stars Unc didn't hear you say that! You'd have been off the training scheme quick as a wink." Alf shook his head. "Whatever do they teach you in school these days? Don't they tell you little 'uns about the Web? There'd be zombies and giants and all sorts tramping about the kingdoms if it weren't for the Web. Can't say as I understand exactly how it works – magic sort of stuff – but it keeps the evil types on this side of the border. Surely you knew that?"

The only answer was a loud sniff.

"Hey! There's no need to cry." Alf gave the very small bat a consoling pat on the back, but the sniffing grew louder. "It's OK – really it is. You'll soon learn better."

The sniffing continued.

Alf tried again. "Even I got things wrong to begin with. Lots of things!"

Billy brightened a little. "Did you really, Mr Alf?"

"Fell down a chimney and into a fireplace once," Alf said cheerfully. "Made a terrible mess. Now, blow your nose, and we'll be offski."

And he set off with a steady wingbeat. Billy, wiping his nose, followed close behind.

In the heart of the forest was a deep green hollow filled with a mist that came and went according to the mood of the occupants of the ramshackle building that lay in the centre. Messengers from the Five Kingdoms often found the mist impenetrable, and wandered for hours before either giving up completely or falling into the Bottomless Swamp. Those of a hardier nature battled on and, if they were fortunate, eventually reached the House of the Ancient Crones.

"Hm. No mist tonight. I'll give the young 'un the full tour," Alf decided as he and Billy flew down, "and

 14

I'll introduce him to our Gracie Gillypot." His devoted heart beat a little faster at the thought. "Start with the best, that's what Unc always says. It'll be downhill all the way once we hit the Five Kingdoms. No Truehearts there, and that's for sure."

Inside the house all was peaceful. Alf, a regular visitor, led the way through the neat little bat flap in the kitchen window. A loud rumbling snore was coming from one of the cupboards, and he grinned.

"That's Gubble," he explained.

"Gubble?" Billy looked anxious. "What's a Gubble?"

Alf's grin grew wider. "He's a troll. The green type. Goes on adventures with me and Miss Gracie and Mr Prince. You'll meet Miss Gracie – her and Mr Prince, they're sweethearts. Ever so romantic." He paused for effect. "We're a team, we are."

Billy stared. "You go on adventures with a Royal, Mr Alf?"

"They couldn't do without me," Alf boasted. "Saved the day time and time again, I have." He swooped round a chair back. "I'm the best hero ever."

"Woweeee!" Billy was breathless. "Fancy me being trained by a hero. Woweeee! Just wait till I tell my mum! The best hero ever... Woweee!"

Alf decided it was time to change the subject. "We're going to see the Web of Power now. No chatting! One of the crones is sure to be weaving … but she'll be too busy to talk."

"Mum's the word, Mr Alf."

"That's my boy." Alf gave his protégé an approving nod and headed out of the kitchen and down a long corridor. There were several doors on either side, and to Billy's astonishment they were sliding up and down. Alf made no comment, however, and Billy was too shy to ask if this was usual.

"Here we go," Alf whispered, and he led Billy into Room Seventeen. Billy took a deep breath, followed Alf to a perch on the curtain rail, and looked round.

An old woman was fast asleep in an armchair, cats piled high on top of her. Beside her another old woman was weaving steadily on the Web of Power, the translucent silver fabric gleaming faintly in the darkness of the room. A glow from the fire was the only other source of light; the thick velvet curtains were firmly closed against the moon. The second loom was set up for the next day, but the shuttles lay empty beside it. All of the Five Kingdoms admired the cloth woven by the Ancient Crones (and paid a suitably high price for it) but as a rule, no weaving of commissions took place at night, unless it was a particularly important order. Royal weddings and pageants left the crones exhausted and cross.

"The one in the chair's the Ancient One. She's the top boss. Gracie calls her Auntie Edna." Alf was whispering so quietly that even Billy had to strain to hear him. "The other one's the Oldest. Real name Elsie."

Billy was staring at the Oldest with fascinated eyes. "She's bald, Mr Alf!"

Alf suppressed a chuckle. "Her wig's on top of the loom. Makes her head hot, she says. Cooler without it. Come on ... we'll go back and find Miss Gracie."

As the two bats slipped silently away, the Ancient One opened her one eye.

"Hm," she said. "Top boss, am I? And part of the tourist route, it would appear." She shifted slightly, and a cat fell on the floor with a yowl. Bending down, Edna scooped it back onto her lap. "There, there." Stroking the cat's head, she looked thoughtfully after the bats. "Hope that little one knows what he's doing, trailing after Alf like that. He's awfully young." She yawned. "Let's hope he doesn't get himself in any trouble..." And her eye closed once more.

Flying out into the bright moonlight, the two small bats circled the House. As they flew higher they could see a row of bedroom windows; in the first the curtains were only half drawn, and a snoring shape was clearly visible humped beneath a heap of fleecy blankets. A pile of empty plates was close beside the bed.

"That'll be the youngest crone," Alf said. "Miss Val. Didn't think she lived here any more ... she must be staying over. Likes her cake, as you can tell."

"The youngest?" Billy looped a loop to have another peep. "Is she very pretty, Mr Alf?"

Alf snorted. "Miss Val? She may be the youngest, but she's still about a hundred. And the Oldest is twice that at the very least. And as for the Ancient One..." Alf whistled. "Unc reckons she's older than Fracture Mountain. She knows EVERYTHING!"

"Woweee!" Billy was impressed. "Does she know about the wolf woman? The one we saw? I didn't even know there was werewolves in the forest till you told me, Mr Alf. You learn ever such a lot when you're a Super Spotter, don't you?"

Billy, wittering as he flew, had reached the next window. At first glance it appeared to be firmly shuttered, but he was almost sure that he could see an eye – a very beautiful eye – peering through a small knothole. Billy flew closer, and the eye winked at him. It was not, however, a cheery kind of wink. It was a cold, calculating snarl of a wink, and a shudder ran down Billy's spine as he flapped hastily away.

"Careful," Alf warned. "Bit of a nasty character in there. Not one of the crones, that one."

Billy was trembling. "I saw an eye! It was horrid, Mr Alf! It was a witch! I know it was—"

Alf shook his head. "Nah. That's Foyce Undershaft." He waved a wing at the shutters as he closed the gap between himself and Billy. "Half a werewolf she is, and bad through and through," he whispered in the little bat's ear. "At least, she was before she came here. The crones'll sort her out though. That's what they do. That Miss Val you saw, she was a holy terror once – but look at her now. All the evil washed out of her. Good as gold, she is. Good as gold."

"Oooh!" Billy looked at the remaining window. "Who's in that one?"

As if it had heard him, the window slid round the corner of the house and out of view. It was replaced by the front door, and the letter box rattled at Billy by way of greeting. Billy squeaked his alarm. "What's going on, Mr Alf? What's happening?"

Alf dodged sideways to avoid a chimney determined to join the front door. "Something to do with magic," he explained. "You should see what the path gets up to – ties itself up in knots, and won't go anywhere. Miss Gracie's the only one it ever takes any notice of – oops!" He swerved again as the chimney changed its mind and headed back towards the roof. "Follow me, young 'un!" And he put on such a turn of speed that Billy was hard-pressed to keep up as the older bat zoomed round the corner of the house and in through the elusive third window. Billy followed blindly, shivering.

Inside the moonlit room a girl stirred, turned over, and sat up in bed.

"Alf? Is that you?" She pushed a wisp of hair out of her eyes. "What are you doing here? Is anything wrong?"

Alf settled comfortably on her shoulder. "Everything's A-OK, Miss Gracie. Fine and dandy – well, as far as I know. Not sure if you've noticed, but the House is rocking and rolling a bit."

Gracie Gillypot smiled, but she was looking at Billy. He was balanced on the windowsill, wings folded tightly over his eyes, and trembling like a leaf in a winter gale. "Poor little bat," she said gently. "Nobody's going to hurt you. Are you a friend of Alf's?"

Alf suddenly remembered what he was meant to be doing, and left Gracie's shoulder to push Billy further into the room. "Billy – this is Miss Gracie Gillypot. She's a Trueheart, and there aren't very many of those around, believe you me. Ever so special, Truehearts are! They make good things gooder, and bad things badder. Isn't that right, Miss Gracie?"

Gracie nodded, trying not to smile.

"And this is Billy, Miss Gracie." Alf gave the tiny bat another push. "I'm training him to be a Super Spotter." He sounded extremely pleased with himself.

Gracie was impressed. "Goodness, Alf! I thought only Marlon trained Super Spotters?"

Alf tried to sound modest. "'S right, Miss Gracie. Quite right. But he's made me a fully paid-up Batster Super Spotter With Full Training Capability!"

"WOW!" Gracie's smile lit up the room, and Billy, peeping over the top of his wing, felt a comforting warm glow creeping through his small body. "That's wonderful!" Gracie went on. "Congratulations! I'm thrilled!"

Alf beamed back at her, dropping all attempts to be cool. "Good, isn't it?"

"It certainly is. And how are you enjoying your training, Billy?"

Billy couldn't answer. He had had little experience of humans, and he was in no way prepared for a girl like this. All he could do was blink at her, awestruck.

Alf regarded his pupil with pride. "Feeling a bit odd, Billy? Quite right. What you're feeling now is what we Batsters call the Trueheart effect."

Gracie laughed, and picked up the little bat. He snuggled into the curve of her fingers and gazed into her very blue eyes. "Miss Gracie," he whispered, "I seed a witch! She winked at me through the shutters! It made me go all weird inside, but it feels better now." He rubbed at his chest. "I went all chilly and cold."

"A witch?" Gracie looked at Alf for an explanation.

"Sorry, Miss Gracie," he said. "He doesn't know any better. It was your – erm – half-sister. Well, not half-sister. Your stepsister – I mean, your stepdad's daughter..." Alf gave up. "Her in the room next door."

"Foyce?" A shadow crossed Gracie's face, and she pulled at the end of one of her plaits. "That's strange. Auntie Edna always makes sure the shutters are closed and locked before Foyce goes to bed – especially when it's coming up for a full moon. Are you quite sure you saw someone, Billy?"

Billy nodded. "It was an eye, Miss Gracie. The window was shut but it peeped at me through a hole."

Gracie sighed. "I hope she's not up to something. She's always more difficult when the moon's very

 22

bright. I had to unpick everything she did on the loom today; it was all lumps and bumps and horrible knots. I wonder if I ought to tell one of the aunties?"

"It wasn't a very big hole, Miss Gracie." Alf fluttered back to her shoulder. "Not even Billy could squeeze through." He put his head on one side. "Seen Mr Prince lately?"

"Marcus was here earlier today," Gracie admitted. "He was escaping a royal parade. Some kind of practice for the Centenary Celebrations."

Alf, who was an old friend of Prince Marcus, and well aware of the prince's dislike of royal puffery and paraphernalia, nodded wisely. "So he ran to the arms of his one true love," he said in his most sentimental tones.

Gracie blushed a fiery red, and concentrated on Billy. "Is Alf going to show you round the Five Kingdoms, Billy? Make sure he introduces you to Queen Bluebell. She's wonderful, and she's a great friend of Alf's Uncle Marlon, so she'll be ever so pleased to meet you." She paused for a moment. "But I'm sure you've been warned that some of the royal families aren't very – um – sensible about bats."

"She means they do lots of screaming and jumping up and down if they catch sight of us," Alf explained.

 23

"Just remember it's because they've never been properly educated," Gracie said. "Try not to let it worry you."

Billy nodded. "Yes, miss."

"We'd better be going, I s'pose," Alf said reluctantly. "Let you get your beauty sleep, Miss Gracie." He giggled. "Although I bet Mr Prince doesn't think—"

"That's quite enough, Alf," Gracie said firmly. "And you're right about my needing sleep." She yawned. "It's been such a long day. We were much later going to bed than usual because of sorting out Foyce's tangles. It probably sounds really lazy, but I think I'll tell Auntie Edna about the hole in Foyce's shutters in the morning." She leant back against her pillows, and tickled Billy's furry tummy. "It was nice to meet you, Billy. Enjoy your trip around the Five Kingdoms, and don't believe everything Alf tells you."

"*Ciao*, Miss Gracie!" Alf dipped in salute, and flew through the window.

"Bye, Miss Gracie," Billy echoed.

Gracie smiled, and snuggled under her blankets. In no time at all she was asleep again.

There was no sleeping being done in the room next door. The eye was back at the knothole, watching, and waiting. It saw the two little figures flittering past, and noticed with evil satisfaction how the smaller of the two kept glancing nervously back before disappearing between the moonlit trees.

"So you saw a wolf woman, did you?" The voice was as cold and sharp as a sliver of ice. "Well, well, well. How interesting. How very, very interesting..."

Chapter Two

Gracie Gillypot woke with a start. A shadow had troubled her dreams, and was lingering on even though sunshine was streaming into her room. As she sat up a bird flew past the window, and the fluttering wings made her think of Alf and Billy.

"Foyce!" The image in her dreams took a sudden shape. "Billy said she was looking at him! I ought to tell the aunties..."

She got out of bed and pulled on her dressing gown. As she did so a goose-feather quill pen, dripping with violet ink, zoomed down from the ceiling and began writing urgently on her whitewashed walls. "*CAREFUL! CAREFUL! CAREFUL!*"

"It's OK," Gracie told it. "There's no panic."

The pen hesitated, then began again. "*CAREFUL! CAREFUL! CAREFUL!*"

Gracie sighed. "You know what?" she said. "It would be really helpful if you could tell me what I'm supposed to be careful of, rather than just being mysterious."

"HER!" scrawled the pen, "HER! HER! HER!" then slid away under the door, leaving a pool of violet ink behind it.

"That's horribly messy," Gracie said disapprovingly. "And I do so wish you wouldn't write on the walls. I spent a whole afternoon last week painting out your silly poem about me and Marcus sitting in a tree K.I.S.S.I.N.G." Even in the privacy of her own room she was blushing. "That sort of thing is none of your business."

The pen reappeared in a rush, wrote "SORRY!" on the one remaining clean wall, followed it up with a badly drawn heart, then vanished as speedily as it had come.

Gracie shook her head. "And that serves me right for telling it off."

She mopped up the ink as best she could with an old handkerchief, then went down the stairs. The doors in the corridor slid towards her in greeting, and she waved hello as she opened the door to Room Seventeen. The Ancient One was still in her chair, and the Oldest was still working away at the loom.

"Dear girl! You're up very early … but you're a sight for sore eyes at any time." The Ancient One smiled at

Gracie. "I don't suppose you fancy making a nice pot of tea? Val hasn't got up yet, and Elsie and I are gasping."

Gracie smiled back. "Of course I will. But there's something I need to ask you – did you know there's a hole in the shutters in Foyce's room?"

There was a sudden silence as Elsie and Edna exchanged glances. Gracie's heart sank.

"Oh no. It DOES matter, doesn't it? I should have told you last night. I'm so sorry … but Alf said it was only a very little hole."

As the steady *clack clack clack* of the shuttle began once more, Edna leant forward in her chair. "It may not matter too much. Hm. Alf didn't mention it when he flew in last night. It seems he's giving guided tours, with me as the main attraction."

Gracie was unable to repress a giggle. "I know! Me too. He's got this teeny little bat called Billy in tow – he's training him to be a Batster spy!"

The Ancient One nodded. "I saw Billy. He's very young to be out on his own with Alf, though. He's a mere baby. He didn't see Foyce, did he?"

The sinking feeling came back to Gracie with a vengeance. "Yes. He was all trembly – he thought she was a witch… Oh, Auntie Edna! She can't hurt him, can she?"

Once again there was a meaningful silence as the two crones looked at each other. Then Elsie said, "You'd better tell her, Edna. She needs to know."

The Ancient One gave a deep sigh. "You're right, Elsie dear."

"Tell me what?" Gracie's eyes were wide. "What is it?"

"Well…" Edna leant back in her chair. "We've been a little worried about Foyce."

Gracie stared at her. "But I thought she was getting better? I mean, I know she tangled all the threads yesterday, but she always does that when it's coming up to full moon. She's not been calling me names nearly as often as she used to. And she hasn't had a temper tantrum for ages."

"That's one of the reasons why we're worried," Edna said. "We'd be delighted with a gradual improvement, with a few backslidings here and there. That's to be expected. But Foyce has changed her behaviour very suddenly and, to be honest, it makes me suspicious. She hasn't said anything to you, has she?"

Gracie shook her head. "She doesn't talk to me unless she has to."

Elsie unhooked her wig from the end of the loom and gave it a shake before putting it on. "I suppose we could be worrying unnecessarily, Edna dear. After all, we've never had a case like Foyce before. What do you think, Gracie?"

"I don't know enough about it," Gracie said slowly. "Auntie Val told me it's never easy when a Falseheart first comes here, though. She told me it was ages before she learnt to behave, and she nearly drove you mad."

"That's true enough," Elsie agreed. "But Val was an angel compared to Foyce. Well, a very bad angel, with a tendency to steal toy trains from small children."

Edna chuckled. "I'd forgotten about the trains. But Elsie's right. Foyce is far worse than Val ever was."

"And do you think she's planning something?" Gracie asked.

The Ancient One nodded. "I've suspected for a while that she's got a way of tapping into a source of evil. If she's been able to look out of her room at the time of the full moon, then that would explain it."

Gracie was puzzled. "But why?"

"Because she's half werewolf, dearie." Elsie tapped the loom with her shuttle. "When the moon's full, the evil part of her can be fed by moonlight. That's why we've always kept her room firmly shuttered at night, and why we have these thick curtains in here."

"I see." Gracie looked up at the velvet curtains. It was true; not the smallest ray of moonlight could find its way through. "But if the hole is closed up, will that make it all right again?"

"I hope so." Edna heaved herself out of her chair, and went to look at the Web of Power. The shimmering silver threads rippled and gleamed like moving water as she came closer, and Gracie rubbed her eyes. "Goodness! I've never seen it look so shiny!"

Edna frowned as she considered the Web. "I've not seen it look like that either. There's no sign of approaching evil … but something's wrong. Have you any ideas, Elsie?"

Elsie scratched her bald head. "Don't ask me. It looked pretty much as usual when I took over last night. I did have a couple of threads snap, though, and that's never happened before."

"I think I'll try a little test," the Ancient One decided. She leant over the loom, and picked up a shuttle laden with shining silver. "Let's see what this shows us. Remind me to tell Val to keep a close eye on the Web when she finally gets out of bed."

"I meant to ask about that," Gracie said. "Is she staying long? Isn't her brother missing her?"

Edna shrugged. "It's because of Foyce, dearie. We thought it best that we were all here until after the full moon. Just in case. Now, what about that tea?"

As Gracie turned to go, there was a loud *bang!* and the door burst open. Gubble was standing in the doorway carrying a large tray.

"Tea!" he announced proudly. "Gubble make tea."

"Now that," Elsie said, "is enough to cheer the gloomiest heart!"

Gubble stomped in and dumped the tray on a nearby table. The cups rattled and the teapot shook, but only the sugar bowl spilled its contents. Gubble licked a grubby green finger and wiped it round the tray. "Tidy," he said as he sucked the sugar off his finger with loud slurping noises. "Gracie pour?"

Gracie was viewing the tray with some suspicion. The milk jug was empty, and the teapot lid was set at a rakish angle. Hoping for the best, she began to pour ... and a curious brown liquid dribbled into the first cup.

"Gubble," she said, "this is VERY kind of you, and VERY clever − but what did you put in the teapot?"

Gubble beamed. "Leaves. Lots of leaves. And water."

"Ah." Gracie put the teapot down. "And am I right in thinking you used cold water?"

Gubble went on beaming. "No hot water for Gubble. Hot water BURNS!"

"Very sensible of you to be so careful," the Ancient One said from her chair. "But I think perhaps we

 33

might make some hot tea as well."

Gracie nodded. "Well done, Gubble," she said, and picked up the tray. As she walked through the door a slim figure came gliding towards her, and with one swift movement tipped the tray and all its contents over Gracie.

"Oh NO! What have I done? Sister dear, I'm so, so sorry!" The voice was clear and musical, but there was a fine-honed razor edge beneath the words, and Foyce's big blue eyes gleamed with pleasure as she viewed the stains down Gracie's dressing gown. "I do SO hope it hasn't burned you. It was dreadfully careless of me."

"Actually," Gracie said, "Gubble used cold water."

"Oh." The sigh sounded disappointed rather than relieved, but the honey-sweet voice went on, "I'm SO pleased. Would you like me to make more tea?"

"I can manage, thank you," Gracie said, and escaped with the tray. For a second Foyce's beautiful face was contorted with frustrated rage, but she regained her equilibrium as she sauntered into Room Seventeen. As she passed Gubble she gave him a sly pinch, but he was still sucking his finger and noticed nothing.

The Ancient One looked at her thoughtfully. "Good morning, Foyce. I hope you slept well?"

"Yes, thank you." Foyce made her way to the looms. "Shall I begin weaving? I'll try harder today."

"If you're ready." Edna stood up, and handed Foyce the shuttle loaded with silver silk.

"Silver?" Foyce was startled.

"That's right, dear," Edna said, and Foyce took the shuttle without further question.

"AAGH!" She dropped it with a cry of pain. "It burnt me!" Nursing her hand, she turned on the Ancient One, and her eyes were harsh yellow, and her rosy lips drawn back into an evil snarl. Then her face changed, and had the two crones not been watching they would have believed that Foyce had never been anything other than blue-eyed and beautiful. Elsie bent down to pick up the discarded shuttle, and saw the silver thread had turned black. Silently she dropped it into the waste basket, and went back to her work.

Edna, as bright as if nothing untoward had happened, patted the stool in front of the second loom. "Start whenever you're ready, dear."

"Of course," Foyce said sweetly, and sat down. A moment later she was weaving thick green wool as steadily as if she had been doing it all her life. Elsie, sitting in front of the Web of Power, saw a shadow darken the gleaming fabric in front of her, and sighed.

Chapter Three

"**G**oosewits!" Bluebell, Queen of Wadingburn, glared at her two grandchildren. "Goosewits, both of you! You haven't a brain between you!"

Princess Loobly and Prince Vincent shifted uneasily.

Bluebell gave the map on the blackboard behind her a hearty thump. "So WHERE exactly would you find the Less Enchanted Forest?"

Loobly gave her brother an agonized look. Vincent coughed. "Erm … I'd say it's best not to know about places like that, Grandmother. Actually. Not the kind of place for PLU, you know."

"PLU?" Queen Bluebell fixed her grandson with a piercing eye. "And what, precisely, does that stand for?"

Vincent coughed again. "People Like Us, Grandmother. You know the sort of thing. Royalty. Blue blood. Cream of the custard."

His grandmother's gaze grew even frostier. "And I suppose you believe that People Like Us are in some way better than everybody else?"

Vincent's eyes bulged. "But OF COURSE we are," he said. "That's the whole point of royalty."

"I see." Bluebell folded her arms. "Well, let me tell you, Vincent, that I know several bats who have considerably more common sense than you do."

Up on the curtain rail Alf nudged his companion. "See, Billy? What did Miss Gracie tell you? That's real royalty, that is, and a real friend of bats. Take a note."

"Yes, Mr Alf, sir. Note taken. She's very grand, though, isn't she?"

"Shh!" Alf raised a warning claw. "A Super Spotter has to obey the rules. Watch and listen. No chit-chat. Best way of checking out what's going on."

Billy nodded, and Alf gave him a conspiratorial wink.

Down below, Prince Vincent was frowning. "Bats? Marcus is always going on about bats. He even says he talks to the horrible things." He gave a sudden shriek of laughter. "Oh! I say! I've thought of a joke! I expect it's because HE'S bats. Bats in the belfry!"

His grandmother shook her head. "Really, Vincent. That's not at all funny."

 37

Vincent went on cackling. "Bats in the belfry! Just wait till I tell Princess Marigold. She'll howl with laughter."

"That," Queen Bluebell agreed, "would not surprise me in the least. She always was exceptionally silly. Just like you, Vincent. Sometimes I wonder what to do with you."

Vincent smiled. His grandmother appeared to have forgotten about her geography lesson, and was now looking resigned rather than angry. "You don't need to worry about that, Grandmother." He gave a little skip. "But there's something I'd like right now this minute! Can I order a cream cake for elevenses? With raspberry-jam filling?"

"That won't do your figure any good." Bluebell inspected him through her lorgnette. "You're already as round as a barrel."

"Yes, Grandmother." Vincent was adept at ignoring any reference to his ever-enlarging waistline. "So can I? Loobly likes cream cake too, don't you, Loobly?"

Loobly nodded, and Queen Bluebell sighed a gusty sigh. "Whenever I look at you two I ask myself WHAT will become of Wadingburn after I've gone."

"Gone?" Loobly looked up. "Where going, Grandmother?"

Her brother dug her in the ribs with his elbow. "Shh, Loo. She means —" he lowered his voice to a sepulchral whisper – "dying."

"Rubbish!" Bluebell rose to her full height and glared at Vincent so fiercely that he took an involuntary step backwards. "I have no intention of dying for a good many years yet. Unless, of course, I am driven so mad by my grandchildren that the only way to escape is to leap off a very high cliff." Her glare intensified. "Now, have you two noticed that this is our centenary year? I hope you have. And I hope you've also noticed that we're having a massive celebration for the founding of the Alliance of the Five Kingdoms." She turned a basilisk stare on Vincent, and he hastily nodded.

"Yes, Grandmother. Exactly. One hundred years! Or is it two? Whatever. Good stuff. Five Kingdoms … united we stand 'n' all that. Yes. Hope we get another hundred. Or two. Erm … yes. Splendid—"

"Vincent! Stop wittering and listen. I've been ruling Wadingburn for more than fifty years, so I've decided I'm going to celebrate as well. I'm going to retire. I'm fed up of ruling a kingdom, and I want to have a little fun in my last remaining years. Travel, perhaps. See what's on the other side of the border… What's the matter NOW?"

Vincent was staring at his grandmother as if she had grown horns and a tail. "The other side of the border?" He swallowed hard. "But ... but TERRIBLE things live there! Werewolves! Zombies! Witches! Trolls! Giants! Dragons! And those Ancient Crones where Gracie lives – they're scary. Really scary." He leant forward, his eyes bulging in his earnest desire to make his grandmother see sense. "Trust me. I've been there, and it was utterly, utterly, UTTERLY ghastly!"

Queen Bluebell beamed. "Sounds utterly wonderful to me. Gracie Gillypot's a dear sweet girl, and I'm a bit of an ancient crone myself. And I think it's high time I met a werewolf. I'm sure it would be far more interesting than poor old King Horace. Or King Frank."

Her grandson was almost speechless. "You ... you ... you're beginning to sound as mad as Marcus!"

"And that's a bad thing?" Bluebell raised her eyebrows. "Has it ever occurred to you, Vincent, that there is more than one way of looking at the world?"

"Yes." Vincent knew exactly where he stood on this question. "There's the right way, and the wrong way. And me and Arioso and Marigold and everyone except Marcus are right. I blame that girl Gracie Gillypot for the way Marcus carries on. He was never as bad before he met her, never!"

Up on the curtain rail Alf nudged Billy. "Did you hear that? That's typical, that is."

Billy nodded solemnly as Queen Bluebell raised her eyes heavenwards.

"Vincent," she said, "I'm not sure I can take any more of your opinions just now. I think we'd better discuss Gracie another time."

Under the mistaken impression that he had won his point, her grandson smiled happily. "So can I order my cream cake now?"

"No." Bluebell began polishing her lorgnette in a businesslike manner. "I haven't finished telling you about my plans. Your cake can wait. I want to retire, but before that can happen, a new queen has to be appointed – and according to the laws of Wadingburn that will be YOU, Loobly."

"Eh?" Loobly's eyes grew very round.

Bluebell gave an exasperated snort. "Ruling the kingdom goes down the female line. I've told you that a thousand times. Always has done ... up until now, that is."

Loobly looked agonized. "Not queen," she said. "Loobly wouldn't like be queen. Not like AT ALL." She pointed to Prince Vincent, who was doing his best to fade into the wood-panelled walls. "Make Vinnie queen."

"Well, Vincent?" The queen swung round. "What do you say to that? Do you really see yourself as King of Wadingburn?"

Vincent opened and closed his mouth, but no sound came out. He knew only too well what his grandmother thought of him.

"Exactly." Bluebell was triumphant. "Just as I said. Goosewits!" She paused, and a thoughtful expression floated across her face. "Hmmm ... do you know what, Vincent? I do believe you've given me an idea."

"I have?" Her grandson was startled into speech.

Bluebell folded her arms. "What if I were to offer the kingdom to 'that girl Gracie Gillypot', as you call her? She's got more sense in her little finger than you two put together."

"Gracie Gillypot?" Prince Vincent turned pale with horror. This was worse than the idea of his grandmother fraternizing with a werewolf. Far worse. "GRACIE GILLYPOT? But ... but she's not ... she's not even NEAR being a princess!"

Queen Bluebell wasn't listening. She was walking up and down the room, muttering to herself. "Am I right? She's a clever girl, but is that enough? Would it be fair to ask her? The rest of the Royals are mostly a pack of numbskulls ... but there's the odd hopeful.

And Wadingburn needs a sensible queen. One with a bit of backbone … If Gracie were willing, it could be the perfect solution. She'd have Marcus beside her as king, of course. Goes without saying. The two of them together … yes! YES! But is it allowed? Is it possible?" Bluebell slapped the table. "That's what I need to find out! And no time like the present. Where's my prime minister? Drat the man! Never around when he's wanted!" And she hurried out of the room, leaving Vincent gasping for breath.

"She's gone mad! Did you hear her, Loobly? She's gone stark staring mad! She needs help! She needs locking up! We have to tell someone – but who?"

Loobly shrugged. "Loobly likes Gracie Gillypot. Is kind and smiley…"

Vincent threw up his hands in horror. "Really, Loo! She's a COMMONER! She lives with a bunch of dotty old witches and she talks to trolls and bats…" He clutched at his head. "Imagine THAT as queen of Wadingburn!"

His twin sister remained unmoved. "Loobly likes bats. And rats."

"But you're a Royal, Loobly! It's OK if you do things like that. It … it's just 'one of Princess Loobly's little ways'. But if someone like Gracie does it, then it's bonkers."

 44

Loobly gave him a sharp look. "Grandmother have funny little ways? Or bonkers?"

Vincent wasn't listening. He was tugging at a bell rope to summon a servant, and as soon as one appeared he gave his orders. "Call a carriage! At once! It's an emergency − I have to go to Gorebreath right now this minute!"

"WHEEEE!" Alf was swinging round and round the curtain rail. "Did you hear that, young Billy? That's our Gracie they're talking about! Our very own Gracie. Just wait until Unc hears about this. Come on − we can hitch a ride to Gorebreath!"

Billy looked blank. "Where's that, Mr Alf?"

Alf didn't answer. He was heading for the window.

Vincent's departure was not as speedy as it might have been. It occurred to him that the journey was a long one, so a well-filled picnic basket was an absolute neces-sity. Then there was the argument with the coachman, who was used to receiving his orders from the queen.

"Her Majesty didn't give no instructions for an outing," he said doubtfully.

Vincent scowled. He was about to argue that HE was giving the order, but second thoughts prevailed, and he managed a fake smile as he explained that there must have been a mistake. "The queen must have forgotten," he said. "She definitely promised that … that I could go and visit my friends. Prince Arioso, you know. And Prince Marcus."

The coachman was still unconvinced, but at that moment the cook's boy staggered out into the court-yard with the most enormous picnic basket. Vincent was inspired.

"See?" he said. "There's my snack for the journey! I wouldn't have that if I wasn't expecting to go, would I?"

Muttering, the coachman gave in. The horses were harnessed, and Vincent and his picnic basket finally settled inside Queen Bluebell's largest travel-ling coach, together with a number of extra cushions and blankets.

"Off we go!" he instructed. "Off we go!"

Alf, comfortably ensconced in the coach hood, nod-ded at Billy. "Get some shut-eye, young 'un. Next stop Gorebreath. I'll wake you up if there's anything you need to see." And he yawned loudly, yawned again and began to snore.

Billy tried to sleep, but couldn't. Every time he closed his eyes for longer than a second the House of the Ancient Crones swam into his mind. The House, and the shuttered window, and the small knothole, and— Billy sat up very straight, his heart hammering. The wink. That horrible, horrible wink. And the eye had been watching him as he flew away. He knew it had; a chill had crept through his body, and his head had felt as if it was full of wasps. And now something was calling to him to come back. He could feel it deep in his bones. It was very far away, but increasingly persistent … not a voice, or a whistle, or any audible noise, but willpower. A mind much stronger than his own was willing him to obey its commands. He made one last effort to resist.

"Mr Alf," he whispered. "Mr Alf? Help me, Mr Alf!"

The only answer was a snore. Billy sighed a small tired sigh, stretched his wings and flew.

Alf slept soundly until the carriage reached the long drive that led to the palace of Gorebreath. He opened his eyes, peered round and remarked, "Here we are! Second of the Five Kingdoms! Take a note, Billy … Billy? BILLY?"

There was no answer, and Alf scratched his head in surprise. "Where's he got to? Billy? We're back in business! Gotta check out what goes on here…"

Alf's voice died away. It was all too evident that the little bat was missing. He flew a couple of circles round the carriage, but without much expectation of finding his small companion. He knew that Billy's hearing was even more acute than his own; he would have heard had he been anywhere near by.

"That's strange," Alf told himself. "Not like the young 'un to flit off for no reason. Keen as mustard, that one! Wonder what—"

Alf's musings were brought to a sudden stop by the screech of brakes as Queen Bluebell's carriage came to a jolting halt outside Gorebreath Palace's front door. "Have to wait 'n' see if he turns up," he decided, and looped down to see what was going on.

"Sorry about that, Your Highness," lied the coachman as Vincent struggled out of the coach, half a chocolate cream eclair squashed in his hand.

"I shall complain to my grandmother!" Vincent said crossly. "My picnic's gone all over the place! It's not good enough!"

The coachman grinned. Vincent, unaware of cherrypie stains down his coat front and mustard smears on his chin, grew even angrier. "You did that on purpose!" he accused. "I know you did! You can jolly well wait here until I've been to see King Frank, and then you can take me home again, and we'll see what Grandmother has to—" He stopped abruptly, remembering that this was the grandmother he had come to complain about. "Well. Yes. Just stay here, and I'll be back in five minutes. Or ten. But don't move."

The coachman bowed. As soon as Vincent had disappeared he clucked at the horses and drove them round to the Gorebreath stables for a well-earned rest.

Vincent, meanwhile, had made his way to King Frank and Queen Mildred's private parlour. He found them sitting cosily together having tea and cake. Prince Arioso, heir to the throne of Gorebreath, was standing by the mantelpiece with his arm round his fiancée, Princess Nina-Rose.

Queen Mildred looked up and smiled as Vincent stomped in, wiping the cream on his fingers onto his trousers.

"Vincent, dear! How lovely to see you!" Anxiously aware that Vincent was about to lower his cream-covered lower half onto a pale pink velvet sofa, she offered him a napkin. "Is darling Bluebell with you?"

Vincent ignored the napkin and sat down. "No. No, she's at home." He saw the cake, and his face brightened. "I say! That looks awfully delicious!"

Queen Mildred, trying not to regret the ruin of her

favourite seat, cut him a large slice. "I hope she's well?"

Vincent shook his head vigorously before attacking his cake. "I'm afraid she isn't. Not at all. In fact, that's why I'm here! I think she's going mad."

"Mad?" King Frank frowned. "Bluebell? Rubbish! There's no one as sane as Bluebell."

"But she IS!" Vincent, his mouth full of cake, waved his arms to make his point more forceful. "She's talking about retiring, and – guess what!" He banged his fist on the arm of the unfortunate sofa, leaving it covered in jammy crumbs. "She wants to make Gracie Gillypot queen of Wadingburn!"

There was a stunned silence, followed by a high-pitched scream as Princess Nina-Rose threw up her hands and staggered dramatically into Arioso's arms. Alf, lurking in a dark corner, winced.

"Arry! I'm going to faint! That ghastly horrible beastly girl … You've got to stop her!"

Arioso, never the swiftest of thinkers, stared at Vincent. "What do you mean, Queen Bluebell's retiring?"

Nina-Rose was miraculously restored to health. "I do wish you'd learn to listen, Arry darling. Vincent said his grandmother is going to retire. That means Wadingburn will need a new queen, and Bluebell's going to choose that dreadful Gracie Gillypot!"

Vincent, delighted with Nina-Rose's reaction, nodded. "Heard it with my very own ears."

"Now, now, now, Vincent." King Frank, recovered from the initial shock of the news, and remembering Vincent's general unreliability, poured himself another cup of tea. "This is all a little unlikely, don't you know? What *exactly* did your grandmother say?"

Vincent opened his mouth, then paused. He had no intention of reporting the full conversation. His grandmother's opinion of him was both misplaced and inaccurate, and was therefore best omitted. "She said," he began, "she was tired of being queen."

"But Vincent dear, we've all felt tired from time to time," Queen Mildred told him. "Nothing mad about that. Rather the opposite, in fact. What else did she say?"

"She said she wants to be an ancient crone, and she wants to meet a werewolf." This made Queen Mildred gasp, and King Frank's eyebrows rise. Vincent was quick to press home his advantage. "You see? Mad! Quite mad! And she said Loobly couldn't be queen and she was going to talk to her prime minister!"

The King and Queen of Gorebreath looked at each other in consternation. Talking to one's prime minister

 51

suggested a seriousness of purpose that it was difficult to ignore.

"That's not good, Mildred," King Frank pronounced. "Not good at all. We can't allow it. Not under any circumstances."

Nina-Rose stepped forward. "I've always said she was a troublemaker, that girl. I mean, who does she think she is? You should ban her from the kingdoms—"

The parlour door opened and Prince Marcus, twin brother of Prince Arioso, but younger by ten minutes, wandered into the room.

"What's up?" he asked. "Who should be banned from the kingdoms? Anyone interesting?"

"Your friend Gracie Gillypot," Nina-Rose snapped. "She's trying to wheedle her way into being a queen!"

Even Vincent felt this was a little harsh. "Hang on a minute!" he began. "That's not what I said—"

"Oh?" Marcus's eyes gleamed with a dangerous light. "So what DID you say, Vincent?"

Vincent had always been frightened of Marcus. He was the one and only member of all the royal families resident in the Five Kingdoms who willingly rode over the border and actively sought adventures. Not only did he seek them; he came back covered in glory. And his companion in these adventures was always Gracie

 52

Gillypot ... and it had become only too obvious in recent months that Marcus had developed a most regrettable affection for Gracie.

Vincent swallowed. In his rush to report the unfortunate state of his grandmother's mind he had completely forgotten that Marcus was involved, and would have an opinion on the matter. A very strong opinion.

He swallowed a second time, and said feebly, "Grandmother's gone mad, that's all. She wants Gracie to be Queen of Wadingburn." A thought struck him. "And you to be king, Marcus. She said that too. Honestly, she did!"

Marcus was prevented from making any reply by Nina-Rose collapsing into hysterical laughter. "MARCUS? A KING? Now I know it's a joke. Goodness, Vincent – you had us all fooled! I never thought you could be so..."

Her voice died away. Three pairs of royal eyes were regarding her with cold disapproval. Arioso, embarrassed rather than disapproving, coughed.

"Ahem. Sweetie-pie. Marcus IS a prince, you know. Second in line to me, actually. If a pig fell on my head, he'd be the heir to the throne."

Nina-Rose did her best to rally. "But darling, DARLING Arry – guess what! I was joking too!

Couldn't you tell?" An expression reminiscent of someone eating an exceptionally sour lemon crossed her
face. "Of course it would be simply fabby if Marcus
was a king when you're a king and I'm a queen. What
fun we'd have! Thousand thrills a minute!"

Arry patted her hand. "There speaks my own
Nina-Rosey-posey."

"Hang on a second." Marcus flung himself down on
a chair. "I don't understand what's going on. Bluebell's
not dead or anything, is she?"

"No!" Vincent shook his head. "No … but she's a
bit … strange. Acting weird." He produced his trump
card. "Says she wants to meet a werewolf, and be an
ancient crone."

"Well, THAT'S not mad," Marcus said, with some
relief. "She'd love the crones, and what's wrong with
wanting to meet a werewolf? I've always wanted to
meet one. And Gracie does too. We were talking about
it only yesterday − it's nearly a full moon, you know.
We thought of riding to the Less Enchanted Forest to
see if we could find a few."

King Frank glared at his younger son. "Don't be
so foolish, Marcus. You'll do no such thing. Most
unwholesome things, werewolves."

Nina-Rose gave a hysterical giggle. A sudden vision

of Gracie Gillypot solving the current problem by being eaten had popped into her head. "OH! Oh, Marcus! What an adventure that would be! Or maybe Gracie would prefer to go on her own? Had you considered that, Marcus?" She gave him her very best irresistible smile. "Dear Gracie! I'm sure she and the werewolves would find such a lot in common—"

Unlike his twin, Marcus had never had any trouble resisting Nina-Rose's fluttering eyelashes. "You're only saying that 'cos you hope Gracie'll get into trouble. I'd never let her go on her own, and you know it."

"Really, Marcus!" King Frank was frowning. "The border was created to keep us safe from such terrible things. I fail to see why you should feel the need to search them out. You'd be much better off staying here in Gorebreath and attending to your duties. I noticed you were absent at yesterday's parade, by the way. Disappointing, my boy! Most disappointing."

"That's right, Marcus old bean." Vincent nodded. "We Royals need to stick together." He looked hopefully at King Frank. "Don't suppose you'd like to have a word with Grandmother, would you?" A pained expression floated across his pudgy face. "She doesn't listen to a word I say."

Marcus grinned. "That's because she's got more

sense, Vincent old bean. Right … I'm off. I'll see you all later."

"Where are you—" King Frank began, but he was too late. Marcus had gone.

"There!" Nina-Rose stuck out her lower lip. "I bet he's gone rushing off to tell Gracie Gillypot she's going to be a queen!"

Arioso put his arm round her. "I don't think he is, my sweetest petal. I think he's going to Niven's Knowe to see Tertius. They were talking about a tournament as part of the Centenary Celebrations."

"A tournament?" Nina-Rose cheered up at once. "Oh, Arry DARLING! Will you wear silver armour? And ride a white horse? You'll look SO wonderful! And I'll give you a white rose, and you can hold it in your teeth and wave it as you gallop past at a million miles per hour to defeat the evil foe!"

Arry, who had no intention of taking part in any such energetic activity, smiled nervously. "Well, I think Marcus and Tertius rather want to act it out together," he began.

Nina-Rose turned a threatening shade of purple. "No, Arry! You absolutely have to take part! And you have to be the winner because you're the heir to the throne, and I really, REALLY think that if you love me like you say you do then you could do just this little tiny thing for ickle pickle me…"

Alf, watching from his curtain rail, shook his head. "No point hanging about here. Think I'll check and see if the little 'un's come back. Be nice to have a catch-up with Mr Prince as well." And he flittered away, leaving Nina-Rose doing her very best to persuade her fiancé to risk life and limb in the interests of demonstrating his undying affection for her.

Chapter Four

Marcus was making his way to the stables when Alf caught up with him.

"Hi, Alf!" he said. "How's things? Heard you got your Batster Super Spotter certificate. Well done!"

Alf flew a surprised, but highly gratified, circle. "Who told you that, Mr Prince?"

"Marlon kept me company when I was riding home last night," Marcus explained. "Said you've got a trainee, as well." He looked round. "Is he with you?"

Feeling that losing his pupil suggested a certain carelessness, Alf changed the subject. "You've been seeing Miss Gracie, I hear, Mr Prince. Me and Billy — that's my trainee — we popped in to see her last night." He gave Marcus a knowing wink. "Went ever so pink when I mentioned your name, Mr Prince."

Marcus laughed, refusing to be embarrassed. "Good."

He swung into the stable yard. "I'm off to Niven's Knowe. Coming?"

Alf dithered. Where was Billy? This was the ideal opportunity to introduce him to Royalty, and continue his education. Surely he couldn't be too far away...

"Erm ... you haven't seen a very small bat out here, have you, Mr Prince? Name of Billy?"

"Has he gone missing? Oh, look! Here's Ger!" Marcus nodded at the stable boy, who was leading out Marcus's pony. "Thanks, Ger. You're a marvel."

Ger handed over the reins and Marcus rubbed the pony's nose affectionately. "Good boy, Glee. Good boy." He turned back to Alf. "So what happened? Did you scare Billy away with stories of trolls and dragons?"

"Would I do a thing like that, Mr Prince?" Alf tried to sound outraged, but part of him was beginning to wonder if Marcus could be right. Had he told Billy too much?

Marcus mounted Glee, and began heading for the gates that led out of the yard. "Maybe he's gone home for a rest. Or could he have gone to see Marlon? He's dozing in the barn if you want him."

"Unc? In the barn?" Alf circled Marcus's head while he did some speedy thinking. Should he pretend that everything was fine? But what if Billy had been found by Marlon, and was in the barn under his supervision? It was probably best to own up. "Coolio. Thanks, Mr Prince. I'll check it out." And he whizzed away.

"Bye!" Marcus called. Moments later the palace of Gorebreath was left behind, and he was on the road that eventually led to Niven's Knowe. Vincent's news was very much in the prince's mind, and he considered it as the pony trotted steadily onwards. "Fancy old Bluebell thinking of Gracie as her successor … makes a lot of sense, of course. All Loobly wants to do is play with her ratty friends, and Vincent's got about as much brain as a bluebottle … but would Gracie really want to be a queen?" Marcus stared at Glee's ears as if they might hold the answer. "And would I want to be a king? Not a lot. Although it would make Nina-Rose as sick as a parrot … might almost be worth it just for that … no. No, it wouldn't. But what about Gracie?" Marcus pulled Glee to a halt. "Should I tell her? Give her a chance to think about it before it all kicks off … if it really happens. I wouldn't be surprised if Vincent had got the whole thing upside down, but if he hasn't then she needs to know. It's only fair… What do you think, Glee?" Glee whickered softly, as if agreeing, and Marcus nodded. "I know what I'll do. I'll see Tertius today, but I'll get up early tomorrow and spend the day with Gracie." His decision made, Marcus urged Glee into a canter and set off once more for the kingdom of Niven's Knowe.

"Unc! Uncle Marlon!" Alf zoomed high into the rafters of the old wooden barn, much to the annoyance of a cluster of elderly bats who had gathered together for a peaceful afternoon's snooze. "Unc? Are you there?"

"Where's the fire, kiddo?" A much older bat, grizzled and grey about the whiskers, emerged from the shadows. "And where's your manners?"

"Sorry, Uncle Marlon." Alf looped a cheery double loop. "How's tricks?"

His uncle was not taken in. "You're up to something, kid. What've you done?"

Alf had been using his acrobatic skills as a cover to see if Billy was lurking under the old wooden beams, but there was no sign of him. "Unc," he said casually as he settled himself beside Marlon, "has Billy been here?"

Marlon snorted. "Lost him?"

"No," Alf said firmly.

There was a pause.

"Well … sort of."

Marlon snorted again. "Careless, kiddo. Careless. When d'you see him last?"

Alf considered. "We hitched a ride from Wadingburn in a coach, but he'd vamooshed by the time we arrived."

"*Vamooshed?*" Marlon raised his eyebrows.

"Erm." Alf wriggled on his perch. "Well … I might have closed my peepers for a moment or two along the way…"

"Snoozing while on duty?" The older bat folded his wings across his chest. "And you a Super Spotter! Thought you were going to do me proud, kid."

"Sorry, Uncle Marlon." Alf drooped.

Marlon took pity on him. "Billy's probably winged it off home to his mum. He's in the kingdoms, so he'll not come to any harm."

Alf, recovering, agreed. "That's right. Hey, Unc – guess what! Our Miss Gracie's next in line to be Queen of Wadingburn! Me 'n' Billy – we heard the old queen telling her grandkids. The fat prince – he didn't take it too well. Hurtled off here to sneak on his grandma, making out she'd lost her marbles." Alf sniffed. "They're all of them madder than Queen Bluebell ever will be."

"Queen of Wadingburn?" Marlon was interested. "Hm. Sure you got it straight, kid?"

"Sure as I'm here. Billy, he heard her too." Alf puffed out his chest. "She – the old queen – she said

 62

she knew bats with more sense than her grandkids. And then she said Miss Gracie was the perfect solution! She'd make a great queen, wouldn't she, Unc?"

Marlon did not share his nephew's enthusiasm. "Could be trouble ahead," he said. "She ain't popular with the crowned lot."

"But she's a Trueheart!" Alf was appalled. "Look what she's done – saved the Royals time and time again."

His uncle shook his head. "Don't mean a duck's quack, kid. Shove a crown on their heads and they'd forget their own ma."

Alf refused to give in to this gloomy view. "Mr Prince – he can tell them!" He wriggled closer to his uncle. "She's the best, our Miss Gracie. You should have seen her sorting Billy out earlier! He said he'd seen a witch and got into a real old dither until Miss Gracie calmed him down." Alf giggled. "Know who it was? Just Miss Gracie's stepsister, peering through her window!"

Marlon froze. "Say again?"

"Miss Gracie's stepsister." Alf was puzzled. "You know, Unc. The one that lives with the crones. Does the weaving 'n' all that—"

"Foyce Undershaft." Marlon's voice was grim. "And you're telling me her window was open?"

"Not open. Just a little hole. Billy said he could see an eye – that's all."

"Hmph." The older bat considered the implications of this. "Might be OK. But she ain't meant to see out ... not at night when it's this time of the month."

"Why not?" Alf asked. "What's the deal?"

His uncle paused. "You don't know?" Alf shook his head, and Marlon went on. "Well. For starters, Foyce Undershaft ain't no relation to our Gracie. Her dad married Gracie's mum, that's all. Biggest mistake the poor dame ever made – she didn't last long, even though she was a werewolf. And that reminds me –" Marlon glanced up into the shadowy rafters above his head – "it's coming up to a full moon."

"WOWEEEE!" Alf's squeak was one of delight. "Will Foyce go hairy? Whiskers all over? Can we watch?"

For a rare moment Marlon was speechless. Alf, unaware, continued to witter on about fangs until the sweep of a wing sent him flying backwards off his perch.

"Ouch! Steady on, Uncle Marlon! What did I say?" The small bat was outraged as he fluttered his way back. "I only asked—"

"Think, kid, think!" Marlon snapped in exasperated tones.

Alf shut his eyes tightly. "Full moon…" he muttered. "Full moon … werewolves … hairy…" He shook his head. "Sorry, Unc. I'm just not getting it."

Resisting, with some difficulty, the urge to cuff his nephew for a second time, Marlon asked, "And WHERE is Miss Foyce Undershaft?"

There was a sharp intake of breath as Alf's eyes widened. "You don't – she wouldn't – she couldn't hurt our Miss Gracie, could she?"

Marlon sighed. "Give her the chance, she'd eat her alive."

"But…" Alf was quivering with shock. "But Miss Gracie's a Trueheart! And what about the crones? And the Web—"

"If she turns werewolf while she's inside the House, who knows what'll happen?" Marlon shrugged. "Not me. Seen a lot of things in my time, but a half-blood werewolf face to face with a Trueheart? Nah. The hopeful money's on the Trueheart, but it ain't a cert. Tricksy things, werewolves. Could go either way."

"We have to stop her!" Alf was now flying in agitated circles round and round his uncle's head. "Come on, Unc! We've gotta go! Right now!"

"Hold your horses." Marlon tapped his head. "Know what's needed right now, kid? Brain."

Alf looked doubtful. "If you say so. But——"

"There ain't no buts," Marlon glowered. "Think about it. We fly in – the dame turns hairy – then what? You got superhero powers?"

Suitably squashed, Alf settled once more beside his uncle. "What about telling Mr Prince?" he suggested.

Marlon stretched his wings. "Better, kiddo. Better. But we don't want the guns goin' off before we've set up the target."

"Guns?" Alf stared. "When did Mr Prince get a gun?"

His uncle snorted. "Figure of speech. Don't want the lad rushing into action before we know where the action is."

"But we do!" Alf protested. "Miss Gracie's in terrible danger!"

"Nah. Potential of danger? Yup. Certainty of danger? Unresolved. So what does a Super Spotter do?"

Alf leapt to attention. "Check the situation. Watch and listen. Grade and assess. Report to higher authority as appropriate!"

"Correct. So – what are you waiting for? Get going!"

Alf looked surprised. "What about you?"

Marlon raised an eyebrow. "Need your hand held?" he enquired, and Alf launched himself into the air with a squeak of protest.

"Alfred Batster – on his way!" And with a flip of his wing he was gone.

Marlon gave him a couple of moments, then followed him out of the barn. Instead of heading for the border of the kingdoms and the House of the Ancient Crones, however, he turned and swooped towards the palace. "Better see what's goin' on," he muttered as he flew. "Our Gracie could be in danger in more ways than one. Pack of werewolves? Or a pack of angry Royals? Hmph. Give me the werewolves every time."

Chapter Five

Marcus was whistling as he rode along. Life was good, he decided. Vincent's news could be dealt with when and if it happened, but for the moment there was a lot to look forward to. Prince Tertius had suggested a royal tournament as part of the Centenary Celebrations, and Marcus had jumped at the chance to avoid the speeches, parades and balls that everyone else seemed to think were necessary. What was more, he was now able to take himself off to see Gracie whenever he felt like it; all he had to do was claim that he needed the time away from home in order to do Serious Tournament Planning, and his parents positively encouraged him to leave the palace.

"Excellent to see you so involved in the Centenary Celebrations!" King Frank had told him with a slap on the back. "Glad to see you're taking part!" Marcus, who was not entirely without a conscience, had mumbled

 68

something about armour, and hurried away to the stables. He had soothed his guilty conscience by having a long discussion with the Ancient One about tournaments; it appeared that she had been present at several, and had supplied him with a good deal of useful information.

Tertius, an old friend, was equally delighted to have an excuse to steal away from his own palace. He explained to Marcus that married life was splendid, absolutely splendid, but a chap needed a break from time to time … and for this reason he happily provided Marcus with an alibi whenever he needed one. In return, Marcus reassured Princess Fedora that her young husband's regular absences were required for practice sessions, and research into the ancient weaponry of Times Past. He would have thought it a terrible breach of trust to reveal that Tertius spent the time fishing, a pursuit that Fedora considered totally unsuitable. Fishing, she believed, was for the Lower Classes. Royalty, she informed Tertius early on in their relationship, did not handle fish.

Recently, though, rather too many questions had been asked about how the tournament was progressing, and Marcus and Tertius had agreed to meet to concoct some kind of plan.

"It won't take long," Marcus told himself. "After all, it's only two guys on horseback bashing away at each other. And Tertius always falls off if his pony goes faster than a trot, so it's not as if we'll have to do much. We can arrange beforehand who's going to win. I expect it'd better be Terty − Fedora would be furious if he lost. And Gracie won't mind a bit. She'll understand. She always does. She's not at all like Fedora and Nina-Rose or that dreadful Princess Marigold..." Marcus smiled as he mentally compared the loud and opinionated Marigold with his calm and sensible Gracie. "Gracie's much prettier, too—"

The loud call of a trumpet broke into his thoughts, and he looked up to see a coach rattling towards him. As it drew nearer a familiar head popped out of a window, and called imperiously to the coachman to stop. Marcus reined in Glee, and waited. A moment later Princess Fedora flounced her way out, followed by a nervous-looking Tertius. Fedora's feet had hardly touched the ground before she began talking, and Marcus stifled a sigh. He could quite understand why Tertius needed to escape.

"So THERE you are, Marcus! Terty said you had a meeting today, but I said it would be FAR better if we came to see you. I've had such a fun idea! I was asking my darling Tootle Toes about your little tournament, and he's in such a muddle that I've decided to take

 70

over. I'm much MUCH better at organizing things than he is, aren't I, sweetie pie?"

Tertius cleared his throat, and threw an agonized look of appeal at Marcus. "If you say so, precious – but you should ask Marcus. Ahem. He's got our plans all worked out, haven't you, Marcus?"

Marcus hesitated, then rose to the occasion. "Absolutely. It's all sorted, Fedora. Nothing left to do. I'm afraid you've had a wasted journey—"

Fedora gave him a steely glare. "So what are these plans, exactly? I want to know, Marcus. I'm quite sure I can think of something better."

"They're – they're secret." Marcus folded his arms. "It would completely spoil the surprise if we told you. I expect that's why Terty sounded confused. He didn't want to give the game away, but he's much too nice to tell you to mind your own business."

It was Fedora's turn to hesitate. Marcus sounded as if he meant every word … but had she caught the suspicion of a wink? She turned on Tertius. "Is this true?"

"Of course! You don't think Marcus would tell you fibs, do you?" Tertius raised his eyebrows in what he hoped was a convincing manner. "Haven't I been telling you it was all sorted?"

"No," Fedora said baldly. "Every time I asked you told

me something different." She swung back to Marcus. "Is Arry going to be part of it? And Vincent? And Albion? Because I think ALL the princes should take part! I don't see why my darling should be the only one in danger of having a horrid spear stuck through his chest."

"What?" Tertius went pale. "Who said anything about spears?"

Marcus, realizing his house of cards was in danger of toppling, took a deep breath. "Spears? No no no. We won't be using spears, Fedora – and we won't be using swords either, will we, Tertius?"

Tertius gulped. "I should say not! Why, the very idea! The girls would be terrified!"

"So what will you be using?" Fedora's eyes were narrowed. "Tell me!"

"Lances," Marcus told her. Tertius was looking like a rabbit cornered by a ferret, and was unlikely to say anything sensible. "Long wooden poles, and they don't have sharp ends, and we'll be wearing armour so we can't possibly be hurt even if we do manage to whack each other – I mean, *hit*. But we'll be aiming for each other's shields, won't we, Terty?"

"Erm … yes." Tertius was so obviously about to fall apart that Marcus jumped off Glee and came to stand beside his fellow prince. He put a supportive arm

round his shoulders, and grinned cheerfully at Princess Fedora. "Tertius thought of the best bit, you know. He's told me all about knights, and jousting – and how important the girls are."

"Girls?" Fedora raised her eyebrows. "I hardly think girls are involved."

"Oh, but they are," Marcus said. In his head he was making a mental note to take the Ancient One a very large bunch of flowers. "A knight always has to have a lady to inspire him."

Tertius's eyes were wide with admiration as he looked at Marcus. "Ha! Exactly what I was thinking. Inspiration! That's you, my precious poochy pie..."

"And when the knight is ready," Marcus went on, "he rides into the tournament arena, and salutes the lady of his choice, and she steps forward to give him her hankie to wear in his helmet. And everybody claps, because..." For a moment Marcus faltered. The Ancient One had been vague on this point. "They clap because she's so inspiring! Oh, and beautiful, of course."

"A hankie? How very unhygienic." Fedora sniffed, but she was beginning to look interested. "And where is the lady when this happens?"

"On ... on a throne." Marcus's brain was working overtime. "On a stage, so everyone can see her."

This went down well. Fedora was almost smiling. "And what does she wear?"

"Her very best dress, of course." Marcus, making sure Fedora could not see him, pinched Tertius hard. "Isn't that right, Terty?"

Tertius had now had time to make a full recovery, and he came back into the fray with enthusiasm. "Absolutely right. Wasn't going to tell you, poppet – but you've wormed it out of us, clever little thing that you are. Ha ha ha! You're going to have the most lovely dress ever, and it'll be a present from me to you 'cos you're the most lovely inspiration ever!"

Fedora melted. "Oh, DARLING Tootle Toes!" She flung her arms round him. "What a beastly girl I am to doubt you. Will you ever forgive me?"

Marcus held up a warning finger. "He'll only forgive you if you don't ask any more questions. And you have to keep it a secret. We don't want anyone else to know, or it won't be a surprise."

"Oh, of COURSE! I won't breathe a word to anyone ... especially not Marigold." Fedora looked smug. "She'll be SO jealous when I have a gorgeous new dress, and she doesn't."

"Marigold?" Marcus asked. "What's she got to do with it?"

Fedora gave him a knowing look. "We all know you've got your eye on my dear little sister … and a little bird told me she might have her eye on you too!"

Marcus stared at her. "You're stark, staring mad."

"I say, Marcus old chap," Tertius protested, "that's a bit much! And my poppet has a point, you know. You'll need a lady fair. What was it I said? An inspiration…"

"But I'll have Gracie." Marcus was astonished that there could be any doubt about his choice. "Why on earth would I want anyone else?"

Fedora and Tertius exchanged meaningful glances, but neither spoke. Marcus looked from one to the other. "What is it?" he demanded. "You've been talking about me and Gracie, haven't you? I can tell!"

Tertius coughed. "Ahem. All a bit embarrassing, this. None of our business really."

"Rubbish, Terty!" Fedora gave her beloved a bracing glare. "You agreed with me! 'Not suitable' is what you said! You know you did!"

The worm finally turned. "No, I didn't," Tertius said. "It was YOU who said she wasn't suitable."

Fedora sniffed. "Isn't that the same thing?"

Marcus put his hand on Glee's neck to steady himself as he tried to keep his temper. "Hang on. Not suitable for what, exactly?"

"Gracie's not suitable for you." It was Fedora who answered. "We all agree. We had a little party, and…" Her voice died away. Marcus's scowl was terrifying.

"And who," he asked coldly, "is 'all' of you?"

Fedora turned to Tertius. "Vincent was there, wasn't he, sweetie? And Marigold. And Albion. And Nina-Rose, of course—"

"But not you and Arry," Tertius put in. "Arry was busy. You didn't answer the invitation," he added, a note of reproach in his voice.

A vague recollection of a gold-crested envelope lying unopened on the breakfast table tweaked Marcus's conscience. "Sorry," he said. "But either Gracie comes to the tournament, or I resign. I think she's suitable for me, and that's that."

He swung himself into the saddle, and glared down at Fedora. "And now I think I'll be going, unless there's anything else you want to tell me? No? Good. Terty – I'll see you soon. You can sort out some armour for us … and get a stage built. And two thrones." With a curt nod of farewell he turned Glee's head towards Gorebreath, and set off at a gallop.

Tertius sighed. "Oh dear. Now he's furious."

"Nonsense, Terty." Fedora opened the coach door and jumped inside. "All we have to do is tell Marigold she's going to be Marcus's lady of choice at the tournament, and make sure she gets there early. Even that Gillypot girl wouldn't dare push in when it's all set up."

Tertius was looking worried. "I don't know, petal…" A thought struck him. "Has Marigold really got her eye on Marcus?"

"Of course she hasn't." Fedora shook her head at her husband's obtuseness. "She likes Vincent. They have tea and cake together every Tuesday. But we've got to get Marcus away from the Gillypot girl somehow. Arry actually likes her, and even Albion said she was all right."

Tertius scratched his head. "You know what, poppet? I don't see why there's a problem."

"Stupid!" Fedora's eyes flashed. "Arry's engaged to Nina-Rose, isn't he? And Nina-Rose is my sister! And Marcus, in case you haven't remembered, is Arry's brother – so if Marcus marries Gracie then we'll ALL be related to her! And Terty – she's WEIRD! She lives with WITCHES! And if she comes here to the Five Kingdoms who knows what'll come with her? Now, hop in, and if you're very good and agree with me I'll let you hold my hand all the way home." Tertius, defeated, did as he was told.

Chapter Six

Foyce Undershaft was humming as she wove. She had been humming all day; there had been occasional pauses when she murmured quietly to herself, but the humming always began again, and Edna, Val and Gracie were sitting over a cup of afternoon tea in the kitchen and wondering why.

"She almost sounds happy," Gracie said. "But I don't think she can be. When I lived with her and her father and things were going well she never hummed." She did not add that Foyce's idea of demonstrating happiness had been to pinch Gracie until her eyes watered, or pull her plaits until she begged for mercy.

Val shook her head. "It's just as you thought, Edna. She's up to something. She's been here for months, and she's never hummed before. And we've all noticed the Web is acting very strangely. One minute it's clear, and the next it's covered in streaks and splotches ... and that means trouble."

"That's true." Edna stirred her tea, and helped herself to a biscuit. "Gracie, dear – has Gubble sorted out the shutters in Foyce's room?"

Gracie put down her cup. "Yes. I'm not sure anyone will ever be able to open them again, though. Gubble used the most enormous nails, and he banged them into the walls with a huge hammer."

Gubble, who was sitting at the other end of the table trying to eat sugar with a fork, beamed. "Ug. No opening now. All dark."

"Well done, Gubble." The Ancient One nodded at him. "I'd say it's a good thing they can't be opened – for the time being, at least. Once this full moon is over we'll see how Foyce behaves. Maybe now she can't see the moonlight things will change."

"She was doing so well to begin with," Val said with regret. "I thought we'd be able to deal with her quite quickly. I mean, I know she made our Gracie's life a total misery before she came here, and she was terribly vicious and evil, but once she got here she did seem to settle into a kind of grumpy acceptance. But then all of a sudden she started smiling, and now she's HUMMING!"

Edna looked thoughful. "I always said she'd be a hard nut to crack. I'd say she's been trying her best to lull us into a sense of security. She's half werewolf, remember, and werewolves are clever. Very clever. They have to be, because their lives are never easy. And often a werewolf is clever in all the right ways, and is a pleasure to know … but from time to time a werewolf goes the wrong way, and a bad werewolf is about as evil and cunning as you can get. Foyce may well have been making plans for a very long time."

Gracie leant across the table and replaced Gubble's fork with a teaspoon. "But where would she go? I don't think her father can help her."

Val gave a loud shout of laughter. "He certainly can't! He'll be paying for his wickedness up until the end of time and beyond, and serves him jolly well right."

"I'm not sure Foyce wants to escape," Edna said slowly. "I don't think that's what she's after."

Both Val and Gracie stared at her in surprise. "Not escape?"

The Ancient One gave a deep sigh. "Revenge. I think she wants revenge."

Val's eyes widened in sudden understanding, but Gracie was still puzzled. "But what for?"

Edna took Gracie's hand. "Gracie, dear – you're a Trueheart. You see the best in people, and if there is good in them you bring that goodness out ... but you also have the reverse effect. You make evil people worse. Think about it. What brought Foyce here? She'll never admit that she deserves punishment ... so who does she blame? Who would she like to hurt more than anyone else in the whole wide world?"

Gracie paled, but before she could answer there was a wild flutter of wings and Alf landed on her shoulder, panting hard.

"Our Miss Gracie," he said. "That's who she wants to hurt! But never fear! Alf Batster is here! And ... and ... and ... me and Unc will look after Miss Gracie, who is very very DEAR!"

"Ug." Gubble came stomping round the table. "Gubble here too." He glowered at Alf. "Gubble bigger than bat. Stronger. Much stronger!"

Edna and Val began to laugh and Gracie, after a momentary pause, laughed too. "That's all right, then," she said cheerfully. "I won't worry."

"Good." Val picked up the teapot. "And I know we're only old women, but we Ancient Crones do still have a certain amount of power. And of course, there's the Web. As long as we keep weaving Gracie can't

 82

come to too much harm, can she, Edna? Now, shall we have another cup of tea?"

Outside the door Foyce, sent by Elsie to ask for tea and toast, froze. "Gracie can't come to much harm? That's what YOU think. The little slug deserves to wriggle on a red-hot pin, and I'll make sure she does." Then, rearranging her face into an enchanting smile, she hurried into the kitchen, where the Ancient One was still sitting over a teapot.

Far away in Wadingburn, Queen Bluebell was also presiding over a tea table. She was enjoying herself immensely. Her very dear friend Hortense, the Dowager Duchess of Cockenzie Rood, had come to visit, as had also Queen Kesta of Dreghorn. They were happily discussing the forthcoming Centenary Celebrations; all three were gratified to discover that they felt the planned marches, parades and exhibitions of martial power were most unnecessary.

"It isn't as if we've ever had to fight any wars," the duchess pointed out. "In fact, in my opinion we don't need an army at all."

Queen Kesta sighed. "Boys," she said. "It's the boys. They just LOVE dressing up and wearing gold buttons and rattling their swords. And at least the marching up and down gives them some exercise."

Bluebell snorted. "Vincent's never marched a step in his life. Totally hopeless, that boy. All he ever thinks about is cake." She looked across the room to where Loobly was sitting curled up in a large armchair, cuddling a remarkably large rat. "And she's not much better. I've done my best to give her a bit of education, but she's just not interested in anything that doesn't have whiskers. Which reminds me. I want to ask your opinion about an idea I've had ... but let's have tea first. I was up early this morning baking muffins, and though I do say so myself they've turned out remarkably well. And Cook's made some of her special chocolate eclairs."

There was a dissenting squeak from the armchair. "No eclairs, Grandmother. Vinnie did take the eclairs."

"What?" Bluebell raised her lorgnette in order to inspect her granddaughter. "Taken them where?"

Loobly looked as if she wished she hadn't spoken. "In ... in his picnic."

"PICNIC?" Bluebell's voice increased in volume. "And what picnic was that, may I ask? Where's he gone?"

Loobly buried her face in a cushion. "Don't know, Grandmother."

Bluebell rose to her feet and strode across the room. Towering over her granddaughter, she removed the cushion, leaving Loobly clutching her rat as if her life depended on it. "You can no more tell a lie, Loobly, than fly. You do know, but you think I won't like the answer. Isn't that the case?"

Loobly nodded.

"Then you'd better tell me at once," Bluebell ordered, "so I can get ready to mop up the mess."

"Is gone to Gorebreath," Loobly said with a wriggle of acute embarrassment. "Gone to tell 'bout Gracie. 'Bout Gracie being queen." As her grandmother's face gradually turned an unbecoming shade of purple she added, "Did tell Vinnie Gracie is good! Loobly likes! Loobly like lots!"

Hortense, who had been unashamedly listening, got up to join her friend. "What is it, Bluebell? What's Vincent been up to? You look dreadful!"

Bluebell, incandescent with rage, was unable to speak.

"Punch the cushion, dear," the duchess advised. "Imagine it's Vincent's head. You'll feel much better."

"Really, Hortense!" Queen Kesta was shocked, but Hortense merely smiled at her.

"You've got girls, dear. Bluebell suffers from Vincent. I suffer from Albion. Sometimes punching a cushion is the only way to relieve one's feelings."

Bluebell took a deep breath and hit the cushion so hard that it burst. As feathers flew in all directions she threw herself back in her chair, and groaned loudly. "That boy," she said. "That stupid, STUPID boy."

"But what's he done?" Kesta was pale with agitation. "I don't understand."

"What he's done," Bluebell told her, "is rush off to Gorebreath to tell King Frank and Queen Mildred that I intend to leave my kingdom to Gracie Gillypot." She gave a mirthless guffaw. "When you come to think about it, it could be quite entertaining. I'd love to be a fly on the wall when he tells them. I bet they'll be in a state of high old agitation – if they believe him, of course." She sat up, looking more normal. "And that's a good point. They'll probably take no notice of him, and I've done terrible things to my blood pressure quite unnecessarily."

Hortense chuckled. "I'm sure you're right, dear. But why would you leave the kingdom to Gracie? Are you thinking of retiring?"

"I certainly am." Queen Bluebell of Wadingburn folded her arms. "I've been ruling this kingdom far too long. I'm fed up with all the rules and regulations, and the way that royalty is supposed to behave. All this parading and showing off – a load of nonsense! I want to have some fun before I'm too old to enjoy myself."

"Quite right." Hortense nodded her agreement. "I often feel the same, but what can I do? Dowby's King of Cockenzie Rood, but he's always busy with his horses, and Albion's got the brain of a goldfish. He could never cope on his own. If I thought he could I'd be with you in a flash."

Bluebell gave her friend a thoughtful look. "Hm," she said. "We ought to talk more about this. Have you ever fancied meeting a werewolf?"

Kesta gave a little scream. "Bluebell! How could you? And what did you mean?" She sounded anxious. "You're not serious, are you? You're not really thinking of leaving Wadingburn to Gracie Gillypot?"

"It was an idea I had, that's all." Bluebell sighed. "No more than that … at the moment, anyway. The more I think about it, the more certain I am that Gracie's got far too much sense to want to be bothered with a kingdom. But I was silly enough to mention it to Vincent, and it seems he took me seriously. Oh well. There's nothing I can do about it now. Let's have our tea. Even if we've been deprived of our chocolate eclairs we've still got the muffins."

The three women drew closer together, and the

conversation became general as the tea and muffins arrived. It was noticeable, however, that Queen Kesta wasn't her usual chatty self; Hortense had to ask her twice if she wanted sugar in her tea, and she kept dropping things. After the third teaspoon had landed on the carpet Bluebell put down her cup and saucer. "What is it, Kesta?" she asked. "Something's up, and it's no good saying it isn't. I can tell."

Kesta went very pink. "Oh, Bluebell! It … it's just the thought of you resigning. What would we do without you? You're so very, very sensible!"

Bluebell gave an embarrassed cough. "Ahem. Sorry. Muffin went down the wrong way. Nice of you, Kesta m'dear, but nobody's indispensable."

"Kesta's right," Hortense said slowly. "You balance us all out. There does seem to be a certain —" she paused while she searched for the right word — "a certain self-satisfaction in the Five Kingdoms. And you challenge that in the most refreshing way."

"You mean our fellow Royals are smug and much too pleased with themselves," Bluebell said.

"I suppose I do," Hortense agreed. "What do you think, Kesta?"

Queen Kesta of Dreghorn had never been a forceful woman. She had brought up a string of daughters, and every daughter had many strong opinions that they never hesitated to inflict on their mother. As a result, Kesta was reluctant to offer a view of her own; she was too used to being shouted down by loud cries of "MA! That's RIDICULOUS!" She screwed up her forehead in earnest thought, however, and did her best to consider Bluebell's remark.

"I'm not really sure," she said at last. "All I know is that I like things the way they are. I mean, we're all very comfortable together, aren't we?"

Bluebell heaved a gusty sigh. "That, Kesta, dear, is one of the reasons that I'm bored. I do envy the young, don't you? Just look at what Marcus and Gracie get up to – adventures with trolls, and witches, and all sorts. If I were younger I'd join them like a shot."

A look of extreme alarm came over Queen Kesta's amiable face. "Oh NO, Bluebell! That's why we have the border! We really, REALLY don't need to know about horrible things like witches. I do so wish Marcus would leave well alone, and be more like his darling brother. I lie awake at night sometimes, worrying that he's going to bring something terrible back with him."

"You make it sound like measles!" Bluebell gave a loud snort. "Haven't you ever realized, Kesta, that Marcus has been helping to keep us safe? Him and Gracie."

 89

"Oh no, Bluebell." Kesta's eyes were wide. "Our ancestors set up the border, and it's that that protects us. And, now that you've mentioned Gracie again, I have to confess that I do rather agree with darling Fedora and Nina-Rose. She's a nice enough child, of course, but I don't think she's a good influence on Marcus. Princes shouldn't go across the border. Not ever … and as for leaving your kingdom to her, Bluebell, you MUST be joking!"

Bluebell took a deep breath, but before she could explode Hortense put a restraining hand on her arm. "Might I have another cup of tea?" she asked. "And another of those delicious muffins?"

After a moment's internal struggle, Bluebell subsided. "Of course. And do let's talk about something else. I'm beginning to worry about my blood pressure again…"

Chapter Seven

The evening was overcast and gloomy. Billy, tired out with his long journey, clung to the eaves of the House of the Ancient Crones and slept. The voice in his head had eased during the latter part of the day, and he had been able to stop and doze a couple of times along the way, but his dreams had been so horrendous that he had been glad to wake up and continue his journey. On and on he had flown, his small wings aching with fatigue; even though the voice was less insistent, the demand was still there. Now he had reached the House, and suddenly his mind was empty. He had no dreams. Nothing.

He woke with a start, and for a moment was quite unable to think where he was. When he remembered, he was miserable. "I want to go home," he whispered. Tentatively he stretched his wings. Could he? Was he free? He flew a small circle, and then a wider one … yes! His way was clear! And his mother would be waiting for him—

"Bat. Take a message."

It wasn't a request. It was an order. The witch woman knew he was there, and she wanted him to do something, and that was why she had emptied his mind.

"Yes."

What else could he say? He was much too tired to make even the faintest attempt to resist.

"In the forest. The wolf woman. Tell her I'm here. *Do you understand?*"

The venom in the voice shook Billy wide awake. "I understand," he whispered, even though his heart was frantically trying to thump its way out of his tiny chest.

"Go, then. *GO NOW!*"

Billy summoned all his strength, and flew. Behind him he heard a peal of silvery laughter that all but sent him dropping to the ground, frozen with terror. "I'll know if you try and fly away," called the voice. "I'll know! And it'll be the worse for you, little bat. I'll skin you alive, and pick at your bones with my sharp white teeth…"

With an agonized squeak Billy redoubled his speed. Over the roof he flew, and the chimneys bent out of his way. Through the wisps of mist, and away from the

 92

hollow … and there, beyond, lay the Less Enchanted Forest, crouched in the gathering darkness. Without the cheery companionship of Alf to drive away imagined terrors it had the appearance of some horrible half-formed monster. Billy forced himself to fly over the first few trees, and then on and on, hardly knowing what he was looking for. He had no idea where he had been the night before, and he zigzagged to and fro, desperately trying to recognize something familiar … but every tree creaked and groaned as if it knew a dark and terrible secret, and the bushes whispered and rustled ominously.

There she was! The tall thin figure was walking swiftly along a narrow path, a basket of fir cones in one bony hand and a bunch of twigs in the other. Billy flung himself towards her, squeaking as he flew. "She said to tell you! She said, tell the wolf woman! Tell her she's in the House!"

Agony Clawbone stood very still. "Who is that?" she asked, her voice harsh and rusty as if she seldom spoke. "Who is speaking to me?"

"It's me, Billy," Billy gasped. "She told me to tell you! She's in the House!"

"Who is in the House?"

Billy fluttered to a thornbush and clung to a twisted spike. "The nasty one! The witch! She peeped at me

 93

through a hole ... she tells me to do things I don't want to..."

Agony, with the lithe movement of a beast pouncing on its prey, twisted round and snatched Billy from his perch. "Does she have a name, this witch?"

"Mr Alf ... Mr Alf said she was..." Billy struggled to remember. He was half dead with fear, but Agony's pale grey eyes bored into his. "Under ... Under ... half?"

There was a sharp intake of breath. "Undershaft?"

Billy nodded. "Yes."

"Tchah!" Agony tossed Billy into the air as if she wanted rid of him completely. "Get away! Get away from here!"

Only too relieved to find himself alive and not crushed to a pulp by iron fingers, Billy did as he was told. As he flew for his life Agony called after him, "House? What house?"

Billy didn't answer. The wind was with him, and he had one thing and one thing only in mind. A vision of Gracie Gillypot and the warmth of her hands kept him in the air ... surely he was getting closer now? Exhaustion was creeping over him, deep into his very bones ... each lift and drop of his wings was harder than the one before.

"Must ... get ... there..." he whispered, and saw the mist lying thick beneath him, filling the hollow to the rim.

"Nearly ... there..." Billy shut his eyes, and dived. Relief lent him speed, and he hit the solid object in his path so hard that the breath was knocked out of his body. Gubble, thinking he had been stung by a wasp, dropped his load of logs.

"OOF!" Gubble sat down with a thump, clasping Billy's limp body in his large green hands. "OOF! Bad bat! Very bad ... bat? BAT?" With a thick green finger he gently stroked Billy's damp and matted fur, but there was no response. "Find Gracie." Gubble struggled to his feet. "Gracie make better." And, forgetting all about his logs, he stomped off towards the house.

Agony Clawbone remained standing where Billy had found her. Her eyes were closed, and she was muttering to herself. "Undershaft. Undershaft ... that was the man." She shivered, overcome by old and bitter memories she had tried her best to bury.

It had been Moon Time and, as always, she had turned. Safe in her human's house it had been nothing much more than fur, and running on all four paws, and a sharpening of her features … and it had never bothered the man before. But then he had come staggering in from a long and beery evening in the Battered Herring, and everything changed.

Once again Agony saw the angular figure of Mange Undershaft, and heard the sound of his harsh breathing as he seized her by the scruff of the neck and threw her out of their house, bolting the door against her frantic howling. He had stood at the window and jeered as she padded round and round trying to find a way back in and, worst of all, she had seen the child climb up to stand at his side and laugh with him. Laugh, and point at her mother, and laugh again while her father clapped and urged her on. That had been the moment when Agony had lost hope, and slunk away to the forest. There she had found a dark cave where she could rest, and weep. When she regained her human shape she had set off to find her wolf family, hoping for comfort, but they had rejected her. They felt, and Agony could only agree with them, that she had made a fatal error in believing that a human being like Mange Undershaft could ever be trusted. His wickedness had tainted her; she was not to be trusted either.

* * *

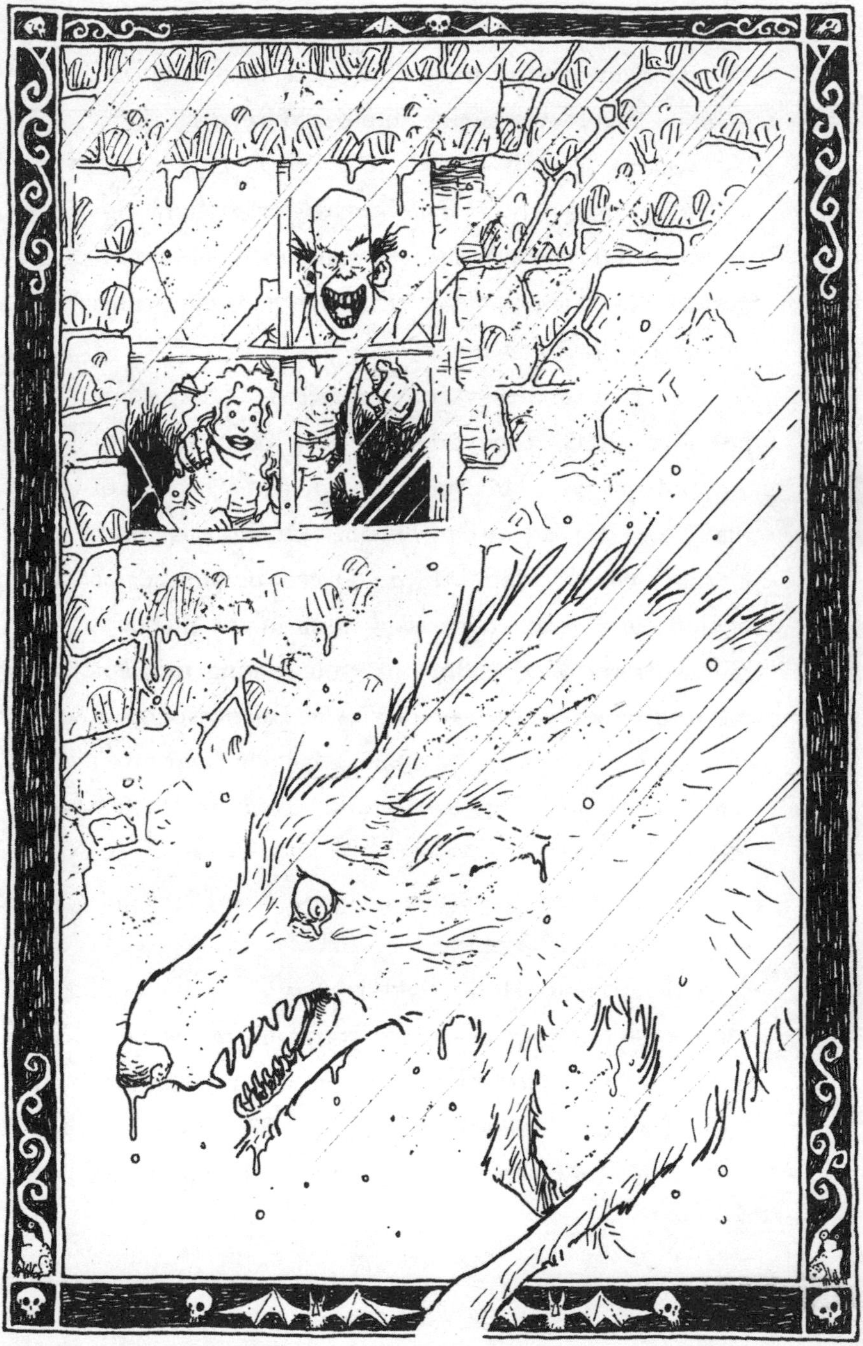

"Who's trying to find you?" The voice came from the shadows, and Agony swung round. "What house?"

"Nothing, Keel. Nobody."

"I don't believe you." The bushes swayed and a figure stepped out … a figure that could easily have been mistaken for Agony's taller shadow. "Someone wants you, cousin. Is it that man?"

"No. He's gone." Agony shivered. "You know he's gone, Keel. You and Jukk have been following me and spying on me long enough to be certain of that." She scowled at her cousin. "Or did you think I hadn't noticed? One of you always beside me, or behind me … watching and waiting in the shadows, but never speaking. What are you waiting for? For me to disgrace you yet again?" Her voice rising, she stepped towards Keel. "Is that what you fear? You really believe I could trust a man a second time? After all that I suffered?"

"Yet someone is searching for you." Keel's eyes glittered. "Who is it? Tell me!"

"I don't know. How could I know? The bat said 'she'—" Agony gave a sudden start, and clutched at her head. "Keel! Could it … could it be my daughter?"

Keel stared at her. "Your daughter? Foyce?"

"It might be! Or then again … it might be the other."

Agony sank down against a tree trunk. "I heard there was another child, later on. Fracture … they lived in Fracture. Two girls and the man. But I never knew the second child, or where she came from." Agony looked up at her brother. "But why would Foyce look for me now? She laughed at me, Keel. She rejected me. I was shut out, and she never once asked her father to let me back in – oh, I could have borne the man's beatings and cruelty if she had only called for me. If she had needed me … just a little."

Keel's gaze softened a little. "Forget her, cousin."

Agony leapt to her feet and seized his arm. "How can I forget my own daughter? And how can I ignore a call that might come from her? Imagine if it's really truly Foyce! She may be like her father, she may be evil … but perhaps not all evil? It could be me, her mother, that she's searching for!" Her grip tightened. "Keel! You can find her! Find her, wherever she is, and bring her to me."

Keel hesitated. "Why not go yourself?"

A tremor ran through Agony's body. "The bat said she was in a house. I can't go near a house … don't ask me! Never!"

The older werewolf heard the appeal in her voice. "I'll try," he said. "But do you know what you're risking? What can she want of you now?"

Agony shrugged her bony shoulders. "Whatever it is, I need to know."

"So be it." Keel nodded.

"Thank you." Agony pushed her hair away from her face. "Thank you, cousin Keel."

Keel shook his head. "It's as well it was me following you, and not Jukk. He would have nothing to do with the daughter of that man."

Agony wasn't listening to him. She pointed at a faint path that wound its way in and out of the trees. "Go that way, Keel. Go to the House of the Ancient Crones. That must be what was meant – there's no other house in the forest that I know of. They're strange, and powerful, but they won't harm you. I've heard good things about them. Go there…"

Keel nodded, and a moment later he was gone, lost in the shadows. Agony sighed, and began to make her way to her shelter.

Chapter Eight

Vincent was feeling extremely pleased with himself. He had left King Frank and Queen Mildred in a splendid state of agitation about his grandmother's plans, and while they were discussing what should be done he had quietly consumed the rest of the cake. He had then been offered a large plate of meringues and, thinking that it would have been rude to refuse them, he had dealt with them in the right and proper fashion. Biscuits had followed, and a substantial apple pie with cream ... but then, rather curiously, Queen Mildred had told the helpful maid that nothing more was required, thank you.

When Vincent finally came to take his leave Nina-Rose had kissed him goodbye, which he took to mean that she agreed with him on the subject of Gracie Gillypot, and he had kissed her back with enthusiasm and a generous dispersal of crumbs. Although he detected a certain lack of heartiness in Arioso's handshake, he put it down to an objection to stickiness rather than any disagreement with his views. Or quite possibly, Vincent thought, Arry was jealous of the favour Nina-Rose had shown him. He had been momentarily disconcerted to find no sign of his coach, but a page had been despatched to track it down, and he was now comfortably watching the moon-bathed landscape roll past the windows while toying with the remains of his picnic. All in all, he decided, it had been a very worthwhile expedition.

"Rather a pity that Marigold wasn't there," he mused. "Nice girl, Marigold. No nonsense about her. Shame it's getting so late … I could have gone to see her at Dreghorn. Maybe I could go tomorrow? I could take another picnic. I'm sure Grandmother won't—"

Vincent sat up. His grandmother. He had forgotten about his grandmother. She would be waiting up for him… Would she guess what he had been doing? She had an uncanny gift of knowing when he had ideas of his own, and her usual reaction was to disapprove. His self-satisfaction drained away, and he drooped against the cushions.

"It's not fair," he told himself. "I've just saved

Wadingburn from a terrible fate. She should be grateful." This remark did not comfort him as much as he felt it ought, and he peered into the picnic basket to see if there was better consolation there. The stale crumbs and smears of grease were unappetizing, however, and he sank back with a groan. "She's going to be angry. I'm sure she is." Vincent began to pout. "I should have stayed the night in Gorebreath. Funny how they didn't ask me. And Queen Mildred almost hustled me out! How does she know if it's past my bedtime or not? Bit of cheek, now I come to think of it. Rude, in fact. There I was, trying to be helpful, and—"

Vincent's monologue came to an abrupt halt as the coach lurched and stopped. There was a loud shout from the coachman, and an answering shout from close by; Vincent flinched, and considered hiding in the picnic basket. Marcus was the last person he felt like talking to – but he was given no choice. The coach door was flung open, and Marcus, Prince of Gorebreath, was staring in at him. His expression made Vincent look again at the basket, and for the first time ever regret his size.

"I want to talk to you," Marcus said. "I've just been home, and I found Mother and Father in a complete stew – well, Father is, and Mother always agrees with everything he says – and he's talking about Royal Precedents and Defence of the Realm and stuff like that in the most pompous way ever. And he keeps going on and on about royalty being special – and he called Gracie a commoner! I nearly hit him." Marcus's brow darkened further. "I would have, too, if it wouldn't have made things worse and upset Mother. And it's all your fault. Father says you told him that Bluebell's been talking to her prime minister, and that means she has to be serious about resigning – but you never said that when I was listening. I know you, Vincent – you make things up so people think you're clever. What I want you to tell me is, is it really true?"

Vincent's very small brain seized up completely. He opened and shut his mouth, but was quite unable to answer.

"Erm..." he said.

Marcus scowled. "I'm waiting."

"Erm ... Grandmother said she WANTED to talk to the prime minister." Vincent put one hand on the picnic basket for moral support. "That was all I said – honestly it was! I never said she'd actually done it – ask Arry! Ask Nina-Rose! They'll tell you! Come and ask Grandmother! She'll tell you as well!"

There was a pause while Marcus studied Vincent's face, and Vincent strengthened his hold on the handle of the basket. At last Marcus said, "You know what? That's exactly what I'm going to do."

Vincent, intensely relieved, managed a smile. "Good thinking! Hop in. Sorry about the crumbs—"

"I'm not coming with you," Marcus told him. "I'm going to ride on ahead. I'll see you there." He slammed the coach door shut and disappeared into the darkness. A moment later Vincent heard the sound of hoofbeats galloping into the distance, followed by a whistle from his coachman as he cheered on the horses. As the coach rumbled on its way Vincent began to wonder what kind of reception he was going to get from his grandmother. Anxiety gave him hiccups, and the discovery of an uneaten ham roll made him feel faintly sick.

Marcus, as he rode, was still brooding over the scene with his father. He and his father had had their differences before; King Frank believed that royalty moved in a very different sphere from the inhabitants of his kingdom, whereas Marcus knew that kings and queens and princes and princesses were no better than anyone else. If asked, he would have said that they tended to be worse. In his view they gave themselves quite unnecessary airs and graces, and their determination to consider themselves superior drove him to distraction. He had always known that his father did not approve of his relationship with Gracie, but it had never been made so apparent before. "Gracie – a commoner!" Marcus fumed. "How dare he? She's the most uncommon person I've ever met. I'd much rather be like her than Father ... and if he thinks I'm going to give her up he's got another think coming. I'll give up being a prince if that's what it takes ... being royal doesn't do me any good. Doesn't do anyone any good ... look at Vincent, and Albion ... total idiots. And even Arry. He's better than they are, but once he's married to Nina-Rose he'll be completely under her thumb. And Tertius ... he's OK when he's away from Fedora, but when she's there he's a wimp." Marcus heaved a sigh, and pulled Glee back into a steady trot. "Sorry, old boy," he apologized. "Didn't mean to take it out on you." The pony whinnied in sympathy, and Marcus looked round. The lights of Wadingburn were shining in the distance, and his mood lifted a little. Bluebell would understand, and sympathize ... unless she had indeed, as Vincent suggested, gone mad.

"Feeling better yet, kiddo?"

Marcus jumped. "Marlon!" The bat was hovering

over his head. "Where did you spring from?"

"Been behind you all the way," Marlon said, "but you were going like the clappers. Saw your face, and thought you'd best ride it off." He chuckled, and landed on Marcus's shoulder. "Liked your style with young Vincent. Really put the wind up him."

Marcus blushed, then grinned. "I feel a bit bad about that now."

The bat shrugged. "Got good reason to be fed up. Your Uncle Marlon heard it all."

Marcus looked puzzled. "Heard what?"

"Barney with yer dad. Alf tipped me off, and I knew there'd be a ruckus." Marlon sniffed. "Can't go upsetting apple carts without a load of rotten apples rolling out. Bluebell's biggest fan, me, but she's started something tricky."

"Were you there all the time?" Marcus asked. "I didn't see you."

"Waved, but you were too busy squaring up for a fight with His Maj. You need to check out your curtain rails, kid. We Batsters like to keep a close eye on what's hangin'."

The sense of injustice overwhelmed Marcus yet again. "He was SO unfair! Gracie's a million times better than any of us. Why can't he see that? 'Not a suitable companion for my son…' How DARE he?"

Marlon, who had observed King Frank's purple face and popping eyes with interest, made a sympathetic noise, then added, "Running scared, I'd say."

Marcus was so shocked at this suggestion that he almost fell out of his saddle. "SCARED?"

"Yup. What does Gracie Gillypot mean to someone like your pa? Life outside the border. And you can do two things about life outside the border. Go and check it out, or keep your peepers firmly shut. Anyone ever talk about werewolves when you were a youngster? Nah. Chat about giants? Never. Mention the fact that there are zombies roamin' round the forests? Not a chance. Pretend they aren't there, and you've got no worries. But if your kid insists on making friends with someone who lives in those great big scary places − then wooeeee!" Marlon whistled. "You can't pretend any more, can you? Think about it. Your kid's girlfriend lives with three weird old women who might or might not be witches and, just occasionally, you wake up in the middle of the night and have a nasty little suspicion that those three old women are keeping the kingdoms safe. What does that do? It makes you feel VERY peculiar. So you turn over in bed and − like I said − keep your peepers tightly shut."

 108

Marcus rubbed his head. "But … but Gracie's a Trueheart…"

"Think that makes it any better? Nah." Marlon shook his head. "Ten times worse."

"So what do I do?" Marcus asked. "I've got to do something. I'm not giving Gracie up, and I'm not going to stop crossing the border either."

"Your call, kid." Marlon folded his wings. "I'm just a bat, remember."

"I think," Marcus said slowly, "I need to see Gracie and the Ancient Crones. I'll forget about Vincent for now. But I'd better hurry, or everyone will be tucked up in bed."

In Dreghorn, Queen Kesta was fast asleep and snoring gently. Her daughters, however, were wide awake and squabbling loudly.

"But WHY, Marigold?" Princess Fedora stamped her foot, and glared at her younger sister. Marigold carefully chose another chocolate from the box Fedora had brought with her to Dreghorn Palace.

"I like strawberry creams best," she remarked. "Don't you? All pink and squidgy and sweet." She giggled. "Like me, Vinnie says."

Fedora went on glaring. "Don't change the subject.

 109

All we want you to do is to arrive really early at the Celebration Tournament and sit with Marcus and be his – what did you call it, Terty darling?"

Tertius, who had taken himself off to an armchair at the other end of the room, looked up. "Lady Fair, my poppet. Just like you are to me. My chosen one. My darling sweetest pudding—"

"Yes." Fedora cut him off with an imperious wave of her hand. "So that's what we want you to be, Marigold. Isn't that right, Nina-Rose?"

Nina-Rose giggled. "You can be Marcus's pudding."

"Shan't." Marigold licked her fingers and chose another chocolate. "I want to sit with my darling Vinnie. He's promised to bring a super-dooper picnic. Besides, Marcus is weird. He doesn't like me. He likes that Gracie Gillypot girl."

Fedora's exasperated sigh echoed round the royal sitting room. "Marigold! You haven't been listening to a word I said! That's EXACTLY why we want you to sit with Marcus. So the Gillypot girl can't!"

Nina-Rose nodded. "If you're there she can't push her way in, can she?"

"She might." Marigold ate the last chocolate and sighed. "Did you bring any more? That wasn't a very big box."

"It was HUGE, and you're a greedy pig—" Fedora began, but Nina-Rose elbowed her sharply, and she forced herself to smile. "Erm ... suppose we buy you a new dress, Marigold? EVERYBODY will be looking at us, and we'll be sitting on dear little thrones on a stage."

Nina-Rose turned and stared at her sister. "On THRONES? On a STAGE?"

Fedora hesitated. She had meant to keep the details of the tournament to herself. It was bad enough having to share the stage with Marigold; if Nina-Rose knew what was planned she would undoubtedly refuse to be left out ... even now her eyes were gleaming.

"You can't sit with us," she said. "Arry's not taking part in the tournament."

"Actually —" Nina-Rose made a mental note to redouble her efforts with the already-wilting Arry – "actually, Fedora, he's promised that he will." She crossed her fingers under the table. "He said he was absolutely LONGING for me to be his Lady Fair. So there."

Marigold sat up. If both her older sisters were going to be on display, the situation was different. "Did you say you'd buy me a new dress?"

"I'm sure Mother will buy us both new dresses," Nina-Rose said, with a careful eye on Fedora's frosty expression. "If we're going to be on a stage she'll want us to look our very best. I bet you're having a new dress, aren't you, Fedora?"

Fedora gave in. She was no match for Nina-Rose. "Darling Terty's buying me something VERY special."

Marigold beamed. "OK. If I get a new dress, I'll sit next to Marcus. Come on, Nina-Rose, let's go and ask Mother right now."

"You can't." Fedora shook her head, pleased to at least be able to postpone her sister's triumph. "She's gone to bed and she'll be asleep now. You'll have to wait until tomorrow – and don't forget, Marigold: you've promised! Hasn't she, Terty?"

Tertius, who had been dozing in his armchair, woke up with a jump. "What was that, my poppet?"

"Marigold's promised to sit with Marcus at the tournament," Fedora explained.

"And I'M going to be on the stage as well," Nina-Rose informed him, "because Arry's going to play at tournamenting too."

"Oh, I say – is he really?" Tertius's forehead wrinkled. "But ... but I don't think he can, actually, Nina-Rose old bean. It's the sort of thing that's done in twos, you see. One prince against another."

The etiquette of tournaments was nothing to Nina-

Rose, and she brushed Tertius's objection aside with a shrug. "You'll just have to make it work."

Fedora decided to pour oil on troubled waters. "Darling Terty," she cooed, "let's see what happens, shall we? After all, Arry has lots of duties, and they might prevent him from taking part. Now, we'd better be getting home." And she swept up her husband and propelled him to the door before any further discussion could be had.

Marigold and Nina-Rose, left together, were silent. Both were plotting to take their places centre stage at the tournament: Nina-Rose was determined that Arioso would be a participant, and was planning a relentless campaign; Marigold had seen an opportunity that she had no intention of discussing with her sister. She knew Nina-Rose would never rest until Arioso had agreed to take part, and Tertius had said that that would be a problem ... but what if she solved the problem by providing a fourth participant? She didn't entirely know what happened in a tournament – something like a tug-of-war, perhaps? – but she had no doubt that if Arry was capable of taking part, then Vincent could too.

"I'll tell him tomorrow," she decided. "Or – I know! I'll send a special messenger tonight. But I'll tell Vinnie to keep it utterly secret, and then Fedora and Nina-Rose can't interfere. After all, I'll still be doing what they want me to do – but I won't get stuck with stupid Marcus." Delighted with herself, she picked up the box of chocolates and had a thorough search amongst the wrappers in case she had missed something. Finding one last nutty crunch, a variety she particularly disliked, she offered it to Nina-Rose with every appearance of sisterly sweetness before heading off to find her box of pink frilly-edged and scented notepaper.

Chapter Nine

Gubble was nearly back at the House when Billy began to stir. The troll stopped to inspect the little bat, and saw he was trembling.

"Cold?" he asked tenderly. "Bat cold?"

Billy opened his eyes. A large green face was peering at him, and a large green mouth was opening wide...

With a faint squeak, Billy flapped his wings in an effort to escape, but he was too tired. He fell back, shut his eyes and waited to be eaten. When nothing happened, he cautiously opened one eye and saw the green face smiling at him.

"See Gracie," Gubble told him. "Gracie make better." And he stomped on.

Gracie was in the kitchen putting the kettle on for a hot-water bottle when Gubble came puffing through the door. "Bat," he announced. "Poorly bat." And he held out his hand. Gracie, with a cry of pity, took Billy from him. "What happened?" she asked. "Where did you find him?"

"Bat found Gubble." Gubble pointed at his large and rock-solid stomach. "Wheeee! *Thump*."

"Poor little bat." Gracie smoothed Billy's fur. "Where does it hurt?"

Billy gave a feeble groan. "Is my head, Miss Gracie."

Gracie glanced at Gubble's substantial body. "Your head, Billy? Did you bump it very hard?"

"Was the voice," Billy whispered. "It told me things, and I had to find the wolf woman, and it was a long, long way … and now my head hurts."

Her mind whirling, Gracie pulled an old tea towel towards her and made Billy a soft resting place in the corner of a kitchen drawer. "You're worn out," she said. "Have a good sleep here tonight, and then you'll feel better. You'll be quite safe."

"No!" The little bat fluttered anxiously. "The witch lady with the eye! It was her, Miss Gracie! She said to tell the wolf woman she was here and I didn't want to but Mr Alf wouldn't wake up 'n' so I had to go … and she said she'd eat me, Miss Gracie!"

"Who did? The wolf woman?" Gracie asked.

 116

"The witch lady!" Billy began to tremble. "The witch lady upstairs!"

"Hush…" Gracie soothed. "You're with me now, Billy. Don't worry about it any more."

Billy lay back in his nest. "If you say so, Miss Gracie…" His eyes closed, and Gracie heard the tiniest of snores. She looked at Gubble.

"Did you see anything, Gubble? What did he mean? What's Foyce been up to?"

Gubble scratched his head. "Not see nothing," he said. "Only bat when fetching wood. Ug! Wood! Gubble dropped wood! Bad Gubble. Gubble get." And he stomped out of the door, slamming it behind him. As this was his usual mode of exit Gracie did not take offence. She returned to the business of the hot-water bottle, but was interrupted by a knock on the door.

"Hello?" she said. "Is that you, Gubble?"

"It's me," said a familiar voice, and Marcus walked in, Marlon flying above his head. Gracie stared at them in surprise, and the prince grinned apologetically.

"Hi," he said. "The back door was wide open, so I came straight through. I'm really sorry it's so late, but I had to talk to you … and is Edna around?"

"She's weaving just now," Gracie said. "Alf's keeping her company. Marcus – what's happened?"

Marcus flung himself into a chair. "I'm fed up. Totally, completely and utterly."

There was the faintest of squeaks from the drawer behind him, and he turned to look. "Is that a bat? It's not Alf, is it?"

Gracie shook her head. "That's Billy."

"Alf's trainee?" Marcus peered at the little bat. "What's he doing here? Alf thought he'd gone home."

Marlon, swinging from his usual spot on the curtain rail, sat up and listened with interest.

"He's had a shock," Gracie explained. "He's not making a whole lot of sense, but he's been in the forest looking for a wolf woman, and −" she lowered her voice − "I think it was Foyce who sent him out there."

"Really? Why would she do that? Oh—" Marcus's eyes began to sparkle. "Hey! Isn't Foyce's mother a werewolf? Do you think she's looking for her?" He leant forward and seized Gracie's hand. "Weren't we saying that we wanted to meet a werewolf? Why don't we go and find her?"

"Find who, dear?" The Ancient One was standing in the doorway.

Marcus swung round. "Foyce's mother! Gracie thinks Foyce is looking for her—"

Edna put her finger to her lips, and Marcus was

 118

silent. The Ancient One glanced over her shoulder, then shut the door behind her. "What makes you think such a thing?"

Gracie pointed at the small sleeping bat. "It was Billy, Auntie Edna. He says he had a voice in his head, and it told him to go and find a wolf woman."

"And the voice belonged to Foyce." Edna stated it as a fact, and Gracie nodded.

"He calls her the witch."

Edna chuckled. "He does, does he?"

"You don't seem very worried, Auntie," Gracie said wonderingly. "Isn't it bad that Foyce is sending messages?"

"I'd be far more worried if she was sending messages to her father," the Ancient One said. "He's appalling, and Foyce grew up exactly like him." A small cough floated down from the curtain rail, and she glanced up. "Quite right, Marlon. She was worse. And as far as I know, Foyce's mother had a terrible time. Mange Undershaft drove her out of her own house."

Marcus was listening eagerly. "So could she be the wolf woman?"

"That I can't tell you." Edna sat down next to him. "It's possible. But there are a good many werewolves in the forest."

"I think we should go and find out," Marcus said. "It's not full moon until the day after tomorrow, so we'd be quite safe, wouldn't we?"

The Ancient One leant back in her chair. "And what, exactly, do you intend to do if you find her?"

Marcus opened his mouth, then closed it again and looked embarrassed. "You're quite right," he said. "I hadn't thought it through. Sorry."

Edna patted his hand. "Dear boy. Werewolves are proud creatures. And sometimes dangerous. You can't go and peer at them as if they were fish in a tank. If you really want to meet one I'm sure it can be arranged."

"Thank you," Marcus said, and he glanced at Gracie. "Maybe we could ask Bluebell to come too. She's longing to meet a werewolf. She told Vincent, and he was so shocked that he dashed over to tell Mother and Father."

Gracie laughed. "Did he? What did they say?"

Marcus began to fiddle with the cups and saucers on the table. "Well … that isn't quite all he came to tell them. There's been a bit of a … a fuss." He picked up a cup, then put it down again. "That's really … that's why I'm here."

"Marcus! Leave my crockery alone, and tell us what's been going on," Edna said. "Breaking cups won't help anything. That's part of a matching set, I'd have you know."

"It's Father," Marcus began. "He's being completely idiotic, and saying all kinds of ridiculous things – and I don't know what to do about it." He flushed as the day's events came back to him, and went on in a rush. "It all started because Vincent was in some kind of mad panic about Bluebell and you and Wadingburn, and everyone got all worked up about it – and Father said…" He grabbed Gracie's hand, and held it tightly. "He said you weren't to come to the Celebration Tournament, and he said that I needed to learn my place in society and I oughtn't to leave the Five Kingdoms and –" Marcus gulped loudly – "and I was letting him down by mixing with commoners." He stopped, put his head on the table and groaned. "I can't bear it."

Gracie made a sympathetic noise and moved as if she was going to hug him, but the Ancient One held up a warning hand. "Really, Marcus! Pull yourself together, and stop feeling sorry for yourself. If anyone has anything to bear it's Gracie, but I don't see her moaning and groaning. Of course you feel your father's being unreasonable – he is – but running away isn't going to change anything. He'll never learn to think differently unless you show him how."

Marcus, gaping like a goldfish, sat up and stared at her. "But—" he began.

"But me no buts! Just behave like the very excellently open-minded prince that you are, and set him an example. Take part in the tournament. Invite Gracie. Make sure that the two of you together show the crowds the way these things ought to be done. If they see Gracie being pushed out of her rightful place, I can tell you here and now that their sympathies won't be with the royal family."

There was a silence, followed by a round of applause from the curtain rail. The Ancient One creaked to her feet and curtsied. "Thank you, Marlon."

Marcus took a deep breath, and stood up. "Yes," he said, "thank you." He moved to stand in front of Gracie, and bowed. "Miss Gillypot, might I request your presence at the Centenary Celebration Tournament? And will you take your place as my partner of choice?"

Gracie was blushing, but she looked steadily into Marcus's eyes as she said, "Thank you. I would be most honoured, and I accept."

"Phew!" Marcus let out a loud sigh of relief. "Thanks, Gracie." He straightened his shoulders and grinned at her. "We'll show them! And now I'd better be going. I've stuff to sort out."

"I'd better get busy as well," said Edna. "I've left Val working on the Web for far too long as it is … and I want to set up the other loom with something special, all ready for the morning. King Horace's tweed can wait."

Gracie looked at her in surprise. "But I thought that was an urgent order?"

"Not as urgent as your dress for the tournament, dear," the Ancient One said, and she opened the door to the corridor to return to Room Seventeen. As she did so Alf came whizzing in, twittering wildly.

"Urgent urgent urgent! She was listening! Listening on the stairs! She followed after you, Mrs Edna. Heard every word!"

Gracie's eyes widened, but the Ancient One remained calm. "That's unfortunate. Where is she now?"

Alf waved a wing. "On her way to bed." He paused before adding with unwilling admiration, "She's got ears like a bat, Mrs Edna. I could tell! She heard everything I did! And she smiled and oh, Mrs Edna! It wasn't a very nice smile!"

"That's her werewolf ancestry," the Ancient One said with a sigh. "Acute hearing. I've noticed it in her before, and I should have remembered. I'm getting old. Marcus – are you going to go now, or do you want to stay and ride back early in the morning? If you're going now, I suggest we send you on the path. Your pony will be too tired."

Marcus nodded. "Yes, please. I'd like to be there for breakfast." He gave Gracie a beaming smile and, much to the romantic Alf's delight, blew her a kiss. "I've got a tournament to plan!"

"I'll see you to the path," Gracie said. "It always behaves better if I tell it what to do."

"Thanks." Marcus linked his arm through hers, and they went out of the door together.

Alf sighed happily. "Love's young dream," he whispered. "Maybe I'll go with—"

"You," Marlon said, and his tone was not friendly, "will stay right here. I've a word to say to you, Alfred Batster. Several words, in fact. Number one? Responsibility! Number two? Responsibility! Number three? Responsibility! Number four—"

The Ancient One chuckled, and left Marlon to it.

Chapter Ten

Vincent had not had a happy return to his ancestral home. Bluebell had been waiting for him, a grim expression on her face, and she had told him in no uncertain terms what she thought of his behaviour.

"I had expressed a mere THOUGHT, Vincent! Now, I know that thinking is an alien concept to someone with a brain the size of a pea, but—" Her grandson's blank expression caught her eye. "You don't know what an alien concept is?"

Vincent tried his best. "Something to do with canaries?"

Bluebell slapped her head. "There you are. A classic demonstration of WHY I am seriously concerned about the future of Wadingburn."

Her grandson attempted to defend himself. "I say, Grandmother! You're not being fair. I'm just as clever as Albion, you know. In fact, I beat him twice at tiddlywinks last time we played, so I must be cleverer!"

Queen Bluebell was, briefly, at a loss for words. She gave an enormous sigh, and sank down in the nearest chair. "Are you TRYING to persuade me to adopt Gracie Gillypot, Vincent?"

"What?" Vincent's eyes popped. "Persuade you? No, no, no, Grandmother. Absolutely not. You've got it all wrong if you think that. Dear me." He sat down beside Bluebell. "What I think is—"

His grandmother held up her hand. "Stop right there, Vincent. I don't want to hear another word about your thought processes. The very idea makes me feel extremely tired. I'm going to bed, and I suggest you do the same. I will see you again in the morning." She rose to her feet, and sailed away to her bedroom, leaving Vincent wondering what he had said that could possibly have upset her.

"Odd," he thought. "But it only goes to show that I was quite right to go to Gorebreath. She's definitely confused. Very confused. Fancy thinking I wanted her to adopt Gracie! Softening of the brain, that's what it is. I've heard about it somewhere." He stood up, and stretched. "I wonder if there's anything left in the kitchen? I fancy a little nibble ... just to help me sleep."

Wandering off in the direction of the kitchen, he was alarmed to hear a loud knocking at the front door. He waited to see if any of the servants were still up, but there was no sign of anyone. The knocking came again, and Vincent tiptoed nervously towards the door. Half expecting to see a furious Marcus, he bent down to the keyhole.

"Who's there?" he whispered.

"Urgent message for His Royal Highness Prince Vincent of Wadingburn from Her Royal Highness Princess Marigold of Dreghorn answer awaited immediate response required," said a voice.

"Urgent message? For me?" Vincent, with some difficulty, unbolted the door and peered out into the night. A dour-looking messenger pushed a small, pink and highly scented envelope into his hands.

"Answer awaited, immediate response required," he repeated.

Vincent turned the envelope over. He recognized Marigold's looping handwriting, and his heart fluttered. "It's for me," he said.

The messenger, who had been hauled from his bed to ride out into the darkness and deliver a letter that, in his humble opinion, could perfectly well have waited until the following day, sighed heavily.

"Yes. Sir. It's for you. And I'm not to come back until I've got an answer. Sir."

"Oh!" Vincent nodded. "I'd better see what it says then, hadn't I?"

Aware that his favoured response would be unsuitable, the messenger remained silent. He watched wearily as Vincent turned the envelope over once more, and finally opened it. His lips moving, and his finger pointing at each word, Vincent read the letter slowly and carefully ... and then read it a second time. The messenger, now leaning against the doorframe with his eyes closed in an effort to catch up on lost sleep, was startled awake by a loud squeal.

"Look at that! Just LOOK at that! What shall I do? I can't ride a horse! I can't. I absolutely can't!" Vincent was quivering with agitation. The messenger hid a yawn behind his hand, and took the letter.

"'Dearest darling Vinnie,'" he read, and stopped. "Not sure as I should be reading this, sir. Personal, and all that."

"No no! Go on ... go on!"

The messenger shrugged, and continued. "'I want you to be a big brave boy and play in the centeenery tornament with Tertius and Marcus and Arry so I can sit on the stage and be your Lady Fare and wear a

 129

pritty dress. I will give you –'" the messenger paused, but was urged to continue by an insistent wave of Vincent's podgy hand – "'I will give you a big kiss and I will make sure we have the bestest picnick ever with rarsperrys and creem. Your very loving Marigold xxxxx PS There will be merangs lots and lots of merangs speshly choclat ones as my darling Vinnie liks them best.'"

Vincent came a little closer. "What was that last bit? What was that about chocolate meringues?"

The messenger repeated the PS, and Vincent began to look interested. "What," he enquired, "what EXACTLY is one supposed to do at a tournament? I mean, of course I know, being a prince and all that – but just remind me."

"A tournament?" The messenger scratched his head. "Well, you get two guys on horses, see, and they each carries a long pointy stick, and they run at each other – leastways, the horses do the running. The guys just have to stay on board – and then they try to knock each other off. I say – are you all right, sir?"

Vincent had gone green. "Go on," he said in a hollow voice. "What do they do then?"

"Then they gets up and shakes hands and says, 'Jolly good show!' to each other. That is, if they ain't dead.

Feeling a bit poorly, are we, sir? You don't look too good, if you don't mind my saying so. Here – have a swig of this!" The messenger pulled a dubious-looking bottle out of his pocket, and held it to Vincent's lips. Vincent took a hearty mouthful, and gasped.

"What … whatever is it?" His mouth was burning, and his eyes watering, but there was no doubt he felt better. MUCH better, in fact. "That's amazing! Stout fellow! Well done! What's your name?"

"Barry," said Barry. "Barry Poodle. Want another swig, sir?"

"Yes, I do," Vincent said. This time the fiery liquid was even more effective, and he began to smile as he handed the bottle back to its owner. "Goodness me, Barry. I must ask Cook to get hold of some of that. What's it called?"

Barry, who was acquainted with the Wadingburn Palace cook, hesitated. He was well aware that she had at least a dozen bottles of the magic brew stashed away in her private cupboard, but he was not at all certain that she would wish this to be known by the heir apparent.

"I suppose you could ask her for a bottle of the Wadingburn Special," he said.

"The Wadingburn Special," Vincent repeated. "I'll remember that. Well I never. Makes a chap feel

hicketty poppetty sooper dooper, doesn't it?" He puffed out his chest and strutted about the hall. "Tell me some more about this tournament stuff. Sounds much jollier than I suspected. By Jove, it does! Running around with long sticks, eh. Anything else? Oh, and I'll have another little sip of the Special, Barry, my boy. Really warms the cockles, don't it?"

Barry watched doubtfully as Vincent helped himself to a rather more than substantial sip. The prince was now very red in the face, and his eyes were beginning to roll.

"About that answer, sir," he said. "The lady was anxious to have your reply as soon as possible."

"My darling little shweee ... shweee ... poppet." Vincent beamed. "Whatever she wantsh she shall have. Giss ush a piece of paper, and the meshage shall be wrote!"

Barry, well prepared by Marigold, whipped a piece of paper and a pen from his pocket. Vincent seized them, and in wobbling capitals wrote, "Yes I will play in the torniment for you and for the razberries and I will give you a big kiss and you are my laddy fair for ever Vinnie. PS bring Wadingburn Speshul too it is the best ever." He handed his answer to Barry, who tucked it carefully into his messenger bag. "Thank you, sir. And now, if you'll excuse me, I'd better be off. Her Royal Highness'll be waiting."

Vincent was now leaning against a wall. "Dearesh Little Marigold," he murmured, and his eyelids drooped. "Do anything for dearesh…" He slid down the wall, and pulled the doormat over his legs. "Time for beddy-byes," he remarked. "Time for beddy … weddy … beddy byes…" A moment later he was fast asleep, and the steady sound of his snoring filled the hallway.

Barry Poodle saluted the prone figure and tucked the much-depleted bottle of Wadingburn Special back in his pocket. Then, with a merry whistle, and leaving the front door wide open, he headed for his horse and the road to Dreghorn.

Chapter Eleven

Up in her room, Foyce Undershaft was pacing to and fro. She desperately needed moonlight; the new ferocity burning in her bones would fade if she could not find a way to feed it and recover her full strength. Over the past months she had felt her passion for evil draining away; the constant presence of the Ancient Crones had weakened her, softened her resolve to escape and, even more importantly, take revenge on the source of all her troubles. She had had to draw on every reserve of anger and resentment to keep her intention clear in her mind; once or twice she had even wondered if it would be better to give in to the forces of good surrounding her, and allow the Crones to win. She had been rescued from these thoughts by staying close to Gracie; when the Trueheart was nearby Foyce's own wickedness was polarized, and the small remaining flame burned more fiercely. And then – after endless nights of searching – she had found the knothole. She had found it just in time; only that morning she had voluntarily offered the Ancient One a plate of biscuits. Retrospective horror at this behaviour had lent urgency to her determination to resist all attempts to change her ways, and she had redoubled her efforts … and that was when she had spotted the tiny weakness in the heavy wooden shutters. A long night's work with a potato peeler stolen from the kitchen had won her a glimpse of the night sky and the moonlight that she craved. At once the darkness deep inside her had surged back, and any inclination to help or do good of any kind was swept away in the welcome torrent of evil thoughts and feelings.

Hope had grown with the knowledge that she had discovered a way to resist the power of the crones, and she had decided to pretend that she was softening day by day while she considered what to do next. Each night she had gloated over her increasing strength and power, and licked her lips as the possibility of revenge became more and more likely. But then her secret had been discovered – and yet again Gracie was to blame.

Foyce ground her teeth, and went on pacing. She had succeeded in bending Billy to her will, but the effort had been exhausting, and the result remained to be seen.

She had been unaware of the presence of werewolves so near the House; Billy's twitterings outside her window had surprised her, and she had acted on impulse. Surely they would want to help her, half werewolf as she was? But, then again, what would they be like? Her memory of her mother was of a craven creature, cowering in a corner to avoid her husband's blows. Her father had seldom mentioned her; when he did it was with a sneer, and the comment that she was lost and gone and good riddance to bad rubbish. Foyce had agreed with him – but she was desperate to make some kind of contact with the world outside the House, and any way was better than no way.

Another thought came to Foyce, and for a moment her scowl lightened. What if it was her mother who emerged from the forest? If she did, pathetically forgiving the past and answering the call of her long-lost child, then, without a doubt, she could be used … and that in itself would be a gratifying state of affairs. But that was only a faint possibility. What Foyce needed at this moment was certainties. She could not even be sure that Billy had done as instructed; her scowl returned, and she resumed her pacing.

"What can I do? How can I hurt the little slug most?" She considered what she had heard while crouched at the top of the stairs, and began to review the information she had gathered.

"A Centenary Celebration. A tournament … and the slimy worm −" Foyce's eyes glowed a furious yellow − "and the slimy worm is to be there. Dressed in silks and satins − hm. Could they be woven with poison? To turn her flesh sour and rotten?" Foyce savoured the idea for a moment, then went back to her first thought. "A tournament, and her precious prince will be taking part. Oh, if only I could be there, to slice him through with his own sword right in front of her big blue eyes! THAT would be revenge indeed. First his arms, then his legs and then his stupid royal head, to lie glassy-eyed in the dust in front of her … surely that would hurt her most." Foyce gave a shrill mirthless laugh as her imagination caught fire. "And the bats. Those tittle-tattling bats. They must be destroyed. Tossed into a cauldron of boiling water, or fried to a crisp, and their ashes poured over the little slug's feet. And the Crones −" Here Foyce hesitated. Her imagination was unable to deal with the Ancient Crones. Even if she were free and fully recovered, what could she do against their power? Remembering several unpleasant encounters with the Ancient One, she hastily put the idea to one side.

"There are other ways," she decided, and then stopped, chewing her lip in frustration. "But how?" she demanded of the empty room. "HOW can I begin? The little worm must pay for what she's done – she must be made to suffer, and go on and on and on suffering until her hair and teeth fall out and her bones rot away – but how? How can I begin?"

She stared at the window, as she had done over and over again since coming upstairs. The new shutters were substantial; she had found no weak point, and her attempts to pull out the nails had been unsuccessful. Gubble had been too thorough. Angrily she flung herself on her bed, and glared at the wall. There was a constellation of cracks that was horribly familiar ... or was it?

Foyce sat up, her eyes narrowed. Above the window were several new, deeper fissures; white flakes of plaster lay beneath on the carpet. Gubble's enthusiasm had had an unexpected result.

Leaping to her feet, Foyce seized a chair, pulled it to the window and climbed up, her long nails picking at the wall above the heavy wooden shutters. A small chunk of plaster came away, quickly followed by another, and another. The girl gave a low growl of excitement and worked even harder. A moment later she was greeted with success. Between the window frame and the

lintel above crept a thin line of silver light; Foyce leant forward, and breathed it in with hungry gasps. So near to the full moon it was wonderfully powerful; she could feel her heart hardening and her mind settling back into dagger-sharpness and steely force. A strange feeling came over her, a feeling she had never had before, and that she didn't recognize. Without realizing what she was doing she flung back her head and howled.

"NO!" She stopped herself. "No!" Her hand over her mouth, she forced herself to be silent. Had anyone heard her? She ran to her door to listen, but there was no sound. Shocked at what had happened, she moved slowly to the window and cautiously climbed back on the chair. The light shone on her face once more, but there was no recurrence. Sighing with relief, Foyce closed her eyes and drank in the moonlight.

Foyce's howl, so quickly silenced, went unheard by the inhabitants inside the House. Even Marlon and Alf failed to hear it. Marlon was too busy listing Alf's inadequacies, and Alf had his wings over his ears in a vain attempt to block out his uncle's hectoring tones.

Outside the sound was clearer; Marcus and Gracie, making their way to the path that lay curled up by the back door, looked at each other in surprise.

"Did you hear that?" Gracie asked.

Marcus nodded. "Must have come from the Forest."

Gracie looked doubtful. "But didn't you think it sounded nearer than that? It almost sounded as if it came from inside the House."

"Can't have done," Marcus said. "Well, not unless Gubble's started howling."

"Ug," said a voice, and Gubble came round the corner of the House carrying an armful of logs. "No howl." He dropped the logs, and studied the sleeping path. "Gubble kick?"

The path hurriedly straightened itself out, and stretched itself invitingly from the back door to the gate.

"SUCH a good path," Gracie told it. "Now, could you take Marcus back to Gorebreath?"

The path gave an obliging wriggle, and Marcus stepped on and sat down. "Thanks," he said, and looked up at Gracie. "Do you think Alf or Marlon would bring Glee back tomorrow? Or —" he looked hopeful — "maybe you could? Then I'd get to see you."

Gracie blushed. "I'll see what I can manage," she said. "Have a good journey."

Marcus nodded. "Yes. See you soon?"

Gracie smiled down at him. "Of course. Very soon."

There was a pause, where nothing happened.

Gubble took a meaningful step forward, and at once there was a convulsive twisting and looping. A moment later Marcus and the path were gone.

"Clever Gubble." Gubble's tone was one of huge self-congratulation.

"Hmm," Gracie said. "I hope Marcus was holding on. I don't think he's used to travelling quite so fast…"

Keel, lurking amongst the thick undergrowth outside the fence that surrounded the House of the Ancient Crones, had also heard Foyce's howl. He had been tempted to reply, but caution had kept him silent, and then Marcus and Gracie had appeared and he had been distracted. He was intrigued by Gracie; there was something about her that made him want to go closer but, knowing nothing of the Trueheart effect, he was unable to explain the feeling. She had a lovely smile, but she wasn't beautiful. She was obviously a girl, and not a werewolf, or any of the other composite beings that could be found in the forest … and usually he avoided humans. He scratched at his ear, and was surprised to find he was using a hand, and not a paw. Having left Agony he had slid from human to wolf; running through the forest was easier when you had a slim body and

 143

four legs. He wasn't aware of having changed back; curious, he thought.

When Marcus and the path disappeared Keel's eyes widened. As Gracie and Gubble made their way inside he began to circle the House, watching to see if there were any other unusual happenings, and wondering if the crones were even more powerful than Agony had suggested. He was intrigued to see the windows shifting from side to side and the front door slithering up the wall; he had stopped to see if the door returned to its original position when a voice spoke in his ear.

"Why are you here, Keel?"

Keel spun round to see yellow eyes glaring at him. Jukk was in wolf form, his teeth bared. "Keel! You swore an oath to the pack! Your cousin was to be watched at all times... Where is she now?"

"Waiting," Keel said. "Waiting for me to discover who is in the House. A message came—"

He stopped. Jukk was growling a low threatening growl. "No," Keel told him. "It wasn't anything to do with my cousin's husband. The messenger said, *she.*"

"It could be a trick."

Keel looked at his companion. Jukk was the leader of the werewolves living in the Less Enchanted Forest, and he was dangerous. His temper was short, and he demanded unwavering obedience, honesty and courage from his followers. If Keel had been allowed to make his own decisions he would have left Agony alone a long time ago; it was Jukk who insisted she had disgraced the pack. She had chosen to put herself into the hands of an evil human and, to Jukk's way of thinking, had made no attempt to defend the honour of the werewolves before slinking away. He also believed that one day Mange Undershaft would come looking for her and that she would not be strong enough to resist him. Deeply suspicious, Jukk's ruling was that Agony must always be kept under surveillance, so should Mange ever be foolish enough to enter the forest he could be dealt with immediately, and the honour of the pack restored.

"It could be," Keel agreed. "But whether it is or isn't, we should find out. Did you hear the call?"

Jukk stared. "That wasn't you?"

"No." Keel pointed to the House. "It came from inside there."

"It did?" Jukk sounded disbelieving. He turned to face the House, and sent an answering howl echoing through the still night air. Foyce, her face pressed to the thin line of light, shivered with excitement.

"The wolf woman's come," she murmured, but then dismissed the idea. The howl had suggested brute strength

 145

and power, and she clutched at the edge of the shutters. "A male wolf … or werewolf. How very fortunate."

Foyce had no doubt about the effect her voice and her blue eyes and golden curls had on the male of whatever species she happened to meet. In the past, if she so wished, she had been able to reduce even the solemnest zombie to a state of drooling infatuation in a matter of minutes. Only a few were able to resist her charms. Marcus, much to her irritation, had never had eyes for anyone except Gracie, and Alf and Marlon were firmly immune. She tossed her curls, and began to sing: a sad, sweet, plaintive song about a wolf maiden lured into captivity by a cruel lover aided by evil witches … and Jukk listened, spellbound.

Keel stared at him in amazement. The song was charming, but he had a keen ear for duplicity, and there was something in the voice that made him uneasy. As long as the song continued he was lulled into a state of dreamy admiration, but each time the singer paused he felt a different sensation, a sensation that reminded him of the time when, as a small cub, he had eaten too much honey and had had to be purged with a large dose of sour nettles. "Be careful, Jukk," he warned, but Jukk took no notice. He was leaning forward in rapt adoration to catch every note.

"Beautiful," he breathed, "so beautiful." He too was now in his human form, tall and dark, with well-muscled shoulders. Keel looked at him warily.

"Jukk?"

"Hush!" Jukk was still listening. Keel shrugged and turned away, wondering what he should do. Agony was waiting to hear what he had discovered, but so far he had found out nothing. He was unwilling to believe the story the singer was telling; he had never heard the Ancient Crones described as evil before, or accused of imprisoning innocent young women ... or, indeed, werewolves.

Up in her room Foyce ended her song, and waited to see if there was any reaction from outside. As she waited she continued picking at the loose plaster round the window frame, trying to enlarge the narrow gap she had already made. "Drat that idiot troll," she muttered. "But I'll teach him a lesson. Oh, WHAT a lesson I'll teach him!" As she spoke another chunk of plaster fell out, revealing brick and part of the wooden lintel, and she pulled the potato peeler out of her pocket. "Let's see ... powdery cement. Old and useless, like everything else here." Scraping and scratching, ignoring the mess she was making on the carpet beneath her chair, she worked away until, to her intense delight, a brick came loose and she was able to pull it away. The hole it left was almost big enough for her head, and she gazed at the night outside in rapture. It took her almost a minute to realize that what she was seeing was not the usual view from her window; she was much nearer ground level, directly opposite the fence that bordered the House and its gardens. A movement beyond the fence caught her eye, and she realised she was staring straight into the eyes of a tall young man. Her immediate and automatic response was to flutter her eyelashes and look demurely down, but before either he or she could say a word the House swept the window back to its usual position beneath the eaves. Foyce was shaken off her chair and onto the floor; the hole above the window was suddenly empty.

The damage, however, had been done. Jukk, his hand on his heart, was gazing upwards.

"Who is she?" he whispered. "She is my soul's one true desire!"

Foyce's appearance had had a similar effect on Keel. His previous doubts had vanished, and his heart was pounding in his chest. He stepped forward, but Jukk flung out his arms.

"She's mine!" he said. "Can't you see? Only the leader of the pack is worthy of beauty such as hers!"

 149

Up in her room Foyce was listening. She smiled a calculating smile as she heard Jukk's declaration, and waited for Keel's reply … but none came. Jukk was the leader. His word was law. Foyce's hopes of a fight for her favours were dashed but, she reasoned, that might be all to the good. She ran her fingers through her curls, pinched her cheeks, bit her lips to make them suitably rosy and climbed carefully back onto her chair. Jukk, watching as she slowly rose up like a saintly vision, held his breath.

Foyce saw his enraptured expression and silently congratulated herself; her face remained impassively beautiful. Raising her eyes to the moon, she began to sing. Once again she sang of her imprisonment and her loneliness, and how the hours dragged as she paced the boards in her bare and cheerless room. A single poignant tear rolled down her cheek and glittered in the moonlight as she told of the cruelty she suffered at the hands of those who held her prisoner, and how a terrible enchantment held her captive unless she gave herself to a cruel prince who she could not ever love … and she begged the heavens to release her, even if only through death.

Jukk listened, and swallowed the bait as if it had been sugar on a spoon. He sent a long mournful howl echoing across the space between them: a howl that promised eternal love and utter devotion. Foyce, who had carefully synchronized a gentle misty-eyed disappearance from the window with the fading of her song, smiled gleefully. "Caught him."

Inside the House of the Ancient Crones, Alf stopped feeling sorry for himself and twitched his ears. A moment later he was airborne.

Chapter Twelve

Queen Bluebell of Wadingburn was up early the following morning. Feeling that she had been a little hard on Vincent the previous night she decided to treat him to breakfast in bed, but as she came down the stairs she was distracted by finding the front door wide open.

"I could swear I locked it," she told herself, and went to investigate. As she got nearer she heard a faint agonized groan, quickly followed by a louder one.

"Vincent?" she said. "Is that you? What on EARTH—"

The sight of her grandson, wrapped up in the doormat and showing every sign of having been asleep in the hallway all night, made Bluebell fish in her pocket for her lorgnette on the assumption that her eyes were playing tricks on her. Finding her first impression had been accurate, she bent over him. "Vincent? What on earth are you doing here?"

There was no response other than another feeble groan, and Bluebell began to chuckle. "Vincent? I do believe you've been drinking!" There was still no answer, and the queen straightened up, but not before she had tweaked the frilly-edged pink letter out of her grandson's nerveless grasp. She had no hesitation in reading the contents, and her chuckle turned to a hoot of laughter. Her aged butler, carrying a large dish of scrambled eggs and bacon across the hallway on his way to the dining room, looked at her in astonishment.

"Is Your Majesty ... erm ... well?" he enquired.

Bluebell waved the letter under his nose. "Never better, Mullins, old chap. My grandson has been asked to take part in a tournament, but it seems the idea was too much for him and he's taken to drink to drown his sorrows."

"There's many another would have done the same," Mullins pronounced, "although I don't hold with it myself. Best to deal with sorrows with a cup of tea, I'd say. And a slice of cake. A goodly slice of Cook's fruit cake can sweep away many a sorrow." He looked disapprovingly over the top of the silver salver at the stout body prone on the tiles. "It ain't good for a young lad to go overdoing it like that. Shall I send the garden boy to heft him up to his bed?"

"I'd be very grateful," Bluebell said. "Give me the eggs, and I'll take them into the dining room myself."

Mullins did as he was told, and as he went off to find the garden boy Bluebell carried her breakfast to the dining room. There she made a hearty meal, refusing to be disturbed by the grunts and groans she could hear in the distance. She reread Marigold's letter a couple of times in a thoughtful fashion as she ate and, after pouring herself one final cup of tea, set out to see how her grandson was faring. She found him lying on his bed, pale green in colour, and clutching a damp towel to his aching forehead.

"I've been poisoned," he announced as his grand-mother swept into the room. "Someone's tried to kill me."

"Nonsense, dear." Bluebell made no attempt to moderate her usual booming tone, and Vincent shuddered.

"I don't suppose you could whisper?" he asked plaintively. "You do have a very loud voice, and my head is killing me."

Bluebell plonked herself down on the edge of the bed, causing the sufferer to close his eyes and whimper. "Now, now, Vincent – do try and man up

 154

a little. I found Marigold's letter about the Centenary Tournament, and I read it as I was more than a little concerned about the state I found you in."

Vincent let out a shriek of anguish, and disappeared under his towel. A muffled voice wailed, "I'm ill! I'm dying! I can't possibly do it! I know I said I would but I can't!"

Surprised, Bluebell raised her eyebrows. "You said you'd take part?"

"It was the messenger made me do it! He said Marigold was waiting for an answer! Oh, Grandmother!" A pair of bleary red-rimmed eyes peered over the edge of the towel. "You've got to help me!"

"I thought I was supposed to have gone mad? Lost my mind? Was a danger to the kingdom?" Bluebell was enjoying herself. "Have you changed your opinion, Vincent, dear?"

"PLEASE, Grandmother! I don't want to be knocked off a horse! Please don't make me! I'll do anything – you can adopt Gracie Gillypot AND a werewolf just as long as I don't have to play in the tournament!"

Bluebell, seeing that Vincent was genuinely distressed, leant forward. "I'm sure we can think of something," she soothed. "I really don't think you'll need to ride a horse. Perhaps you could lead Tertius

 155

and Marcus into the arena?" Knowing her grandson as well as she did, she added temptingly, "You could wear a special uniform..."

The bleary eyes brightened. "And I wouldn't have to ride on a horse? Or be bashed with a long pointy stick?"

"Not at all," Bluebell promised. "And maybe Albion would like to walk with you? Then it would be the princes of Wadingburn and Cockenzie Rood, side by side."

Vincent considered this. "I suppose. But it might be best if I was on my own, actually, Grandmother. Leading the way, don't you know."

Recognizing the signs of recovery, Bluebell heaved herself to her feet. "I'll leave you to think about it, dear. Now, I suggest you have a little sleep. You'll feel so much better when you wake up."

"Green with gold buttons," Vincent murmured dreamily as his grandmother tucked him in. "Or maybe scarlet? With silver braid..."

Bluebell sighed, and made her way back to her office. There she sat down at her desk, but did not, as was her usual habit, dive straight into the endless pile of paperwork. Instead she sat still, gazing out through the window. "What to do?" she asked herself. "What to do? I'm tired of looking after a kingdom. Very tired. It's time to move on … no doubt about it. But how?" She sighed again, and drew a gold-crested envelope towards her. "Such a fuss they all make. Such a fuss." A thought came to her, and she put the invitation to one side in order to give her thoughts due consideration. "The Ancient Crones. Hm. Why not?" A slow smile spread over her face, and she rose from her chair with the air of a woman on a mission. "Mullins? Mullins – could you do me another favour? Ask the stable boy to harness the pony and trap. I'm going on a journey, and I'll be driving myself."

In Gorebreath, Marcus was doing his best not to lose his temper. He had spent some time thinking about the best way in which to announce his intention to invite Gracie to the tournament, and had decided that waiting until after breakfast would merely prolong the agony. With this in mind he had arrived at the table and, before anyone else could say anything, had delivered his ultimatum. He had then set his jaw and waited, with a fast-beating heart, for his father's reaction. To his astonishment, there had been no reaction at all. His father had ignored him, and continued to sip his tea. Marcus glanced at his mother, but she merely

 157

smiled and asked if he would prefer tea or coffee.

Marcus took a deep breath. "Did you hear me, Father? I'm going to invite Gracie—"

"Yes yes yes." King Frank waved a dismissive hand. "No need to make a fuss about it. I've talked it over with your mother, and she's of the opinion that it won't do any harm if dealt with in the right way. If the young person sits behind Princess Fedora the crowd will assume she's a maid, or some such. I do, however, feel that there are a number of very important matters that I would like to draw to your attention!" And before Marcus could say a word in protest at his father's belittling suggestion, the king launched into a long and pompous lecture on the duties of royalty while consuming an impressive number of poached eggs. Even Arioso began to look less than enthusiastic as his father buttered his seventh slice of toast, and their mother, Queen Mildred, began to yawn behind the large silver teapot.

"So you see," King Frank boomed, "you are not like Other People. You must rise above your own wishes, and think of Royalty and Dignity and Example." He gave Marcus a meaningful glare. "This tournament will be, I trust, a splendid example of the Superiority of Princes. You will, of course, wear the Arms of Gorebreath upon your shield, like your brother."

Arry choked on his toast. "Like ME? But … but I won't be carrying a shield, Father. Marcus and Tertius arranged it all, you see. It's a jousting match, and in jousting matches it's just two jousters." He giggled feebly. "Did you hear that? 'Just two jousters!' Ho ho ho…"

"Nonsense!" King Frank held up his fork. "I've been considering the whole nature of tournaments, and I've come to an important decision. The heir to the Kingdom of Gorebreath must take his proper place. The Common People will expect it, and so do I. And so does the Princess Nina-Rose." The king pulled a scrap of heavily scented pale-blue notepaper out of his dressing-gown pocket. "A delightful girl. Extraordinarily thoughtful, and showing a very proper respect. She wrote to tell me how very much she is looking forward to seeing you ride into the arena and rise triumphant over all your opponents!"

Arioso went pale. "She did?"

"She expects nothing less of you." King Frank tucked the note away. "And so does your mother."

Queen Mildred looked surprised. "Do I, dear?"

"Yes," King Frank said firmly. "You do. And I've looked out the armour that your great-grandfather and your great-uncle Frizzley wore when they defended the kingdom of Gorebreath against the Great Terror."

Marcus opened his eyes very wide. "What Great Terror was that, Father?"

"I think it was a plague of rats, dear," his mother said. "Very nasty."

"And they needed suits of armour?" Marcus sounded incredulous, and his father frowned.

"The rats might have been a precursor of something far, far worse. And it's always best to be well prepared. You will find the armour waiting for you in the great hall. It's been cleaned and polished. I suggest you try it on after breakfast."

Arry tried once more. "But, Father——"

"Arioso! Surely you aren't thinking of disappointing me!" King Frank looked genuinely hurt as he gazed at his oldest son, and Arry, always anxious to oblige, stood up and bowed.

"Sorry, Father. Your wish is my command."

"Good boy. Good boy." King Frank settled down to attack yet another egg. "Come and show me when the two of you are ... erm ... encased."

As Marcus and Arry left the room Arry clutched at his brother's arm. "Marcus! What am I going to do? I can't joust! I can't even stay on a pony for more than five minutes! I'm bound to fall off, and everyone will laugh, and Nina-Rose will——" Arry's face

 160

morphed into the expression of a rabbit mesmerized by an extremely bright light. "Nina-Rose! What was she thinking of? Did you see? She wrote to Father ... but she KNEW I didn't want to take part!"

Marcus shrugged. "What Nina-Rose wants, Nina-Rose gets, and she doesn't mind how she does it."

There was a pause, then Arry said in a thoughtful voice, "Do you think she'll ever change?"

"No." Marcus was on sure ground. "All those girls are exactly the same. Look at the way Fedora bosses Tertius!"

There was a second pause, then, "Does Gracie ever boss you?"

Marcus turned and looked hard at his twin. "Why do you want to know?"

"I was thinking," Arry said unhappily, "that I really don't want to spend the rest of my life being told what to do."

"You don't have to." Marcus put his arm round his brother's shoulders. "Stand up to her. For a start, you could say you're not going to take part in the tournament."

Arry wriggled like a fish on a hook. "But then Father'll be angry. And – even worse – disappointed. I can't bear it when he's disappointed."

Marcus withdrew his arm. "Sorry, bro. You've got to decide for yourself."

"I know." Arry walked through the door into the great hall, and stared gloomily at the piles of gleaming armour heaped on the floor. "Look at this stuff! It must weigh a ton!"

"Mmmm," Marcus agreed, but he was not paying attention. He was inspecting the armour, sorting out the different pieces. "Were Great-Grandfather and Great-Uncle Frizzley twins like us? Everything's identical, except for the helmets, and even then it's only the feathers that are different." He picked up a silver helmet with a red feather plume on the top and put it on. Flipping up the visor, he peered out. "Hey! Can you see me?"

"You look as if you're peering out of a letter box," Arry told him.

Marcus closed the visor. "And now?"

Arry frowned. "You could be anyone."

"Exactly!" Marcus pulled off the helmet. "So – if you really want to please Father – say you'll take part. I'll help you." He gave his brother a rueful grin. "Father's always going to be disappointed with me, so we may as well make sure you keep him happy. And you never know … if he's happy with you, maybe he could be persuaded that Gracie Gillypot's the right girl for me."

Arioso stared at him. "You know what? You're the best brother ever. And I'll tell you something else. I like Gracie. I really do. Actually, I think she's much, much nicer than Nina-Rose— " He stopped, appalled at what he was saying. "I mean … that is … I didn't … oh dear!"

Marcus grinned. "It's OK. I'll forget you said it. Just remember to put in a word for me when you can."

His twin nodded. "You have the word of Prince Arioso." He sounded so serious that Marcus swallowed his laughter, and shook his brother's hand. Then, embarrassed by this unexpected display of brotherly solidarity, they swung away from each other to look at the armour.

Arry sighed. "It's decent of you to offer to help, old bean, but I don't really see how you can."

"Easy!" Marcus tickled his brother's nose with a plume of feathers. "We'll both be wearing armour, and there's no difference except for the helmets. This one's got red feathers, and that one's got blue ones – so all we have to do is swap!"

Arioso, Prince of Gorebreath, had moments when the world seemed a deeply confusing place. This was one of those moments. "But why would we do that?"

Marcus sighed. "You were the one who got high marks when Prof Scallio taught us! Don't you see? I can ride for both of us! I'll joust against Tertius, and then we'll swap helmets so I can pretend to be you – and I'll ride again. Easy peasy! Now, hurry up and make yourself look like a tin can so we can go and show Father. Do you want to be red or blue?"

"Blue," Arry said. "Nina-Rose likes blue."

There was a silence.

"No." Arry's voice had changed. "Red. I want the red feathers."

"Good man," Marcus told him. "That's the spirit! And if you do my buckles up, I'll do yours."

Chapter Thirteen

Foyce was weaving steadily, an expression of sweet girlish innocence on her face. Every so often she would turn to the Youngest and tenderly enquire how she was feeling. Val, who had been criminally devious herself in her youth, was not taken in. She responded to the enquiries politely enough, but as she threw the shuttle to and fro on the Web of Power she was wondering what Foyce was planning.

Foyce had been up early patching the hole above her window. The House had made no further twists and turns and her window remained under the eaves; this was to her advantage, as there was a heavy shadow that would hide anything suspicious from observers outside the building. Inside her room she replaced the brick and then, after some thought, tore a strip of wallpaper from a dark corner. Snipping it neatly to shape with a pair of scissors stolen some weeks before from the workroom downstairs, she fixed it over the damage with a couple of dress pins from her secret hoard. Then she went to work on an area near the door, so that anyone coming to investigate would identify that as the centre of her activities. By the time she had finished it would have taken very sharp eyes to see what she had been up to during the night.

She had gone down for her morning's work with a spring in her step. She knew as clearly as if the words had been spoken that Jukk would come to the House again that evening, and she intended to set her plans for revenge in motion as soon as she saw him. A little more information was needed, however, and she was timing her remarks to Val with care. Smoothing the soft blue silk on the loom in front of her, and suppressing a burning desire to spit on it, she asked brightly, "Did we finish the tweed for King Horace, then?"

"Near enough," Val said.

"And this lovely silk is for Gracie?"

"Yes." Val said no more, but Foyce was not to be discouraged.

"So when does it have to be done by? Is the tournament very soon?" Foyce laughed a silvery laugh. "We do want our Gracie to look her very best, don't we?"

 167

Up until very recently Foyce had never referred to Gracie as anything other than Little Slug, or Slimy Worm. Val noted the change, and gave Foyce a quick suspicious glance, but the girl was smiling and her weaving was impeccable. For a moment the Youngest wondered if Foyce's concern could be genuine. It seemed almost impossible that she could be acting a part; everything about her questioning look and steady gaze seemed real.

Foyce had seen the flicker of uncertainty. "I expect you think I'm only pretending to be nice," she said sadly, and drooped over her loom. "I've been so terribly horrid to Gracie, haven't I? Do you think she'll ever forgive me?" She saw confusion on Val's face, and mentally congratulated herself. "Oh, Val! I do feel dreadful!" Concentrating hard, she made herself think how she would feel if she failed to make the rest of Gracie's life a complete misery. A tear trickled down her cheek, quickly followed by another. A swift sideways glance reassured her that Val had noticed, and with a loud sniff she wiped her tears away.

Val, almost persuaded, handed her a handkerchief.

"Thank you, dear kind Val. But I mustn't cry on Gracie's beautiful dress," Foyce murmured, "must I?"

"No way!" It was a chirpy Marlon.

The mood was shattered. Foyce, tears forgotten, glared at the intruder, while Val shook her head to clear it of sympathetic thoughts. The bat flew round the looms, and landed near the Web. "Sorry, girls," he said, sounding anything but apologetic. "Did I interrupt something? Gotta message … erm … nah. It's gone. Old mind's playing up these days. Forget my own moniker next. Toodle-oo!" And he was off.

Val looked after him, her brow furrowed. "That's not like Marlon. He never forgets anything."

"He was spying," Foyce hissed. "Nasty little—" With a start, she remembered her plan, and forced herself to laugh. "Dear me! That wasn't very kind of me, was it? I'm so sorry. Now, what were we talking about? Oh yes. You were just about to tell me when the tournament was."

The Youngest crone, distracted by Marlon's sudden appearance and disappearance, was caught unawares. "Wednesday afternoon," she said.

"Goodness!" Foyce nodded. "So not long at all. We'd better stop nattering, fun though it is, and get on with our work." She bent over her loom to hide her delight, and straightened a tiny thread. Val, realizing she had been outwitted, was silent.

* * *

In the kitchen along the corridor Marlon was proudly describing how he had foiled Foyce's efforts to win Val round. "Cried real tears," he said. "Can't help but admire the dame. Good enough to fool anyone. Not me, natch."

"She must have found some way of catching the moonlight again," Elsie said. "She'd never be that perky if she hadn't."

Gracie, who was tidying Gubble's cupboard, looked up. "Do you want me to go and see if there's another hole in the shutters?"

Before Elsie or the Ancient One could answer, Alf came fluttering in.

"Hello, all!" he said cheerily. "Anyone got some breakfast for a hungry Super Spotter?"

His uncle raised an eyebrow. "Stopped sulking in the hallway, kiddo? About time too."

Alf sniffed. "Actually, Unc, I've been busy. Only just got back. Got a bit of info…" He glanced at Gracie, and lowered his voice. "Did you hear the howl, Miss Gracie? Last night?"

"Yes." Gracie pulled at the end of one of her plaits. "I've been wondering where it came from. Marcus and I both heard it. We thought it sounded really close to the House."

Alf shook his head. "Nah. This was later – after you came back inside." He gave his uncle a frosty stare. "Unc was asleep, but I was awake, and I heard it. So I went to check it out. Want to guess what I saw?"

"Surprise us, kiddo," Marlon told him.

"Werewolves!" Alf was triumphant. "I saw them running away into the forest, side by side, so I followed until one went one way and one went the other."

The Ancient One leant forward. "Did you hear them talking?"

"Not much. Didn't seem too friendly. Snarled at each other, they did. Think the big one was some kind of leader, though. Told the other one to get back to his duties, and to leave the House alone. Said he'd be in trouble if he went anywhere near, and looked like he meant it."

"To leave the House alone? Interesting." The Ancient One looked thoughtful. "He didn't say why?"

Alf shook his head. "Nah. Sorry, Mrs Edna. The other one looked mightily peeved, though. Went off muttering. I was going to follow him further, but I reckoned I'd better report in first. Ahem." He threw his uncle a meaningful glance. "Wanted to be responsible, see."

"You didn't do bad, kid," Marlon conceded. "But sounds like we'd best carry on where you left off. Time to spend time in the deep dark woods!" He stretched his wings. "Ready?"

"Sure thing, Unc!"

Alf flew a happy zigzag, and headed for the door. As he flew a small voice squeaked, "What about me, Mr Alf?"

Alf paused midflight. "Billy? At last! Where did you spring from?"

"I think Billy had better stay here," Gracie said gently. "You need a good rest. You can go adventuring with Alf tomorrow, maybe. Or −" she paused − "maybe you'd like to come out with me?"

Billy struggled out of his tea-towel nest and flew to her shoulder. "Yes, please."

Gubble, who had been watching the cleaning of his cupboard with undisguised disapproval, stumped to Gracie's side. "Gubble go too."

"Of course," Gracie said. "I was just about to ask you."

"Where are you going, duckie?" Elsie asked.

Gracie put down her duster. "I was thinking of taking Glee back to Gorebreath."

Alf circled over her head. "I'm sure Mr Prince'll be THRILLED to see you, Miss Gracie. His heart'll go pitter pitter pitt—"

"Okey doke – made your point." Marlon pushed his nephew towards the door. Alf, still twittering, didn't resist, but his voice could be heard fading into the distance.

"Stupid bat," Gubble remarked. "Heart goes thump. Not pitter. Go now?"

Gracie nodded. "You don't mind, do you, Auntie Edna?"

The Ancient One smiled at her. "Of course not. Take care … and give our love to Marcus. We'll expect you back tomorrow – it's too far to go there and back in a day."

"I will." Gracie kissed her adopted aunts, then took Gubble's arm. As the door closed behind them Edna let out a long sigh.

"Just as well to have her out of here, I'd say."

Elsie looked at her in surprise. "I'd have thought this was the safest place she could be."

"Haven't you noticed?" Edna asked. "Every time she gets near Foyce it makes Foyce worse, and as Foyce gets stronger so the effect is greater. Which reminds me – I'd be really grateful if you could have a look at that young lady's bedroom."

As Queen Bluebell of Wadingburn encouraged the pony along the narrow winding path that led to the

House of the Ancient Crones, she was thinking how very pleasant it was to be away from her palace and the irritations of royal life, and what fun it would be when she retired. "I'll be able to drive out whenever I wish," she told herself. "I might even ride from time to time. Must remember to ask Dowby to look me out a nice—"

"AAKK! AAKK!" An agitated pheasant, disturbed by the sound of wheels, flapped out of the bushes. The pony shied violently, took the bit between its teeth and bolted. Bluebell hauled on the reins, but the pony took no notice. Convinced it was escaping from terrible danger, it galloped madly between the trees until the inevitable happened. An outlying root caught a wheel, the trap overturned and Bluebell found herself sitting in a clump of nettles. Swearing in a manner that would have shocked and appalled her subjects, she extricated herself with some difficulty and made her way back to the path to inspect the remnants of the trap. There was no sign of the pony, the broken ends of the harness drooped despondently and several vital sections of the trap were missing.

"Blast," Bluebell said with feeling. "Oh well. No help for it, I'll have to walk. Hopefully it isn't too much further." She checked to see that her lorgnette had not

 175

been damaged in the accident and, finding all was well, set off at a brisk pace in the direction she had been travelling.

She had not gone far when there was the sound of hooves in the distance; for a moment she felt a faint flicker of apprehension but telling herself not to be a foolish old woman she strode on. As she rounded a corner she realized to her delight that it was Gracie coming towards her, mounted on Marcus's pony. Gubble was stomping solidly alongside, and a very small bat was perched on Gracie's shoulder.

"Gracie, my dear! I can't tell you how pleased I am to see you!" Bluebell beamed.

Gracie was equally delighted to see the queen. "Are you all right?" she asked. "What happened?" She looked round. "You haven't walked here?"

"I was driving," Bluebell explained, "and the stupid animal was frightened by a bird and took off at a gallop. We had a bit of a smash. Ruined my dear little pony trap, I'm afraid." She shook her head sorrowfully. "I was enjoying myself so much I wasn't paying attention. On my way to see your Ancient Crones, as it happens. I could do with a spot of advice from someone sensible."

"Really?" Gracie tried not to look surprised. "I

know they'd love to meet you – they've heard so much about you from me and Marcus." She paused. "And Alf. He's a big fan of yours."

Bluebell let out a bellow of laughter. "Glad to hear it! I'm a bit of a fan of Alf, as it happens."

She patted Glee's neck as Gracie swung herself out of the saddle. "Now THIS is a sensible kind of beast. Belongs to Marcus, doesn't it?"

Gracie nodded. "He left Glee at the House last night, and I'm taking him back to Gorebreath."

"Left him behind?" The queen raised her eyebrows. "So how did the boy get home?"

"Oh – he travelled back on the path." The memory of Marcus's abrupt departure made Gracie giggle. "Rather faster than he meant to. I'm hoping he didn't fall off along the way."

Bluebell's eyebrows rose even higher. "Travelled by path? Well, well, well. What a lot I have to learn!" A thought came to her. "So … would I be able to make the return trip to Wadingburn by path?"

"I don't see why not," Gracie told her.

"Splendid!" The Queen of Wadingburn beamed at her. "Although I'm sure I could find my way. I used to be a bit of a hiker in my younger days, as it happens. Of course, I don't have my boots, and I daresay there are a few things lurking in the forests that might need a stern word or two."

Gracie was just wondering whether to mention the possibility of werewolves, when Gubble stepped forward. "Wolfies." He nodded. "Lots of wolfies."

"Wolves, you say?" The queen of Wadingburn's smile widened. "Don't tell me they're werewolves! I've always fancied meeting a werewolf. I've heard they can be splendid company. Best avoided at full moon, of course."

"Ug." Gubble pointed upwards. "Big moon soon."

Billy, who had been listening and watching wide-eyed, gave a sudden twitch. "Badness," he whispered.

"Sssh," Gracie soothed. "You're safe with me."

"Gubble keep Gracie safe." Gubble frowned up at Billy as if the tiny bat had threatened to usurp his position.

"So you do," Gracie agreed, "but maybe you could keep Queen Bluebell safe instead? Could you show her the way to the House?" She turned to Bluebell. "It's not always easy to find. There's a thick green mist that comes down; King Horace's messenger wandered about for ages and ages, and ended up in the Relentless Thorns. We had to make him a new pair of trousers by way of compensation."

"But what about you, dear?" Bluebell asked.

"I'll be fine," Gracie assured her. "I'm more than used to the journey, and Gubble will catch up with me later."

Bluebell was puzzled. "But will he be able to? Isn't he — please forgive me, Mr Gubble — rather slower than your pony?"

Gracie chuckled. "Not the way he goes. Gubble's a great believer in travelling in a straight line. He's been known to walk through a brick wall if it happens to be in his way."

Gubble was still considering Gracie's suggestion. "Ug," he said at last. "Gubble take queen."

"I'm extremely grateful," Bluebell told him, and she tucked his arm through hers. "We'll have a good chat as we go. I expect you know all about the forest, don't you, Mr Gubble?"

It was all Gracie could do not to burst out laughing as the queen and the troll set off up the path together arm in arm.

"Don't they look funny?" she said, but Billy didn't answer. He was listening; his acute hearing had picked up the sound of stealthy footsteps in the undergrowth bordering the path. As the pony made its way onwards towards Gorebreath the footsteps kept pace; when Glee trotted, they went faster too.

"Miss Gracie," he whispered, "something's following us."

Gracie's heart beat faster, but her hands were steady on the reins, and no one watching would have noticed any alteration in her expression. "Would you be able to go and see who or what it is?" she asked softly.

Billy nodded, and a moment later he was circling over Gracie's head. Remembering his Super Spotter instructions he did not immediately fly in the direction of the follower; he gradually widened his circle and then, as if on some casual quest of his own, dropped in-between the trees.

A moment later he was back, quivering with excitement. "Miss Gracie! Miss Gracie! It's the wolf woman!"

There was an instant whirl of conflicting thoughts in Gracie's mind. Should she stop? she wondered. Could it be a trap? After all, wasn't this the woman Foyce had sent Billy to find? And there had been howling outside the House the night before ... and Alf had seen not just one, but two werewolves. But he'd said they were male...

Gracie made up her mind. She pulled Glee to a halt, and looked into the shadowy depths of the Less

Enchanted Forest. "Please don't be frightened," she called. "And please come out, whoever you are. I won't hurt you."

For a long minute nothing happened. Gracie found her hands were sweating and her mouth was dry, but she made herself look calmly about her. At last the bushes parted, and the tall thin figure of a woman stepped cautiously out. She stared at Gracie, and Gracie looked back at her, her fear fading.

I'm sure she's a werewolf, she thought, *but she looks as if she's more frightened of me than I am of her.* Holding out her hand, Gracie introduced herself. "Hello … I'm Gracie Gillypot. I don't think we've ever met."

Agony Clawbone continued to stare, and made no attempt to take Gracie's hand, or to answer. Just as Gracie was beginning to wonder if she should introduce herself again, Agony moved nearer. She put a thin bony hand on Glee's neck and peered up into Gracie's face as if searching for some recognizable feature.

"You were never called Foyce, child?" she asked, and there was such longing in her voice that Gracie's heart ached for her.

"I'm so sorry," she said. "But no."

Agony gave a long weary sigh. "Oh."

Gracie hesitated. "I do know Foyce," she said. "She

… she lives in the same house as I do. The House of the Ancient Crones."

"What?" Agony went rigid. "You both live there? And who else? What others are there?"

"It's just me and Foyce and the crones," Gracie told her. "And Gubble, of course. He's a troll – oh, oh – please don't do that!" The wolf woman was pulling at her own hair with a terrible ferocity. "What do you want to know? If I can help you, I will – I promise!"

Agony stopped, and once more stared at Gracie as if committing each and every feature of her face to memory. Then she said, "I believe you. You are good, and there is no evil in you. I can see that. Gracie Gillypot, I need to know the truth."

"If I know the truth, I'll tell you," Gracie promised.

"Then –" Agony came even closer, so that Gracie could see the deep lines etched on her face, and the purple hollows beneath her eyes – "put me out of my misery. Is Foyce a prisoner in the House?"

"Yes," Gracie said.

"Has she done much wrong?"

Gracie took a deep breath. "Yes."

"Thank you." Agony Clawbone dropped her gaze and stared at the ground. "Keel – my brother – told me there was a prisoner in the House, but he said she is fair, and beautiful, and good. He said she has a voice that twists cords around a man's heart, and he loves her, but that she is not for him. He said she is kept prisoner by enchantment and sorcery, but —" Agony's voice dropped to a whisper, and Gracie had to strain to hear her — "but I do not believe him. If the girl is good, why would she be kept prisoner by the Ancient Crones? That is not their way. So it seemed to me that she must be evil, but I hoped — oh, how much I hoped! — that it was not Foyce. Surely, I told myself, it was some other girl, some girl who had learned dark wicked ways to trap a listener with poisoned words. Not Foyce. Not my daughter—"

"Your daughter?" Gracie looked at the wolf woman in wonder. "Foyce is your daughter?"

Agony began to pace up and down the narrow path. "Her father was Mange Undershaft, an evil, evil man."

"Yes. I know..." Gracie stopped. What else could she say? That Mange was her stepfather and had made her life miserable from the very first moment he had set eyes on her as a small child? That he and Foyce had starved her and bullied her and humiliated her in every way they could? That until she met the Ancient Crones, she had never known love and kindness?

The wolf woman had an animal's instinct for

suffering, and she read a little of Gracie's unhappiness in her face. "I see," she said. "You and I – we know him for what he is. The thought of his return makes us both tremble."

Gracie shook her head. "Oh no. He won't be coming back. He's the servant of the Lady Lamorna now – and she'll never let him go." She gave Agony a rueful smile. "Besides, one of his feet is enclosed in an enormous block of stone, so he can't exactly go anywhere."

"Is this true?" The bushes had been pushed aside, and to Gracie's astonishment another figure stepped out. "You speak of Mange Undershaft? You say he is imprisoned? Will you swear it?"

Before Gracie could answer Agony spoke for her. "Can't you see, Keel? She doesn't need to swear. The truth is in her face."

"Wait!" Keel was staring at Gracie. "I saw you at the House of the Ancient Crones."

"That's right." Gracie was beginning to feel uncomfortable. Keel had come closer than she liked, and there was a strange glazed look in his eyes as if he was only half aware of what he was doing and saying. Had Gracie been able to see Jukk, she would have observed the same expression; such was Foyce's power of enchantment.

Glee, who had been standing peacefully while Gracie spoke with Agony, grew suddenly restive, pawing at the ground and shaking his head. Gracie put a hand on his neck to calm him, even though she was nervous too. She could tell that Keel was a wolf man … but what did he want? Was he planning to rescue Foyce?

She turned to Agony. "I'm very sorry to have given you bad news, but the Ancient Crones will look after Foyce. They really will! They look after everyone…"

Agony was playing with Glee's mane, twisting and turning a lock of hair. "Will you take her a message?"

"No!" It was Keel. "There will be no messages." He was scowling at Gracie. "You have met my cousin. What you do not know is that she has disgraced us. Whoever you are, you will not go to the crones on her behalf. The House is forbidden to her as it is to me. Jukk has spoken, and we must obey. Come, Agony." He seized Agony's arm, but before he pulled her away he gave Glee a stinging slap. The pony, already jittery, set off at a gallop and Gracie, taken entirely by surprise, was forced to grab his mane and hang on for all she was worth. It was several minutes before she could bring the pony back to a trot, and by that time any hope she might have had of finding Agony again was gone.

"Wow!" she said. "What did you make of that, Billy?"

There was no answer. Billy was not on her shoulder, and neither was he flying above her. It was Alf who circled down and landed on her shoulder.

"Afternoon, Miss Gracie!" He gave her an admiring look. "You didn't half travel when that wolf man hit the pony. I could only just keep up with you — and they call me the Super Speedster!"

Gracie shook her head. "I just hung on to poor Glee's mane and hoped for the best. Alf, Billy's gone missing again. I think he must have got left behind when Glee bolted."

"Too small for speed," Alf said. "He'll catch up."

"Did you see the wolf people?" Gracie asked. She shivered. "The wolf man — I think his name was Keel — he was weird. His eyes were … I can't explain it. As if he wasn't quite awake."

"Certainly did." Alf puffed out his chest. "Me and Unc, we searched the woods until we found the werewolves that went running away from the House last night. Unc followed the big one, but I've been on the tail of that one all day." He glanced over his shoulder as if werewolves might still be watching, and lowered his voice. "He was following the lady one, and she was following you, Miss Gracie."

"She's called Agony, and she's Foyce's mother," Gracie told him. "She wanted me to take Foyce a message, but she never said what it was. She was very sad, Alf. I do wish I could help her…"

Alf gave her a fond look. "That's 'cos you're a Trueheart, Miss Gracie. But you're right about her cousin. Weird as weird can be. I heard him telling her she couldn't send a message. He's a nasty piece of work, if you ask me."

Gracie was looking thoughtful. "But one thing was good. He said he wasn't allowed to go to the House, and nobody else was either … so it doesn't sound as if they're thinking of trying to rescue Foyce. He said someone called Jukk had ordered them not to. Is he the other one you saw?"

"Big guy," Alf agreed. "He's the leader. Unc's on his trail right now, seeing what he gets up to. Sometimes he's got two legs, then *woop!* he's covered in fur and running on four."

"I feel so sorry for poor Agony." Gracie sighed. "But maybe she and Foyce can get together after the aunties have cleared the evil away… I'll talk to Auntie Edna about it when I get home. But now we'd better get on to Gorebreath – unless you think we should go and look for Billy?"

Alf stretched his wings. "Leave it to me, Miss Gracie. I'll take a turn, find the kid and be back before you know it. I'll be there to see you rush into Mr Prince's arms, no worries."

Gracie decided to ignore this remark. "Thank you, Alf. I'll see you soon."

And as Alf soared up into the late-afternoon sky, she urged Glee forward in a steady trot.

Chapter Fourteen

King Frank of Gorebreath had called out the army for an evening inspection. He was distressed to see how few of them there were. There had never been any wars in the Five Kingdoms; although there were guards, and a small platoon of soldiers who spent their time sitting around in the guardroom at the end of the palace drive, when you put them all together they were less than impressive – especially if you were worrying about the defence of the kingdom. Vincent, red in the face and puffing hard, had arrived from Wadingburn with the shocking news that Queen Bluebell had driven away from her palace without telling anyone where she was going, and that the pony had returned without her. What was worse, it had arrived dragging the larger part of an extremely battered trap.

 190

"She's been kidnapped!" Vincent had announced. "Kidnapped by werewolves!"

King Frank was of the private opinion that any werewolf attempting to kidnap Bluebell would soon discover the error of its ways, but he had not said as much. He had told Queen Mildred to calm Vincent down, and gone outside to consider the situation. There was every possibility that she would come striding home unharmed; driving accidents were by no means rare in the kingdom of Wadingburn, and Bluebell was well known to be an enthusiastic but erratic horsewoman. There was also no proof that she had crossed the border; Vincent had not thought to check if she had been seen by any of the border guards, but ... then again, what if she had? Strange and dangerous things lurked on the other side of the border; things that might be stirred into action by the arrival of a queen. What better hostage could there be than a reigning monarch from the Five Kingdoms?

It was this thought that had sent the king of Gorebreath out to check his own security arrangements.

"Preparing for the celebrations, are we, Your Majesty?" enquired a large and grizzled sergeant major.

"Erm ... yes. Are you sure there aren't any more of you?" King Frank stared at the massed ranks of fewer than a hundred. The buttons were shiny, and the boots well polished, but the general impression was more fancy dress than serious intent to do damage.

The sergeant major leapt to attention and executed a smart salute. "No, sir! All present and correct, sir!"

"Ah." The king stroked his chin. "But I expect you've a number of new recruits somewhere, Sergeant. Lots of healthy strapping boys in training?"

The sergeant major bristled. "No need for that, Your Majesty. No need at all. Good lads, these. Do their duty every day." He drew himself up to his full height and glared down at the king. "There's no cause for complaint, I hope, sir?"

King Frank was taken aback, but also reassured. A man who stood up to a king was surely capable of defending a kingdom. He did his best to look as if he was in command of the situation. "No, no, Sergeant Major. I have every faith in you. Every faith. I'm sure the – er – lads are splendid chaps." He paused. "You'd say the border was well protected, wouldn't you?"

The sergeant major relaxed. So THAT was what it was all about. Yet another stupid rumour about zombies, or dragons, or witches. It happened all the

 193

time, and he was used to ignoring such things. He and his troops had had many cheery discussions about the foolishness of the royal families, and their fond belief that the border was kept safe by guards. The military knew better. They had seen for themselves what happened when a geographically confused zombie hit the force field of the Web surrounding the Five Kingdoms; their role was simply to pick up the pieces and leave them in a safe spot where the owner could reassemble himself once the shock had worn off. Where the force field came from was of no interest; it worked, and the guards were grateful. They could happily play cards, or knit socks, or pop elsewhere to visit a friend without a care in the world. This was not, however, something that they advertised. If royalty chose to pay them a respectable salary for guarding the kingdom and marching up and down from time to time, who were they to query a mutually satisfactory arrangement?

The sergeant major gave the anxious king a comforting pat on the back. "No worries at all, Your Majesty. Safe as houses. Guards on duty night and day."

"Excellent. Good show. Keep it up!" King Frank nodded, and went back to the palace to see if there was any news of Bluebell. No messages had arrived, and he made his way to his private parlour, where he found Vincent sitting with Queen Mildred.

It was an indication of the prince's state of mind that the piece of cake in front of him was quite untouched. He looked up as the king came in, his face even paler than usual. "Has she been eaten?"

"What? Eaten? Certainly not!" King Frank sounded more confident than he felt. "She'll come rolling in, full of beans as usual. Just you wait and see."

Vincent was not convinced. "But what if she doesn't? What'll happen to the kingdom? Loobly doesn't want to be queen; she told Grandmother so. And –" Vincent's face crumpled, and for a moment he stopped looking pompous and turned into a little boy who had lost his way – "I don't know how to be a king. Would Marcus do it for me, do you think?"

"Do what?" Marcus, carrying a long wooden lance, swung into the room. "I say, Father! This lance is ANCIENT! Haven't we got anything better? I'll never knock Tertius off his horse with this."

There was a loud wail from Vincent. "The tournament! I'd forgotten all about the horrid tournament! What am I going to do? Grandmother promised I wouldn't have to play! She said she'd arrange for me to walk in front of you and Arry instead – but she's not here any more, so what am I going to say to Marigold? I can't ride a horse! I can't wave a spear!"

Marcus looked at him, baffled. "Who said you were going to have anything to with the tournament? It's me and Tertius. Oh, and Arry."

King Frank was listening with interest, and now he nodded. "Just a minute, Marcus, my boy. You really mustn't be so selfish, you know. Of course Vincent must be there! All the princes of the Five Kingdoms taking part – that's the way to do these things. You'll have to ask Albion just as soon as possible – can't imagine why you didn't think of it. His father'll be delighted. Absolutely delighted. Amazing horseman, King Dowby."

It was common knowledge that Albion turned a nasty shade of green if he so much as saw a picture of a pony, but Marcus was wise enough to keep this information to himself. Instead he made a noise that could be taken for agreement, and turned back to Vincent. "What are you doing here, Vinnie? Come with more stories about your grandmother going mad?"

Vincent stared at him. "Don't be horrid." He sniffed, and rubbed his eyes. "My grandmother might have been eaten by werewolves."

"What? Bluebell? Eaten by werewolves?" Marcus gave a dismissive snort. "Never."

"But she's missing!" Vincent wailed. "Her pony came back without her and the trap was chopped into little tiny pieces!"

Marcus, taken aback by this news, looked questioningly at his father, who nodded. "It's a serious situation, Marcus. You should be more considerate of Vincent's feelings."

"Sorry, Vincent." Marcus gave his fellow prince a sympathetic slap on the shoulder, but there was an interested gleam in his eyes. "When did she go missing? And which direction did her pony come from?"

Vincent looked at him in astonishment. "How should I know? I had ever such a bad night and I had to have an extra little sleep this morning and when I woke up she was gone! And then her pony came back without her, and I jumped in the carriage and I came here." His lower lip began to tremble. "I was so upset I didn't even think about bringing a snack with me, and I never, ever go anywhere without a little snack..."

"Really, Marcus." King Frank gave a disapproving tut. "You can't go bothering the poor boy with questions when he's so anxious about his grandmother."

"Sorry again, Vincent," Marcus said. "Erm ... if you'll excuse me, I've just thought of something I must do."

His father frowned. "I trust you're not up to anything foolish. It's getting late, and it'll be dark before long."

Marcus shook his head. "Don't worry, Father. See you soon, Vincent..." And leaving his lance propped up against the wall, he hurried out of the room and headed for the stables. It was only as he turned into the stable yard that he remembered that Glee had been left at the House of the Ancient Crones.

"Blast! What am I going to do now?" He walked down the line of loose boxes to see which other horses or ponies were there, and found Arioso's pony Hinny looking hopefully at him over her half-door. "Brilliant," Marcus said. "Fancy going on a little adventure, Hinny?"

The pony whickered softly, and Marcus grinned. "You don't get out much, do you? Poor old girl. But today's your lucky day. There's a queen gone missing, and I'm going to find her ... even if it takes me all night." He paused, and rubbed his head thoughtfully. "If only Gracie were here. Adventures aren't the same without her."

Hinny wasn't listening to Marcus. Her ears were twitching, and she was looking eagerly over his shoulder.

"What is it?" Marcus asked, but it was another moment before he too heard the sound of hooves.

Going to the stable door, he saw Gracie riding into the yard on Glee, her blue eyes shining with pleasure as she caught sight of him.

"Hi," she said. "I've brought Glee back. Erm … are you going somewhere?"

Marcus caught her as she swung herself off Glee's saddle, and gave her a quick hug. "You're just in time! Bluebell's been knocked out of her trap and gone missing, and Vincent's in a terrible state, and I was just about to go and look for her – but now you can come too, so it'll be much more fun."

"Oh!" Gracie, her cheeks very pink, looked up at him. "But she's not lost! She's having tea with the Ancient Crones – I met her just after her accident. Gubble went with her to show her the way to the House."

"Really?" Marcus's disappointment showed in his face. "Are you sure?"

"Quite sure," Gracie told him. "I'm very sorry. I did meet two werewolves, though."

Marcus brightened. "You did? I wish I'd been there. Hang on a moment while I put Hinny's saddle away, and then you can tell me all about it."

Chapter Fifteen

Foyce had been weaving all day. She had been careful not to draw attention to herself; she had noticed the murmured consultations that had resulted from her humming the day before. She was also aware that the Oldest had been upstairs to snoop around her bedroom, but as nothing had been said she assumed that the careful camouflaging of her night-time activities had been successful. Now, as she wove, her mind was whirling. She knew that Marcus was to take part in a tournament at the Centenary Celebration Day, and that Gracie would be present. Crowds from all around the Five Kingdoms would be attending; this, Foyce had already decided, would be the ideal time to strike. Her cold heart beat faster at the thought of Marcus lying bleeding and broken in the dust while Gracie looked on ... and perhaps there could be even more carnage? Foyce's fingers moved faster on the loom in her excitement, and she dropped the shuttle. As she picked it up she was imagining princes and princesses falling in heaps, while the crowd pointed accusing fingers at Gracie. "It's your fault!" they would howl. "All your fault!" And Gracie would cower away, but still the shouting would go on, and hands would reach out to tear at her silk dress, and bring her screaming to the ground and rip her limb from limb...

Foyce stopped weaving and stared, unseeing, at the silk on the loom in front of her. She had to be there. It would be no kind of revenge unless she could watch every blow, every taunt. But how? How could it be done?

The Youngest sighed. "Foyce – you're not paying attention to your work."

With a jolt, Foyce came back from her dream and reluctantly took up the shuttle again. As she did so she became aware of a voice in the distance, and what she heard made her lean towards the loom to conceal her expression as she listened with every part of her being.

"So tell me about this Web you weave. Keeps the Five Kingdoms safe, you say?"

Foyce risked a quick glance at Val, but the youngest crone gave no indication of hearing anything out of the ordinary. She was weaving steadily, and the silver sheen of the Web rippled and flowed under her fingers. Several shadows were darkening its gleaming surface, and Val was studying them thoughtfully; it was evident that no word of Bluebell's had reached her.

The Ancient One's reply was not loud enough even for Foyce's acute hearing, and she bit her lip in annoyance, but then Bluebell's voice rose again. "So the Web creates a protective wall? My goodness! Clever stuff indeed. Has it ever been broken?"

Once more the Ancient One's answer was lost, but from Bluebell's loud guffaw Foyce guessed that the reply had not been serious. She waited for the next comment.

"So it protects you and your house as well?"

Foyce froze. She had always assumed it was the power of the Ancient Crones that held her captive. She had often tried to escape, especially when she first found herself under their guardianship, but every time she had made an attempt she had been defeated. As she drew near to any outside door a feeling of weakness would seize her; her arms would lose strength, her legs would give way and her head would be filled with a mindless buzzing that sent her reeling. But if it was the Web, that was different. Surely it would be possible to—

"Foyce!" Val had noticed her preoccupation. "You're not paying attention! Just look at those tangles. It'll take at least an hour to put that right. I really think you'd better give up for today. Go to your room, and I'll bring you something to eat later after I've sorted out this mess."

Hoping for the opportunity to hear more from Bluebell and the Ancient One, Foyce threw down her shuttle, jumped to her feet and headed for the door. Her hopes of lingering outside the kitchen were, however, frustrated, as she met the Oldest coming to take her turn on the Web.

"Off to your room, dear?" Elsie asked and, much to Foyce's annoyance, stayed to watch the girl make her way slowly up the staircase. She continued watching until Foyce had gone into her room and slammed the door behind her.

"Hm," Elsie said to herself. "She's scowling. Is that a good sign or a bad one? Could be either, I'd say. Certainly more her usual style, so maybe it's good." And she went to take up her place at the loom in Room Seventeen.

Foyce, meanwhile, was considering her next move. Should she uncover the hole above the window? The Youngest had promised to bring her supper; would she notice anything if the curtains were drawn, hiding the missing bricks? Foyce thought not. Val had never been as observant as Edna or Elsie, and the curtains were thick and heavy. Even if it was windy outside they would be unlikely to stir. Deciding she was safe, Foyce began to methodically undo her work of the morning. She was careful to make sure no plaster flakes fell on the carpet, and she kept the curtains all but closed in case of a surprise visitation. In no time she was once more breathing in the evening air; as she looked out she could see the evening star twinkling high above her. Something fluttering towards the house caught her eye, and she leant forward to see what it was.

"The little bat!" she breathed, and as she smiled she showed her sharp pointed teeth. "Billy! Come here! Come here this minute, or you'll wish you'd never been born!"

It was Billy's worst nightmare coming true. Having lost Gracie, he had dithered between flying home or following along the path to see if he could catch up with her, but the speed at which Glee had taken off had made him doubt that he could fly fast enough. In the end he had decided to go back to the House. He knew he would feel safe in the warm kitchen, and he wanted to wait there until Gracie returned − but now Foyce's cold eyes were staring at him and he was unable to resist her order. Quivering, he flew nearer.

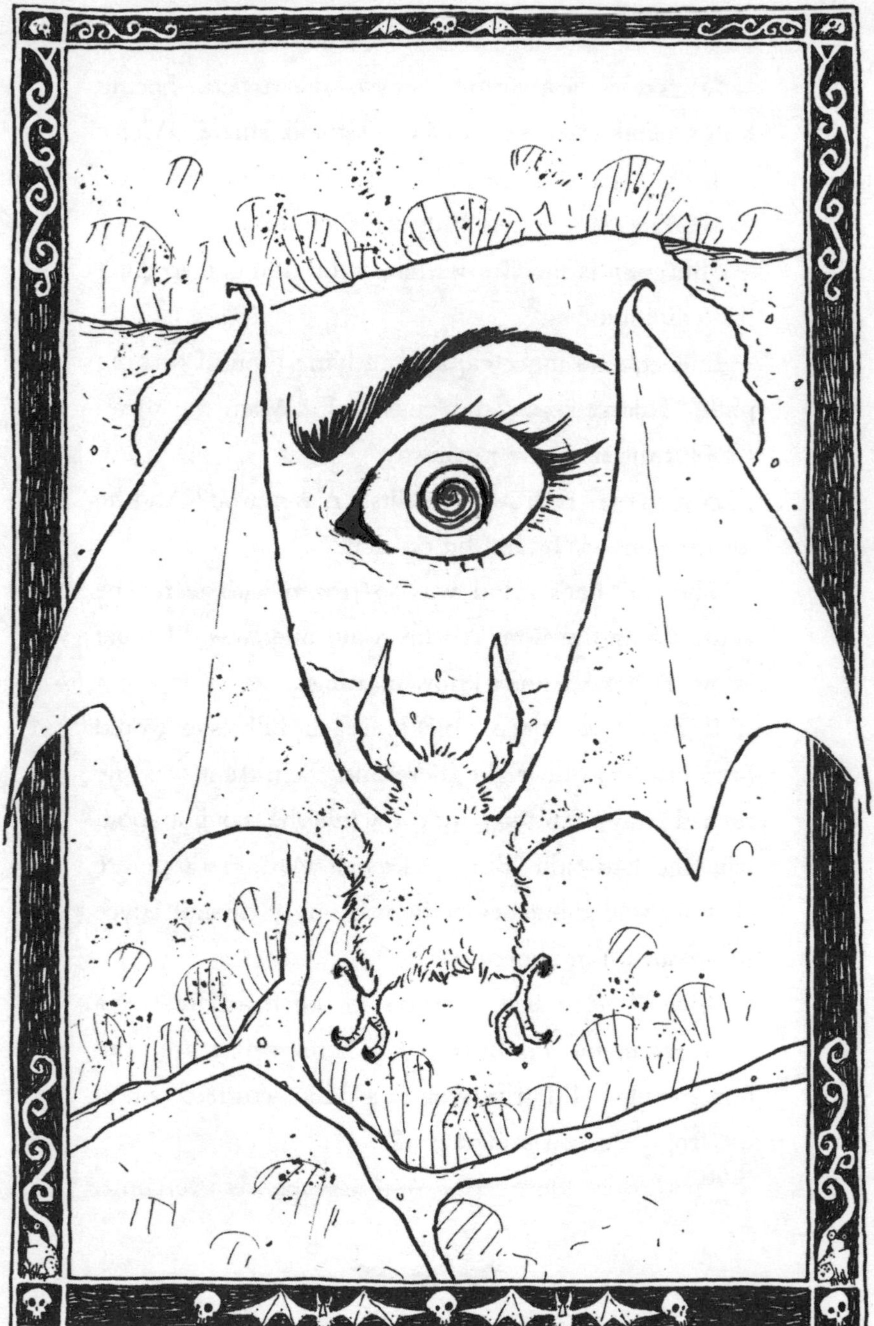

"Where's the worm?" Foyce demanded. Seeing Billy's blank stare she added, "Gracie, stupid! Where is she?"

"Riding on a pony," Billy whispered.

"But *where* is she? In the forest? I'll find out, so don't try telling me lies."

Billy was no more capable of lying than of turning pink. "I don't know," he quavered. "When the were-wolf hit the pony, he ran away."

Foyce's eyes narrowed to slits. "A werewolf? And he hit the pony? Why did he do that?"

The tiny bat's mind was so frozen with terror he could find no answer. All he could offer was, "I don't know. Please – I don't know nothing..."

If Foyce had been able to reach Billy she would have crushed him right there and then. As it was she turned away from the window, while she thought about what he had said. Billy, released, made a desperate dash for safety, but before he was out of earshot Foyce summoned him once more.

"Billy," she hissed, "if you so much as breathe a word about me I'll find you, wherever you are, and boil you alive. I'll grind you to a paste, and feed you to the frogs. Do you understand?"

"Yes," Billy squeaked. "Yes!" Completely overcome,

he fluttered helplessly in a downward spiral, whirling round and round until he fell in among the thick leathery leaves of a laurel bush. There he lay still, his eyes closed.

Foyce drummed her fingers on the windowpane. So … there was a werewolf in the forest, he'd met Gracie and he'd sent her and her pony running … but what did that signify? Evidently he hadn't fallen under Gracie's Trueheart spell, and that was pleasing. It also suggested he wasn't afraid to confront a human, and that pleased her even more. But could it have been the magnificent creature that she had seen the previous night? Somehow she found it hard to imagine him engaging Gracie in conversation … but, certain that he would be coming back to the House very soon, she abandoned that line of thought and concentrated on removing another brick from the wall.

Marlon had sent Alf after Keel while he followed Jukk. Hovering above the pine trees he had watched him walk deep into the forest and make his way to a cave half hidden by ferns and bracken. Marlon, flying close, had hoped to discover a gathering of werewolf conspirators, but instead he found himself in a bare but serviceable room.

For a moment Jukk stood in the doorway. He appeared to be staring out into the night, but his eyes were glazed and lacking focus. Marlon shook his head. "Looks mad. Off his head, or been eating dodgy mushrooms."

As he watched, Jukk heaved a heavy sigh, and flung himself onto a large couch. In seconds he was fast asleep.

Marlon flew a swift circle of the room in case he was missing something, but discovered nothing more suspicious than a large collection of bones. Hearing a succession of faint snores coming from the couch, Marlon decided that conspiracy was not on the agenda for the time being.

"Might as well catch a quick kip while I can." He yawned, and settled himself on the top of a convenient coat rack. A moment later the werewolf's snores were echoed by his own.

Marlon woke to find he was alone. Impressed by the werewolf's silent exit, he looped swiftly out of the empty cave. Several circles later there was still no sign of Jukk. Feeling faintly guilty for not having stayed awake and alert he headed for the House. There he found Queen Bluebell and the Ancient One

 208

deep in conversation in the kitchen. A lot of tea had been drunk, judging by the number of teapots and cups on the table, and as he arrived through the bat flap Edna was pouring out yet another brew while Bluebell expounded her problems.

"So you see –" the queen waved a teaspoon in the air to make her point more forcefully – "another few years and the Five Kingdoms will be in chaos. All of us older rulers will be gone, and if you added up the combined brain cells of Loobly, Albion, Vincent, Tertius and Arioso you'd probably have enough for a very small guinea pig. And what about Dreghorn? Fedora's married to Tertius – so does that mean Dreghorn will have to be linked with Niven's Knowe? Or will one of the other daughters be queen instead? Nina-Rose will be married to Arry by then, heaven help him, so that leaves Marigold – and she can't see further than the next pair of satin slippers." Bluebell pulled out her lorgnette and polished it fiercely. "I think we're coming to the end of the Five Kingdoms. I really do."

"But the end of one thing can make room for the beginning of something different," Edna said. "Change isn't always a bad thing. It can be … enlivening."

Bluebell gave her loud booming laugh. "We could certainly do with a spot of that in the Kingdoms."

 209

The Ancient One chuckled. "Maybe change will come about in its own way." She glanced up at the picture rail. "What do you think, Marlon?"

Marlon shrugged as he settled himself for a chat. "*Qué será, será* 'n' all that jazz." He scratched his head. "Never quite got the point of kings 'n' such, excuse me for saying. I mean, how come someone gets to call the shots just 'cos they've got a crown?"

"You're quite right, Marlon." The Queen of Wadingburn beamed at him. "It's a ridiculous idea. Now tell me, who do you think should be in charge of the Five Kingdoms?"

There was a pause. "Tough ask," Marlon said at last. "With us bats, it's the guy –" he saw Bluebell's expression, and hastily added, "or the gal who's been around a bit and knows what's what, and who looks out for the little ones, and doesn't get big-headed 'cos they're the big chief."

"An excellent summary of the necessary virtues," Bluebell told him.

Marlon coughed. "Thought of something else. Gotta listen. Important, that. Not too good at it, myself. At least, that's what my daughter tells me, and she's a good girl."

"But a willingness to admit to the occasional

mistake is also of prime importance." Bluebell clapped her hands. "So – we know what we need. But where will we find such a perfect leader?"

The Ancient One and Marlon exchanged a glance of complete understanding and agreement. "Looks to me like you, Your Maj," Marlon said. "And if you can hang on a bit longer, you might get young Marcus and Gracie trained up in time to follow you on."

Bluebell looked hopeful. "You don't think they'd be able to manage now?"

"Nah." Marlon was very definite. "Too soon. Too young."

"I'm afraid I agree with Marlon," Edna said.

"Oh dear," Bluebell said, and she sounded weary. "Oh dear."

The Ancient One heaved herself up from her chair, and came to lay a hand on Bluebell's shoulder. "You can do it, my dear. And I promise that whenever you need a rest, you'll be more than welcome to come and stay here. In fact, I think I should offer you a bed for the night tonight – it's getting very late."

"I do feel tired," the queen agreed, but then a sudden alarming thought made her sit bolt upright. "But what about Vincent? He could be up to anything by now! I should get back—"

Elsie shook her head. "Gracie will have told them that you're here. And I've had an idea. Why don't you stay tomorrow, as well? You look as if you could do with a little break. Marlon will take a message, won't you, Marlon?"

"Be my pleasure," Marlon said, and he stretched his wings. "I'll be offski *toute suite*, pardon my Italian. *Ciao*, ladies both!"

Bluebell and Edna watched as he took a short cut behind the curtains and out through the window. "He's a character, that one," Bluebell remarked. "I'm honoured he considers me his friend."

"I'm not sure what we'd do without him these days," Edna told her as she began to clear up the tea things. "His past doesn't bear a lot of investigation, to be honest, but ever since he met Gracie he's been on the straight and narrow. Now, would you like a hot water bottle?"

As the two old women made their preparations for the night, Foyce was far from thinking about sleeping. She had extended the gap above the window by the width of another two bricks; she stood back and inspected her work with pride. There had been a bad moment when the Youngest had come in without knocking;

 213

fortunately she had been concentrating so hard on the tray of stew and dumplings she hadn't seen anything significant. The curtains had all but covered the window, and once the tray had been put down Val had hurried away.

Foyce licked her lips, and chuckled – or tried to chuckle. To her alarm the sound that came out was more of a satisfied growl; she clutched at her throat, and moved swiftly away from the moonlight pouring into the room.

"Full moon tomorrow night," she told herself, and was conscious of an unusual feeling of anxiety. The howling … and now a growl. What was happening to her?

A sound from outside made her move cautiously back to the window. Jukk was standing outside, gazing up at her window. In his arms was a bunch of roses; in the light of the moon they looked black, but as he tossed them one by one into her room she saw they were as red as blood.

"Stupid fool," Foyce muttered. "How can I explain away roses?" And once again a small guttural growl escaped her. Now seriously alarmed, she studied her hands and arms, but there was no sign of wolfish hair or claws. As the final rose fell at her feet she looked

 214

up at the sky, and saw the moon slide behind a bank of clouds. Much relieved, she stepped forward so the watching Jukk could see her. "What sweet flowers!" she trilled. "Who are you, that you bring such kindness to a poor prisoner?"

"I am Jukk, leader of the pack." Jukk's voice rang out, and Foyce put a finger to her lips.

"Hush! My guards may be listening! And if you are discovered, I will be lost to you for ever." Foyce allowed a tear to roll down her cheek as she hung her head.

"Not so!" Jukk was whispering now. "You must never be lost to me. I will call my brothers, and we will storm the house and set you free—"

"No ... my dear sweet friend. That must not be. But there is a way, a way you could do me such service that I will be in your debt for ever and ever..." Foyce was calculating madly. Her burning desire to see Gracie humiliated and destroyed was growing stronger and stronger, but to act too soon would send her plans crashing into ruins.

Jukk, so deeply caught in the net of Foyce's wiles that he would have promised her anything, stood up straight and held his hand to his heart. "I swear your wish shall be my command, whatever it might be!

Only ask, and I will obey, oh, breath of my soul, and song of my heart."

Foyce repressed a snort of derision. "Fancy-pancy speak" she muttered, but out loud she said, "Kind sir – all I ask is that you destroy my enemy, and the friends of my enemy. Then, and only then, will I be freed from my chains..."

The werewolf bowed. "I swear. Tell me when and where, and it shall be done, if I die in the attempt."

Coming closer to the window, Foyce began to hiss her instructions.

"There is to be a tournament in the Five Kingdoms, and my enemy will be riding out. Challenge him! Challenge Marcus, brother of the heir to the kingdom of Gorebreath! He wishes me to be his bride; I am prisoner here until I promise I am his – or until he dies. Throw him to the ground, and then – kill him!"

At the thought of a rival Jukk's lovesick mind filled with a furious red mist, and he snarled and bared his teeth. "It shall be done! And you will be mine, fair lady – mine, and mine alone!"

Deep in the darkness of the laurel bush Billy opened his eyes for a moment, and shivered. He was having a dream. That's what it was. A terrible, terrible dream.

 216

When he woke up he would be safe in the kitchen drawer, and Miss Gracie would be moving gently round the kitchen, and all would be well...

He closed his eyes once more.

Chapter Sixteen

The news that Queen Bluebell of Wadingburn had gone to have a cup of tea with the Ancient Crones had left King Frank of Gorebreath in a quandary. He was unable to decide if he was relieved or horrified or both, and the confusion made him tetchy. Urgently needing to take control of something he could understand, he decided that Marcus's tournament required a firmer hand and stricter rules.

He got up early the following morning, and sent a flurry of messengers riding off to Niven's Knowe, Cockenzie Rood and Dreghorn to announce that he was now in charge, and that the venue would be Gorebreath. With a swirl of his pen he wrote a further instruction: all the princes of the Five Kingdoms were to take their place in the tournament. Refusal would not be tolerated.

The Prince of Wadingburn was the first to be informed of this directive. Vincent had stayed overnight at Gorebreath, and came face to face with King Frank at the breakfast table. Here he was terrified into a state of trembling collapse – so much so that even the king had to admit it was highly unlikely that this particular prince would ever be seen on a horse. Growling to himself, he sent orders for a uniform to be found, firmly ignoring Vincent's feeble requests for something custom-made with a good deal of gold braid and buttons. After the reply came through from Cockenzie Rood the king's growling got louder. The dowager duchess had done her best to send a tactfully worded reply, but had not entirely succeeded. "Allergic to horses?" King Frank muttered. "What are these modern-day princes made of? Candyfloss?" And the order went out for a matching uniform for Prince Albion, together with instructions that he should arrive early on the Wednesday morning.

"Thank heavens for Tertius and Arioso," King Frank told himself as he put down his pen. "And Marcus, of course. Stout fellows. Sure to put on a good show. And the girls will give it a touch of glamour. The peasants like a touch of glamour. Reminds them that we're the Royals, and they're not." For a moment he allowed himself to smile, but then he remembered that amongst "the girls" would be Gracie Gillypot. The smile vanished, and he snatched up the pen and began to chew the end. It seemed only too obvious that Gracie was the reason that Bluebell had abandoned her senses and her kingdom—

King Frank stopped.

Could that be true? Had she abandoned her kingdom? When Marcus had come hurrying in to report that the queen was safe and sound he had said nothing about her plans to return. What if she had decided to move in with the Ancient Crones? The king jumped up and began to pace to and fro. He felt as if his world had taken a sudden alarming lurch, and all the rules and regulations that knit the Five Kingdoms into a safe and harmonious whole were in danger of unravelling. Striding across the room, he rang the bell, and when a page boy came running to see what was wanted he demanded that Marcus and Gracie be sent to him at once.

Gracie had not appeared at breakfast. Marcus had persuaded her to stay the night, arguing that it was too late to return to the House of the Ancient Crones, and Gracie, conscious of King Frank's

 220

increasing coldness towards her, had agreed with much reluctance. Queen Mildred, uncomfortably aware of things not being as smooth as they might once have been, had tactfully suggested that Gracie have her breakfast in bed. Gracie had been surprised, but had enjoyed the unaccustomed luxury of a silver tray heaped with plates of porridge, scrambled eggs and toast. The king's summons found her carrying her tray down the stairs to the kitchen; the page took it from her with a broad smile. All the servants at Gorebreath Palace were fond of Gracie. As they regularly told each other, "She never gives herself airs, that one. Nice as pie to everybody, she is. Not like them princesses, with their 'Do this! Do that!' and never a please or a thank you."

"Mind your step, Miss," the page whispered. "His Majesty's in a right old mood."

"Thanks," Gracie said, but her heart sank. She was cheered by seeing Marcus running towards her, and even more so when he swept her up in a hug before kissing her soundly.

"Let's go and see what the old grump wants," he said as he took her hand. "And whatever it is, don't worry. He can't chuck us in a dungeon."

Gracie privately thought that there might be worse

221

things than being thrown into a dungeon, but she didn't say as much. She and Marcus walked together down the long marble corridor, and into the king's private office. King Frank was sitting behind his desk, and he made no attempt to get up and greet the young couple as they came in.

Gracie stepped forward, and bobbed a curtsey. "Good morning, Your Majesty."

The king frowned, but before he could reply the door opened again.

"Morning, Father! Mother said Marcus and Gracie were here, and I thought you might be talking about the tournament, so I thought I'd pop in as well." Arry beamed, and settled himself in an armchair. "Hello, Gracie. I'm so pleased you're going to be there. It's going to be super fun, isn't it?"

King Frank had not expected this. He cleared his throat while he tried to rearrange his thoughts. "Ah. Yes. The tournament." He coughed again, and went on, "Yes. I did want to talk about the tournament..."

"Was it about the stage?" Arry asked helpfully. "Mother says it's going to take place here now, and not at Niven's Knowe."

"No. No, it wasn't about the stage." Momentarily deflected from his purpose, King Frank looked at the

 222

notes on his desk. "That's all sorted. There's a wagon bringing it over from Niven's Knowe this afternoon. It'll be all set up by tomorrow."

"Ready for the tournament!" Arry gave Marcus a quick glance. "Tertius and Marcus battling it out first, and then Terty against me." He saw Marcus's tiny nod of agreement, and went on beaming. "Ha! Can't wait!"

"What?" The king raised his eyebrows. "No, no. You're the oldest. You'll go first. And then Marcus will ride out against the winner. I'm sure that'll be you, Arioso!"

If the king had not been staring at his desk he would have noticed the sudden disappearance of Arry's smile, and his agonized look at his twin. Marcus opened his mouth to protest, but a second thought made him close it again without saying anything, and wink at Arry instead. "It's OK," he mouthed. "We'll sort it."

Unaware of the silent communication between the brothers, the king went on, "But now I have something else I need to say. You may as well stay, Arioso. I'm sure you'll agree with me. Ahem." He fiddled with the papers on his desk, then took a deep breath and looked up. Faced with Gracie's clear

 223

blue gaze he faltered for a moment. "Erm ... that is ... yes." In sudden need of reassurance, he put up his hand to settle his crown more firmly on his head. Feeling the comforting weight of royalty heavy on his brow, he was able to continue. "I've called you here, Miss Gillypot, because I want to ask something of you. I want you to go home, and not return to the Five Kingdoms." There was a sharp exclamation from both Marcus and Arry, and the king held up his hand. "No! Hear me out. I know I agreed that Miss Gillypot could attend the tournament, but I've changed my mind. The circumstances are different now."

Marcus was very pale. "What circumstances? Explain. What circumstances?"

His father was finding the situation harder than he had expected. "Really, Marcus! I do NOT expect to be spoken to in that tone of voice! How dare you?"

"Because I want to know." Marcus was keeping his temper with difficulty. "I think it's only fair to give Gracie the facts before you ask something like that."

"I'd be glad if you could tell me, Your Majesty," Gracie said gently.

King Frank swallowed. "The thing is, Miss Gillypot, that you're in a very unusual situation. I've been giving the matter a lot of thought. It – it's not at all usual for a young lady of your background to set foot in a palace, let alone make advances to a prince of the realm."

Marcus gave a loud gasp, but Gracie put a restraining hand on his. "Let's hear what your father has to say."

"Thank you, Miss Gillypot. As I was saying, you have been behaving in the most unusual way. And your influence has led my son Marcus to behave in an unusual way for a prince. In fact, I'd go so far as to say he has been behaving for some time in what can only be described as a thoroughly – er – thoroughly unusual manner. Not the kind of thing his mother and I expect. No. Not at all. And … and other members of royalty are also being led astray. Our own dear Bluebell, Queen of Wadingburn, for example. I believe she is, at this very moment, either with the strange old women who you call aunts, or on her way back—"

The king stopped. Gracie, her eyes very bright, was standing right in front of him.

"Excuse me, Your Majesty. Are you saying that I am responsible for the actions of both your son and the Queen of Wadingburn?"

"Well … perhaps not personally responsible," King Frank admitted. "But if it wasn't for you, Miss Gillypot, Marcus wouldn't be wittering on all the time about dragons and zombies and werewolves – and we don't need to know about these things!" The king's voice was rising, and he began to stab the air with his finger. "You see, it was all so COMFORTABLE before you came along! Here in the Five Kingdoms we've always known what's what, and who's who, and how we like things to be – and that's the way we've ALWAYS been – but now I keep wondering what might be lurking outside the border and—"

"And you're scared." Gracie nodded. "I can understand that."

The king was, momentarily, speechless.

"But there have always been those things outside the border, Your Majesty," Gracie told him. "Pretending they aren't there doesn't make them go away, you know. But not all of them are scary. And the Ancient Crones will always be there to protect you—"

This was too much. King Frank stood up, his face scarlet with rage, and glared at Gracie. "What nonsense are you talking? Get out of here, young

 227

woman, and never come back. NEVER! Do you hear me? NEVER!"

Gracie, hoping that the trembling of her knees would not betray her, moved closer to Marcus. "I think I'd better go. But if you still want me to be your – what was it you said? – your Partner of Choice at the tournament tomorrow, then I promise that I'll be there."

Marcus took her hand. "Just a minute. I've had enough of this. I'm coming with you." He gave his father a cold look. "I'll be back for the tournament. I'm not going to let Arry down, or Tertius. But I'm not going to stay here. You can't talk to people like that, Father. You really can't. Gracie's just the same as you, or me, or the little boy who stirs the soup in the kitchen. Just because you wear a crown on your head doesn't mean you have the right to think you're better than everyone else."

Eyes popping, King Frank stared at Marcus, then turned to Arioso. "What? What? What's he saying? Is he mad?"

Arry shook his head. "I'm afraid Marcus is right, Father. Gracie's a great girl. No doubt about it. Just as good as us." He sighed. "In fact, do you know what? I'd say she's better. Rather a lot better, actually."

 228

"Well said, bruv." Marcus gave his brother a slap on the back that sent him reeling. "Well said indeed! Come on, Gracie. We'll say goodbye to Mother, and then we'll be off."

"Wait!"

Marcus would have ignored his father, but Gracie heard the hidden appeal in the king's voice, and held the prince back. "Yes?" she asked.

"Just … just give me a moment." King Frank held on to his crown as if he might find some help in the feel of it. Gracie and Marcus stood waiting, and Arioso held his breath.

"I suppose—"

The remainder of the king's speech was lost in the sound of splintering wood and a loud crash as the door fell in.

"Ug." Gubble's flat green face was glowing with triumph at his achievement. "Find Gracie!"

He was immediately followed by a small bat, who flew in a circle over the troll's head, squeaking loudly.

"I told him not to, Miss Gracie! I did! I really did!"

"Cool it, kiddo!" A second bat was right behind. "A troll's gotta do what a troll's gotta do, that's a fact. Morning, all!"

King Frank made a curious gobbling noise, then

rushed for the broken-down door. "Guards!" he yelled, "Guards! Guards! GUARDS!"

Ten minutes later, Gracie and Gubble found themselves locked in a dungeon. It was chilly, but not entirely unpleasant. As nobody had been imprisoned there for over a hundred years the royal household had taken to using it for storage, and all kinds of miscellaneous items were piled up against the walls. Gracie and Gubble were able to make themselves reasonably comfortable on a couple of velvet sofas, one of which was surprisingly new, apart from copious smears of jam and cream. Gubble, who had wasted at least an hour attempting to force his way through the steel-reinforced dungeon door, was now lying back with one of Gracie's hankies tied round his bruised and battered head. He was sucking his thumb, and from time to time a green tear trickled down his dust-smeared cheeks.

Gracie sighed. "It's all right, Gubble. You weren't to know it was the king's private office."

Gubble took out his thumb and gave Gracie a mournful look. "Gubble bad. Gubble VERY bad. Gubble bring TROUBLE."

"Marcus will get us out of here very soon," Gracie told him, with rather more hope than conviction.

 230

* * *

The king had been very angry indeed, and had refused to listen to any arguments or pleading from either Marcus or Arioso. Gracie and Gubble were taken to the dungeon, and Marcus, fighting all the way, escorted to his room and locked in. It had not helped when he inadvertently poured fuel on the flames by telling his father that Bluebell was staying on in the Less Enchanted Forest, and would only be returning the following day for the Celebration Tournament. King Frank had taken this as a personal affront and something akin to a declaration that the queen had gone over to the enemy; after seeing his tormentors dealt with he had stormed off to send urgent messages to King Horace of Niven's Knowe, the dowager duchess of Cockenzie Rood and Queen Kesta of Dreghorn. So far there had been no response, and this was not improving his temper. Vincent, who had been foolish enough to remark that at least his grandmother hadn't been eaten by werewolves, was told that it might have been better if she had.

"Rack and ruin!" the king roared as he marched into his parlour to see if Queen Mildred would lend him a sympathetic ear. "Rack and ruin! Am I the only sane person left in the Five Kingdoms, Mildred?

Whatever next? Revolution and uprising, that's what it'll be. You mark my words!"

The queen said nothing, but silently handed him a cup of tea. Marlon, watching from the curtain rail, nudged Alf. "Letting him get it out of his system," he observed. "Sound move."

Alf was fidgeting up and down the rail. "Hadn't we better see how Miss Gracie's doing?"

Marlon held up a reproving claw. "Need to check out the action," he explained. "Need to get the full picture before you report back."

"Me?" Alf asked. "Report?"

"Clear the fluff outta your brain, kid," his uncle snapped. "We've got Gracie in a dungeon, Marcus locked in his room and a king that's mad as a box of frogs. Gotta report back to the heavy guys, 'n' that means your pal Bluebell and the crones. Now shut it and listen."

Rightly judging that Marlon's irritation was caused by worry, Alf did as he was told.

King Frank had downed his tea in a couple of gulps, and was now consuming cake while Queen Mildred refilled his cup. "Thank you, Mildred. A firm hand – that's what's needed. A firm hand. If there's a firm

 232

hand in charge, we may yet restore the Five Kingdoms to the way it was, and always has been. If we can get the celebrations out of the way without any trouble, then we can start again. I'll get together with Horace and Kesta and Dowby – no, not Dowby. He'll only talk about horses. We'll get Hortense, and we'll bash out a few new rules. That should do it. Everyone to stay inside the border. Nobody in, and nobody out, except by special permission. That'll be MY permission, of course." The king stopped to swallow. "Hm. That's better. Nothing like a nice cup of tea. In the meantime, I've made quite certain that the Gillypot girl and that DREADFUL troll can't cause any more trouble, and we'll keep Marcus in his room until it's time for the tournament, however much he shouts about it." King Frank shook his head. "I have to say, my dear, I was strongly tempted to shut him in the dungeon as well, but he and that Gillypot gal are best kept apart, as I'm sure you'll agree. Might there be another cup of tea in that pot?"

There was, and the queen poured it out. She had her own opinions about Gracie, but now was not the moment to mention them. Instead, she topped up the teapot with hot water, and handed the king his third slice of fruit cake. He took it without noticing what he

 233

was doing, but Queen Mildred saw that he was now leaning back in his chair, and the hectic purple tinge had faded from his cheeks.

"I'm sure you'll do whatever is right and proper, my dear," she said soothingly.

The king nodded. "I always try to do my best. Responsibility comes with the crown, you know. Hm! Very fine cake, this. Very fine indeed." He heaved a massive sigh. "Shame our boys don't have more of a sense of responsibility."

The queen was shocked. "Frank! Arry's always been a perfect model of responsibility!"

"Not any more. Do y'know, he actually tried to tell me Gracie Gillypot shouldn't be put in a dungeon? He's fallen under her spell, I'm afraid—" The king suddenly choked on his cake. "Mildred! Do you think that's it? Witchcraft?"

"No, no, no." Queen Mildred put a reassuring hand over the king's. "She's a perfectly ordinary girl." Judging that she could risk a little persuasion, she added, "I've always found her extremely sensible, as it happens, and I know Hortense thinks the same. Rather a sweet child, in fact. I'm sure she won't make a fuss when you let her out to watch the tournament."

"Let her out?" King Frank's eyebrows shot up. "No, no, Mildred. I'm keeping her safely under lock and key until the celebrations are well and truly over. You can be quite certain of that! Now, let's have another cup of tea and talk about something much more pleasant. What are you going to wear tomorrow? I've found some splendid uniforms for Albion and Vincent, and our boys and Tertius will look magnificent in their armour – and I believe all Kesta's gals are having brand-new dresses. But what about you, my love?"

Up on the curtain rail Marlon nudged Alf. "Time to go. Report to thc House. Fast as you can. I'll pop down and check on our Gracie."

Alf nodded. "Sure thing, Unc. Erm … what about Mr Prince? Shouldn't you see him too? Torn apart from his lady love, 'n' all?"

"Gotta point there, kid," Marlon conceded.

"And there's the other Mr Prince who isn't our Mr Prince," Alf went on. "Fighting for our Miss Gracie too, he is."

Marlon gave his nephew a cold look. "Think I'm past it, kiddo? On my list. Now, scram!"

Alf gave his uncle a cheery claws-up, and made a

silent departure through the open window. Marlon, aware that it was more than likely that Marcus's window would be shut and barred to prevent escape, headed for the fireplace. He was well acquainted with the maze of interconnected chimneys within the palace, and he made no mistakes as he flew through the darkness. Moments later he landed, only a little sooty, on the back of an armchair in Marcus's room.

"Wotcher, kid. I wouldn't, if I was you!"

The prince, who was standing by the window holding a large and unflattering bust of King Frank, jumped. "Marlon! Marlon – I'm going mad! I've got to get out of here. If I smash the window I think I can swing down onto the wisteria—"

"Nah." The bat shook his head. "Wouldn't hold you. End up with a broken arm or leg, and then what good'll you be?"

"Are you sure?" Marcus swung the bust to and fro in front of the glass.

"Certain. Sorry, kiddo, but you need Plan B."

Marcus slumped down on the chair. "And that is?"

"Door unlocked." Marlon waved a wing in the general direction of the outside world. "Any chance your bro can help out?"

 236

"He's been banned from talking to me," Marcus said gloomily. "He had to promise, and Arry never breaks his promise."

Marlon's eyes brightened. "No need for the old chit-chat. Just slide a key under the door."

"I wish it was that easy. Father's got the key in his pocket. Have you seen Gracie? Is she OK?"

"On my way. Gotta message?" Marlon was circling the room as he spoke, looking for any possible alternative escape route. Marcus's room was in the oldest part of the palace, and the walls and door were substantial; it was unlikely that even Gubble would be able to force an entrance.

Marcus saw what he was doing, and shrugged. "I've been over all the walls, tapping and banging. They're solid as a rock. There's no way out. Give Gracie my love, and tell her I'm really sorry my father is such an idiot. Tell her I'll make it out of here somehow, and we'll get away together."

"Willco." Marlon nodded.

"And Marlon–" Marcus was anxious – "can you come back and tell me what she says? I wouldn't be surprised if she never wants to speak to me again."

"Sure," Marlon said. "Be back soon as. Keep your spirits up, kiddo. It ain't all over 'til the fat lady

 237

sings." And with a flutter of his wings he shot back up the chimney.

Marcus watched him go. A moment later he was kneeling in the fireplace, staring upwards. "Who's the idiot?" he asked himself. "Me, that's who. How could I have missed it?" And with a wriggle and a squirm, he began to climb.

Chapter Seventeen

"**D**on't you think I look absolutely gorgeous in purple?" Princess Marigold was twirling in front of her sisters. It would have been hard for them to have looked less interested, but Marigold was used to their indifference. She twirled nearer, tweaked Nina-Rose's nose and simultaneously pulled Fedora's hair. They squealed and looked up, and Marigold beamed at them. "I said, *Don't I look gorgeous?*"

Nina-Rose sniffed. "You look like a shiny purple plum. No wonder Vincent likes you so much."

"I know." Marigold took the remark as a compliment. "He adores me! And tomorrow he's going to lead the parade into the Celebration Tournament, and I'm going to wave MADLY at him from the front of the stage!"

Fedora glowered. "Actually, little sis, you're wrong.

 239

My darling Terty will be MUCH the most important person there, and as I'm his wife AND the future queen of Niven's Knowe it'll be ME at the front of the stage!"

"Just a minute!" Nina-Rose was scowling now. "What about me? I'm going to be queen of Gorebreath, and Gorebreath is MUCH bigger than potty little Niven's Knowe! And tomorrow Arry's going to be JUST as important as Tertius."

"Girls, girls, GIRLS!" Queen Kesta put down her sewing. "You'll sit in a row, and you'll all look beautiful – but if you keep on quarrelling you'll get nasty little frown lines, and then you won't be pretty at all."

Marigold stuck out her tongue at her older sisters. "See? So I WILL be at the front of the stage." She turned to her mother. "Ma – what's happening about that Gillypot person? Suzy in the kitchen says her boyfriend – whose gran is one of the cooks at Gorebreath – told her she's in a dungeon!"

Fedora stared at her sister. "Why would anyone put a cook in a dungeon?"

"No, stupid! It was Gracie they put in a dungeon!" Marigold giggled. "And that fat green troll she goes about with is in there too! Suzy says her boyfriend says his gran says he flattened five guards before they got him locked up!"

Nina-Rose began to smile. "Really? Gracie's in a dungeon? How long for?"

Marigold shrugged. "I don't know. Suzy says her—"

"That's enough, Marigold!" Queen Kesta said sharply. "How often have I told you not to gossip with the servants?"

"But Ma – it's the only way I ever find out anything!" Marigold was indignant. She giggled again. "Suzy says Vincent got ever so drunk the night I asked him to the tournament. She says—"

"That's enough, I said." The queen looked flustered. "Poor Vincent! He's got a lot to cope with at the moment, so you must be very kind to him."

"Because Bluebell's gone totally mad, you mean?" Fedora asked.

"Certainly not! She's done no such thing!" Kesta did her best to sound as if she believed what she was saying, even though she had private doubts. "Wherever did you get an idea like that?"

Fedora hesitated. She had, in fact, overheard the information, but saw no reason why it shouldn't be true; the coachman had been talking to the footman, and the groom had agreed with them, adding that he'd heard the same story from the postman.

"Everyone's talking about it," she said vaguely.

"They say she's gone to be one of those witchy women in the forest outside the border. The ones Gracie lives with."

Queen Kesta was remembering Bluebell's behaviour at their little tea party, and her doubts were in no way removed. Unwilling to admit as much to her daughters, she said brightly, "Well! Let's wait and see, shall we? I'm sure darling Bluebell will be here for the celebrations, whatever she may be up to just now."

Had Queen Kesta been able to see the Queen of Wadingburn at that precise moment, she would have been appalled. Bluebell was sitting at one of the looms in the House of the Ancient Crones having her very first weaving lesson, and enjoying every minute.

"Very soothing," she was saying. "A delightful activity! And I can pop back any time I want?"

"Yes, indeed." Edna straightened a wobbly thread. "I think you've got a natural aptitude. That silk will make up into Gracie's dress for tomorrow, and it's looking wonderful."

"And that other loom holds the Web of Power?" Bluebell looked across to where Elsie was working. "What colour is it? I thought it was silver, but I'm not so sure now. Looks a bit patchy, if you don't mind my mentioning it."

"Something evil's stirring," Elsie told her. "It's been patchy off and on for quite a while now."

Bluebell pulled out her lorgnette and peered more closely at the Web. "Can it tell you where the evil is?"

Elsie shook her head. "Sadly, no. Sometimes it's a long way away, and doesn't really affect us. We can usually tell if it's threatening the Five Kingdoms, though."

"I see." Bluebell put her lorgnette away. "And are you able to prevent the evil from doing any damage?"

"That depends." Edna began to tidy away the shuttles of blue silk. "We keep the border as strong as we can, and if it looks like an undesirable is trying to get across we can increase the protective barrier." She paused, staring down at the loom. "Sometimes I wonder if we do too much."

"Could do the Five Kingdoms good to meet a few undesirables, I'd say," Bluebell agreed. "Especially the Royals. Stop them being so terrified. All too easy to be scared of something you've never met."

The Ancient One nodded. "That's quite right." She gave the queen a sharp look. "Would you say the spirit of adventure is lacking, generally speaking, amongst the royal families?"

Bluebell began to laugh. She laughed until she was whooping and coughing, and Elsie began to wonder if she was about to have some kind of attack.

"Spirit of adventure?" Bluebell mopped at her eyes. "My dear Edna – I may call you Edna? – there's more spirit of adventure in the smallest of those little bats than there ever will be in the palaces of the Five Kingdoms. Marcus is the one glorious exception, and his father is doing his level best to crush him. He won't succeed … but if he's not careful, he'll lose the boy entirely."

"That's what I thought." The Ancient One nodded. "Marcus reminds me of his great-grandfather. He used to call in here quite often to talk about this and that." A reminiscent smile spread across her face. "I remember he liked chocolate cake. I think Marcus does too."

Mentally readjusting her assessment of the Ancient One's age, Bluebell smiled. "What boy doesn't?" she began, but any further thoughts were halted by the sudden arrival of Alf, panting hard and squeaking his news before he had even got through the window.

"… and it's EVER so dark, Mrs Edna, and we've got to get her out!" He landed on the top of the loom, wobbled and fell into Elsie's lap. "Ooops! Sorry, Mrs Elsie. Bit out of breath." He fluttered his way back, and waved a wing at Bluebell. "Hi, Mrs Queen! Isn't it dreadful?"

"Alf!" The Ancient One pointed a gnarled finger at him. "Take a deep breath, and begin at the beginning. We don't know what you're talking about!"

"But I told you—" Alf stopped. "I mean, it's Miss Gracie! She's in a dungeon! And Gubble is too – and Mr Prince is locked in his room, and his dad is raging mad at them all! And he's not letting Mr Prince out until tomorrow, and he says he's not letting Miss Gracie out because it's all her fault and oh, Mrs Queen, he's going to make a law so nobody can ever go over the border without his permish .. permish … permission!"

The three old women looked at each other. "I think this is what's called a crisis," Bluebell said. "That silly, SILLY man. Oh dear." She pulled herself up to her feet. "I'd better be going, and see if I can make Frank see sense."

"Yeah! Mrs Queen to the rescue!" Alf clapped his wings together.

"Just a minute," Edna said slowly. "Suppose we wait a little longer, and see what happens?"

Alf's eyes opened wide, but Elsie put her finger to her lips and he was silent.

Bluebell sat down again. "Tell me what you're thinking, dear."

"I'm thinking," the Ancient One said, "that we are

very old. And the Web is very old. How much longer can we go on protecting the Five Kingdoms when they behave like this? When they don't even believe in us?"

"I see." Bluebell took out her lorgnette, polished it and put it back in her pocket. "Well, apart from poor Gracie being most uncomfortable, I don't see that waiting for a little while can do any harm."

"No…" Edna sank back in her chair. "And this needs serious consideration. I might need to sleep on it … but for the moment, I do believe we should leave the Five Kingdoms alone."

Alf, outraged, took to his wings and flew an angry circle round the room. "But Mrs Queen! Mrs Edna! You can't! You can't not help Miss Gracie!" He saw Elsie's expression and, suspecting an ally, flew down to her shoulder. "Tell them, Mrs Elsie!"

"Hush, Alf." The Ancient One was taking the silk off the loom and laying it out on a table. "Don't let's rush into anything. For the moment, the most important thing is to get Gracie's dress made." And she picked up a pair of scissors with a flourish.

"But Edna, pet, how will she be able to take part in the tournament if she's shut up in a dungeon?" Elsie wanted to know.

"Tomorrow is another day," Edna said cheerfully.

"And besides, our dear friend the Queen of Wadingburn will be returning in the morning. That's right, isn't it?"

Bluebell nodded. "I can take Gracie's dress with me, if it's finished." She raised an eyebrow at the Ancient One. "Unless you were thinking of coming to the tournament yourself?"

Edna shook her head. "I think not. But if you can give the dress to Gracie, that would be most helpful. Now, how would you like to learn how to use a sewing machine?"

"But –" Alf was on the point of bursting – "but – but – how CAN you talk about sewing machines when Miss Gracie's in a dungeon and Mr Prince is locked away?"

Bluebell gave him a conspiratorial wink. "Don't fret, Alf. Gracie's a brave girl, and what's more, she's clever. And so is Marcus. Why don't you have a little rest, and then you can pop back and tell Gracie I'll be bringing her dress tomorrow."

"But what am I going to tell Unc?" If bats could turn pale, Alf would have been white.

"You'll tell him that everything is fine," the Ancient One said firmly. "Now do as you're told. Go to sleep."

* * *

It took Marcus until late in the evening to escape from the palace. The chimneys interlinked one with another, and each time he thought he had found an escape route he found himself frustrated, either because the chimney narrowed to such an extent that he was unable to squeeze through, or because he found himself at a dead end. He was considering giving up when he finally came across a flue wide enough to allow him to wriggle his way up to the very top; it was exceptionally sooty, and worryingly warm, but at last he was able to crawl out onto the palace roof.

"Atchoo!" Soot was up his nose. "ATCHOO!"

Marcus rubbed at his face, unaware that he was plastered in thick black soot from head to foot. Cautiously he crept to the edge of the roof, and looked down.

"Wow!" he said. "WOW!"

From his vantage point the prince could see not only the full extent of the kingdom of Gorebreath, but all the way to Dreghorn. Squinching up his eyes he almost believed he could see the twinkling lights of Dreghorn Palace; swinging round he could clearly see the dark rim of the forest edging the border of the Five Kingdoms, and the mountain peaks that lay beyond. "It's all so SMALL," he breathed. "The way everyone carries on you'd think we were part of some mighty

empire … but we're not. Father ought to come up here. It might do him good."

Thinking about his father reminded Marcus that he needed to find a way down as soon as possible, and he began moving carefully round the roof. At the far end a massive beech tree spread its branches tantalizingly close; it was a tree Marcus knew well from his younger days, when climbing trees had been a way of escaping lessons … but could he reach it?

"Only one way to find out," he told himself. He took a deep breath, and jumped. There was a heart-stopping moment when his fingers slipped away from the smooth bark and he fell another couple of metres – but then was brought to an abrupt and jolting halt.

"OUCH!" Wondering if there was any skin left on his hands, Marcus clung on to the saving branch and gave himself a moment to recover his breath, and check his arms and legs to see if he had done himself any irreparable damage. Everything seemed to be in place and working, so with a grateful glance up at the tree he scrambled his way down to the ground. There he discovered that his right knee was horribly sore and his right hand was dripping blood; fishing in his pocket, he found a grimy handkerchief and did his best to wind it round his hand, grimacing with pain as he did so. Once this was done he set off for the back of the palace as fast as his aching leg would allow.

"Hope everyone's in bed," he muttered as he came round the corner and reached the kitchen door. "The lights are all off... Now, where's that key?"

Years of sweet-talking the Gorebreath Palace cook had left Marcus in possession of a good deal of useful information about the internal workings of the building; his adventures had often necessitated secretive arrivals and departures at times when his parents were safely tucked up in bed, and he knew that a spare key was usually kept under the doormat. Much to his relief it was there, and a moment later he was tiptoeing down the corridor towards the less-frequented regions of the palace. The marble corridors took Marcus through to a thinly carpeted passageway, and this led in turn to a dimly-lit stone-flagged walkway ending in a flight of steep stone steps, with a heavy iron-bound door at the bottom. There was no guard at this time of night; the door was strong enough to withstand any attack from the inside, and the old furniture and rubbish had always been peaceful occupants. Attack from the outside had never been a problem; in the entire history of Gorebreath not one revolutionary had ever made an attempt to storm the palace and rescue the heaps of ancient mattresses and broken chairs.

Marcus studied the door. Grasping the enormous iron handle, he did his best to turn it, but it remained immovable. Bending down to the keyhole, he tried to peer through; was there a tiny light glimmering in the distance? Rubbing his eye, he looked again, and was sure he was right.

"Gracie!" he called, "Gracie! Are you there?"

"Marcus?" The voice was a long way away, but a moment later there were hurrying footsteps. "Marcus?" Now the voice was right on the other side of the door. "How did you get here? I thought you were locked in your room!"

Marcus grinned. "I escaped. And we've got to get you and Gubble out – he is there, isn't he?"

"He's asleep. Marlon's here too. He gave me your message." There was a tiny pause. "It cheered me up a lot."

"Good. I meant it," Marcus said gruffly, and then, "How did Marlon get in? Is there a window? Could you get through it?"

There was a sigh. "It's tiny. Even Marlon had trouble squeezing through."

"Trouble? *MOI?*" Marlon was evidently on Gracie's shoulder. "Piece of cake, kiddo. Piece of cake. But that door's one solid piece of work. You need the key."

"But where is it?" Marcus asked. "Who's got it? Did the guard take it away?"

"Yup." The bat sounded surprisingly cheerful. "Hang on in there, kid. Had an idea. I'm coming round soon as."

Marcus did as he was told, and after a couple of minutes he saw a small familiar figure flitting down the steps towards him.

"Wooeee! Cool disguise, kid! Even yer mother wouldn't know you done up like that!" Marlon sounded admiring, but Marcus was puzzled.

"Disguise? I'm not disguised!"

"Could have fooled me," the bat said. "Take a look at yourself!"

Marcus glanced down. "Oh! You mean the soot! I had to climb a chimney to get out."

"Could be useful if anyone sees you," Marlon told him. "Although if it's night-time, they won't. What's with the war wound?"

"I got scratched falling into a tree. Marlon, how are we going to get Gracie out of here? Where does the guard keep the key?"

Marlon tapped his nose with his wing. "Trust old Marlon. Happened to be checking this place out when Mr Briggs went home. Saw him put the key in his pocket."

"In his pocket?" Marcus leant against the wall. "Where is he now? Does he live here?"

"Back on duty at six in the morning." The bat wheeled up the stairs and back again. "Heard him muttering – mutters a lot, does Briggsy. Lack of company, if you ask me."

"So do we have to wait until then? Can't we find him, and steal the—"

"No dice." Marlon was very definite. "Listen to your Uncle Marlon. He'll be here at six, plus brekkie for the prisoners. That'll be your chance, kiddo."

It took another five minutes to convince Marcus that this was their best plan; Gracie was consulted through the keyhole, and it was her decision that finally saw him settling down in the small guardroom that provided Mr Briggs with somewhere to spend his days when he wasn't occupied with furniture. There was not much more than an empty fireplace and a large armchair, but Marcus was so tired after the events of the day that it was not long before his eyes had closed and he was fast asleep. Marlon nodded approval, and made his way back to the dungeon, where Gubble was peacefully snoring. Gracie was sitting by a guttering candle, patiently waiting for information.

"Wotcher, kid. You best get some sleep too," Marlon told her. "Keep away from the door, mind. Remember, you've heard nothing. When Briggsy comes in with brekkie, act casual."

Gracie smiled. "He's not a bad man," she said. "But he's a bit nervous of Gubble. He thinks Gubble's going to bite him."

Marlon, imagining the substantial form of Mr Briggs in flight, sniggered. "No harm done if he's nervy. Now, tuck yourself up, and I'll wake you when Briggsy's on his way."

"Thank you." Gracie yawned, then gave the bat a shy sideways look. "Is … is Marcus OK? I heard you say something about a war wound, but I couldn't hear what had happened to him."

"Fell into a tree," Marlon told her. "And he's covered in soot from his bonce to his toes. Needs to get his chimneys swept, if you ask me. But that's royalty for you. As long as the fires burn, no need to check the chimneys." With which philosophical thought the bat swooped across the dungeon and vanished through the slit of a window, leaving Gracie to wonder about Marcus until she too fell asleep.

 255

* * *

While Marcus was climbing chimneys, Foyce was planning her own escape. Queen Bluebell's arrival had distracted the thoughts of the Ancient Crones in the most satisfactory way; Foyce had been able to remove another brick from the top of the window, and was certain that she could squeeze through if circumstances allowed. These consisted of two things; the first was to catch a moment when the house was performing one of its acrobatic tricks and spinning her window down to ground level, and the second was to be rid of the terrible feeling of lethargy that swept over her each time she leant out through the gap she had made. She tried again and again, but each time she was sent reeling back into her room with her head spinning and an urgent desire to lie down. Frustration overcame her, and she pulled at her hair and screamed ... and the scream became a thin wail of pent-up fury that echoed into the moonlit forest.

Alf woke with a jump, wondering what had disturbed him. Bluebell, Edna and Elsie were discussing the last details of Gracie's dress and heard nothing. Val, who had been having a day in bed, was working on the loom in Room Seventeen and singing so loudly she was oblivious to any other noise. Alf assumed it was her falsetto that had woken him and, with a grin, went back to sleep.

Jukk, lurking on the edge of the forest, heard the cry clearly, and within minutes he was leaping the fence and standing beneath Foyce's window.

"My love!" he called. "My love! What ails you?"

The tears in Foyce's eyes as she stood by the window were, for the first time, genuine. "I want to escape," she whimpered. "I want to be free!"

"And you shall be," Jukk promised. "Just say the word, and I will carry you away——"

"No!" Foyce, with a huge effort, pulled herself together. "No. Do as I've asked you, and that will set me free. Tomorrow, at the tournament. You know what you must do."

"You have my promise, sweet lady. It will be done. But have you no word of love for me, your devoted slave? Not one word?"

Foyce smiled sweetly. "My hero," she cooed. "My heart is yours for ever."

Had Jukk known that his sweet lady's heart was colder than ice and harder than iron, he might not have bowed so deeply, or blown so many kisses. Foyce, gritting her teeth, waved and nodded in reply, but as her lover turned away to vanish in amongst the trees a thoughtful look crossed her face.

"Now … how can I find a way to get out of here in time for the tournament? Maybe—"

The sound of voices outside her room made her stop, and listen. The crones and the queen were chatting amiably as they made their way to bed; Foyce's lip curled as she heard that Gracie's blue silk dress was finished, and considered a triumph.

"I'll take it with me tomorrow morning," Bluebell boomed. "And you say I can travel on your path? Can't tell you how much I'm looking forward to it!"

"Would you like to go straight to Gorebreath?" Elsie asked. "Or to Wadingburn?"

"Hm … Gorebreath, I think. If I go to Wadingburn I'll get entangled in too many whys and hows and what-have-you-been-doing type questions. Plenty of time for that once the tournament is over…" Bluebell's voice gradually faded as she moved away along the corridor.

Foyce stood very still. So the path was going to take the queen directly to Gorebreath? In the past she had been able to run like the wind, but it was a long time since she'd had her freedom, and it was possible that the lack of exercise would slow her down. Was there a way she too could use the path? She had seen it leaping away from the House many times, and had watched it returning and curling up against the wall of the House after its journeyings were over. She also knew that it had strong opinions, and could be highly unreliable; she had overheard stories of various expeditions that had been curtailed or ruined by the path's decision to take a direction of its own.

But I still have to find a way of leaving the House, Foyce thought. *A way to break the Power.*

A vision of the Web came into her mind, and she wondered, as she had so often done before, how it could be destroyed ... knowing, even as she considered one wild idea after another, that she was incapable of doing such a thing. The Web was too powerful and – although Foyce would not admit it, even to herself – it frightened her. When she touched it her fingers burned, and shivers ran up and down her spine. What was worse, her thoughts, normally crystal clear, slid one into another in an alarming jumble before dissolving into a numbing fog of nothingness that was more terrifying than any pain.

Biting her lip, she walked back to the window. A small rustling outside caught her attention, and she looked down, every sense alert. The leaves of the laurel bush below were trembling, and a small dark shape was slowly crawling out ... a shape she recognized.

 259

"Billy!"

"Miss Gracie... ?" The tiny voice was hopeful.

Foyce had a flash of inspiration. Concentrating on keeping her voice soft and gentle, she whispered, "Yes, Billy! It's me, Gracie! You poor, poor little bat... Just fly a little higher, and I'll catch you and look after you ... and you'll be safe..."

Billy, confused after his long sleep, did as he was told. Up he flew, wobbling as he went. Up and—

"GOTCHER!" Foyce had him in her hands, and she was squeezing him in glee at her triumph ... squeezing until Billy was unable to breathe.

"Mum!" he squeaked as his world went dark – and Foyce realized what she was doing.

"Oh no," she snarled. "We don't want you dead. Not yet. You're going to be SO useful, little bat..." With a fiendish smile, she opened the lid of a small box, dropped the gasping Billy inside and shut the lid. "Just wait there until the morning. Tomorrow will be a special day, little bat. A very, VERY special day..."

Another ear had heard Foyce's cry of frustration. Agony Clawbone had taken to wandering night after night through the trees that surrounded the House, her terror of human dwelling places overcome by the hope that she might one day catch a glimpse of Foyce. At first Keel had remonstrated with her, reminding her of Jukk's orders, but after she had promised she would make no attempt to contact her daughter he left her to her own devices. He had believed Gracie's promise that Mange Undershaft was no longer a threat and, still smarting from Jukk's claim to Foyce, had taken himself off to another part of the forest to think mournful thoughts about unrequited love.

Agony drew as close to the House as she dared, and watched. She saw Jukk arrive, and trembled as she hid from his view; she heard his declaration of love and, at last, saw Foyce's face.

"But she's beautiful!" Agony breathed. "SO beautiful!" It was all she could do not to rush out and claim her daughter as her own, but she forced herself to stay where she was.

And then Foyce spoke. Her words to Jukk were honey-sweet, but Agony could hear the cold-blooded calculation underneath, and her heart chilled. *Her father's daughter*, she thought. *But* – and she straightened herself – *she's my daughter too. There might still be a little hope. She could change...* She stayed where she was, her eyes never leaving the window; when Billy was caught she gave a muffled cry of distress, but she did not

 262

move until Foyce had finally blown out her candle, and the window was dark. Only then did Agony slip into her wolf shape, and find a dry spot sheltered by a beech tree. There she curled up, and dozed for the rest of the night ... one ear always open.

Chapter Eighteen

Gracie woke early to find Gubble missing. Alarmed, she sat up on her sofa and called for him.

"Ug," said a voice and, squinting into the half-light, Gracie saw that the troll had managed to pile up a selection of chairs and tables in front of the door. Gubble, looking far from comfortable, was balanced precariously on the top.

"Gubble! What are you doing?" she asked.

Gubble gave a toothless grin. "Man come with breakfast. Gubble jump – Gracie and Gubble escape." His grin grew wider. "Clever Gubble?"

"Erm…" Gracie tried to think of a kind way of pointing out that Mr Briggs would now be unable to open the door. She also had reservations about the wisdom of the troll jumping on him. Even though Mr Briggs was more than substantial in build, Gubble

 264

was solid through and through. There would be little of the jailer left undamaged, and it would undoubtedly cause problems.

Before she could think of a solution, Marlon flew in through the window.

"You awake, kiddo? We've got—" Noticing Gubble's tower, Marlon stopped mid-sentence. "What—"

There was a rattling at the door. Mr Briggs, unsure what he should provide for breakfast, had arrived sooner than expected to check on his prisoners and to ask if they would prefer eggs or porridge. The rattle was enough to shake the tottering tower; chairs and tables fell with a mighty crash, Gubble in the midst of them. Mr Briggs opened the door to find the troll lying flat on the stone floor surrounded by broken furniture. Gracie was crouched beside him. His head had rolled away, and she was carefully putting it back.

"'Ello, 'ello, 'ello," Mr Briggs said. "What have we got here, then?"

Gracie looked up, tears in her eyes. "Oh, Mr Briggs! I think he's really badly hurt!"

Mr Briggs was not a hard man. When he had accepted the position of head jailer he had not expected to have to do more than rearrange furniture, and attempt the occasional spot of light dusting. When

Gracie and Gubble had been unceremoniously thrown through the door by several burly guards he had been astonished, but being a man who knew his duty he had buckled on his jailer's belt – complete with truncheon – and taken responsibility for his charges. Now one of them appeared to be headless and dead, and the other was crying. What was worse, the one who was crying was young and pretty, and Mr Briggs was already worried about the suitability of his dungeon for young and pretty girls.

He bent over Gubble. "Beg pardon, Miss, but I'd say he was a goner."

"It's OK," Gracie said. "He's still alive. His head falls off quite often, but he banged it a lot last night, and now he's done it again, and—"

"Burdies." Gubble opened one eye. "Gubble see burdies. Burdies goin' round and round and round and…" His eye closed again.

Mr Briggs looked over his shoulder as if expecting to see flocks of seagulls. "Birds?"

Gracie blew her nose, and smiled at him. "I think that means he's recovering."

"If you say so, Miss." Mr Briggs was disbelieving. "He's still a bit of a funny colour, if you don't mind me mentioning it."

Gracie was beginning to explain that Gubble was constitutionally green when the door swung open with a crash, startling them all. Before they could see what was happening a sooty figure had flung itself on Mr Briggs.

"Let her go!" it demanded, and then, seeing the prone figure of Gubble, "WOW! What's going on?"

Recognizing Marcus underneath the layers of coal dust, Gracie pulled him away from Mr Briggs. The jailer had been so surprised by the sudden attack that he had made no resistance, but keeled gently over onto his side, where he lay like a grounded whale.

"I'm so sorry, Mr Briggs," she said. "Marcus – that is, Prince Marcus – must have thought you were someone else. Someone quite different. Here, let me help you up. Marcus – you help Mr Briggs too."

Between them they righted Mr Briggs, who stared at Marcus with a puzzled expression.

"You? A Prince? One of the twins?"

"That's me." Marcus bowed in his most dignified manner. "Prince Marcus, second in line to the throne of Gorebreath. But I must ask you to let Miss Gillypot go. There's been a dreadful mistake, you see, and she's not meant to be here. She's expected to take her place at the tournament—"

"Aha!" Mr Briggs took a step back so that he was firmly positioned in front of the dungeon door. "Now, that I can't, young sir. My instructions was to keep the young lady and her friend safe in here until the tournament was properly over. Those was my instructions, and it was the king himself that gave them." He gave Gracie an apologetic look. "I'm sorry I have to do it, as this is no place for a nice young lady like yourself, but orders is orders as I know you'll understand."

Marcus began to protest, but Gracie interrupted him. "You're quite right, Mr Briggs. Orders are orders." She smiled her sunniest smile at the jailer. "But nobody − not even the king − could blame you if you'd been hit by a whole lot of falling furniture." She pointed at the heap of smashed chairs, splintered tables and shattered cupboards. "It's lucky you weren't killed."

Mr Briggs looked thoughtfully at the ruins. "Ah," he said.

"And then you were attacked," Gracie went on, "by a ferocious figure so covered in soot it was impossible to see who or what he was, and in the struggle you lost your keys, even though you defended yourself most bravely."

Up in a corner, Marlon silently applauded.

"Just a minute, Miss." Mr Briggs shook his head. "You're wrong there, though in a way I wishes you wasn't. I haven't lost my keys, you see, so although it's a fine story—"

Gracie held up the keys. "But you did, dear Mr Briggs. And I'm really sorry, but Marcus and Gubble and I are going to escape. Right now, this minute. But Marcus will make sure you get a medal for your bravery in defending the dungeon, won't you, Marcus?"

Marcus was staring at Gracie, open-mouthed in admiration. "What? Yes. Yes, of course I will."

Mr Briggs sat down heavily on a sofa.

"I think it might be best if we locked you in," Gracie said as she and Marcus began heaving Gubble out through the door. "It'll look so much better. You'll find that sofa very comfortable. And we'll make sure you don't have to stay here too long. Thank you so much, Mr Briggs."

With a final heave they were through the door. As Gracie locked it behind them, Gubble began to stir. "Ug?"

"It's all right, Gubble," Gracie told him. "You're free now." She turned to Marcus. "Where shall we go? I'd better not be seen, nor Gubble."

"No," Marcus agreed. "Gracie … how on earth did you do that?"

Gracie blushed. "Get the keys? I took them out of Mr Briggs' pocket when you knocked him over. Is that very bad?"

Marcus began to laugh. "Bad? You're amazing! Now, let's see. Why don't you hide out in Mr Briggs' room for the moment, just until Gubble's feeling better? It's reasonably comfortable, and Mr Briggs won't be needing it. And as soon as I've cleaned up a bit I'll come and collect you."

Marlon came swooping down. "Good work!" he said approvingly. He circled Gracie's head. "Nice to see the Trueheart effect in action again, kiddo."

"Ug. No burdies … where did burdies go?" Gubble sat up, and looked round.

"They've all flown away," Gracie told him. "Do you think you could walk a little way? We're going to have a rest, and then Marcus will take us to the tournament – oh!" She glanced down at her torn and dusty dress. "But what will I wear?"

"No worries, Miss Gracie! Mrs Queen is bringing your dress over this morning!" Alf, looking pleased with himself, was hovering in the doorway. "You'll be as pretty as a picture. All will be well, so ring on that bell. Mr Prince will be – Mr Prince? Is that you?"

Marcus, his teeth very white in his grimy face, grinned. "Yes! So are you saying Bluebell's on her way here?"

"Sure as eggs is eggs." Alf flew a little closer. "Where have you been, Mr Prince? You're ever so dirty."

"Up a chimney. But I'm off to have a bath now – I'll be back as soon as I can. See you all later." Marcus headed for the passage, then stopped and turned back to Gracie. "And as soon as the tournament's over we'll be off. You and me." His voice was confident, but his eyes were anxious. "That's OK with you, isn't it?"

Gracie's smile shone out. "Yes."

"YES!" Marcus punched the air. "See you soon!" And he was gone.

Alf heaved a satisfied sigh. "True love," he remarked. "True love. Doesn't it make you feel all warm inside? Like a sunny day when all the birds are singing!"

Gubble looked pleased. "Bat hear burdies too? Ug."

Chapter Nineteen

Foyce had laid her plans carefully. Although she was up and dressed she made no move when she heard the sound of the Ancient One going downstairs to take over from Val at the Web of Power. Elsie and Queen Bluebell followed soon after, and a strong smell of toast suggested breakfast. The patter of Val's footsteps meant Edna was now safely at work, and this was confirmed when a nearby door opened and shut. The Youngest had retired to take her morning's rest.

"Not long now," Foyce told herself. "Not long…"

It was easy to hear what Queen Bluebell was up to, as her voice could clearly be heard all over the House. Foyce heard her discussing what she should have for breakfast, her remarks on the day to come, and – most importantly – the fact that she would like to reach

Gorebreath an hour or so before the celebrations were due to start.

"Got to give Gracie time to get dressed in her best," she said.

Elsie had been quietly fretting. "What if she's still locked in a dungeon?" she asked.

"She won't be after I get there," Bluebell said grimly.

Foyce, listening, smiled mirthlessly. *No,* she thought. *She's needed in front of the crowd. She has to watch the hideous death of the prince of Gorebreath...*

"I'll make sure Frank knows what an idiot he's been," Bluebell went on. "But first I need to get there, of course. How do I ride on this path?"

"I'll take you out to meet it," Elsie said, and Foyce jumped to her feet.

"Now," she told herself. "Now it begins!"

She was dressed in her most attractive dress. It was not what she would have chosen herself; she was forced to take what was given her. Nevertheless, she had no doubt that she was still beautiful; Jukk's adoration was proof enough. She swept across the room, and opened the box that contained Billy. He was crouched in a corner, whimpering; she picked him up and shook him.

"This is your moment, little bat," she hissed. "This is when you become useful. Very useful. You, and only

 273

you, are going to take me to the kingdom of Gorebreath, and there we'll see the end of Gracie Gillypot."

Billy shut his eyes. "Let me go," he whispered. "PLEASE let me go!"

Foyce threw back her head and laughed before flinging open her door. With Billy in her hand she made her way to the bottom of the stairs, arriving at the bottom step as Elsie and the queen were walking past on their way to the front door. Bluebell was carrying a basket, and Foyce raised her eyebrows.

"Gracie's dress, I presume. Such a lucky little worm to have such a itty pretty dress."

"You're very late, Foyce, dear," Elsie said reprovingly. "You'd better hurry and have your breakfast. The Ancient One is waiting for you to start work."

"No." Foyce's eyes were glittering. "I'm leaving. I'm leaving the House now."

"Nonsense!" Elsie's voice was very sharp. "The power of the Web won't allow you to leave, as you very well know."

Foyce held Billy up by one wing, and as he squeaked alarm she sneered at Elsie. "But I've got a little bat here. A friend of your dear sweet darling Gracie, I do believe. Wouldn't it be a shame if I were to crush him in front of your eyes?"

Billy was crying bitterly in between piteous calls for help. Foyce swung him to and fro above her head. "I mean it."

"Put him down right now this minute," Bluebell boomed, and she stepped forward. Foyce took a step back, and gave Billy a sharp pinch.

"Little bats mean nothing to me," she hissed. "Let me go … or I'll tear his wings off, first one and then the other."

Elsie put a warning hand on Bluebell's arm. "Don't say anything. Wait here. I'll fetch Edna." She scuttled off, and a moment later the Ancient One appeared.

"It's no good," Foyce snarled. "You can say what you like. I'm going … or the bat dies."

The Ancient One looked at Foyce, her gaze calm and considering. Foyce, summoning all her powers, stared back.

"Help," Billy squeaked faintly. "Please…"

Foyce pinched him again. "Shut up, or I'll pull off your feet and stuff them down your throat."

Edna nodded. "You are evil, Foyce Undershaft," she said. Her voice was cool and calm. "Very evil. I see now that we've failed. That being the case, there is no place for you here. You may go. I'll stop the Web."

"Promise! I want your promise!"

 276

For a moment the air crackled with anger, and the Ancient One's blue eye flashed. "How dare you doubt my word?"

Alarmed, Foyce tightened her hold on Billy, and he gave a high-pitched squeak of pain.

The Ancient One composed herself. "It's a sign of your nature that you doubt me, Foyce, and much to be regretted. But because this is all that you are capable of understanding, I will say to you that I promise. I will stop the Web, until the full moon rises."

"Edna!" Bluebell was aghast. "How can you possibly let her go? She's dangerous! What about Gracie?"

"Gracie is a Trueheart," Edna told her. "Hopefully that will be enough. There's nothing more I can do." She drew Bluebell to one side, and lowered her voice. "If blood is spilt in the House of the Ancient Crones – any blood at all, be it bat or human – we'll have no powers ever again."

The Queen of Wadingburn nodded. "You're an old, old woman, my dear, and very wise. If that's the case I'll say no more."

"Stop the Web!" Foyce's voice had deepened to a growl, and Bluebell was shocked into staring at her. The girl still looked beautiful, but as she spoke there was the glimpse of a long red tongue and the gleam of sharp white teeth.

Edna pointed down the corridor, and the door to Room Seventeen swung open. Elsie was sitting in front of the Web of Power, but her hands were folded in her lap.

"Then let's go," Foyce ordered. "You first. I'll follow."

"As you wish." Edna led the way out through the door, Bluebell by her side. Foyce walked behind them, her eyes darting from side to side, and her ears pricked.

The path was waiting ready, as if it knew it was needed, but as Foyce crossed the threshold it shot away to the other side of the gate and tied itself into a quivering knot.

The Ancient One sighed. "I did wonder if we'd have trouble," she said. "We'll have to try and persuade it. Foyce, step out of sight for a moment."

Foyce's eyes glittered. "It's a trick," she said angrily. "You're trying to trick me back into the House."

"I wouldn't have you back even if you begged me to," Edna told her. "But if you want to get to Gorebreath—"

Muttering, Foyce did as she was told. As she passed Bluebell she knocked the basket out of the queen's arms with a sly nudge of her elbow, and kicked it neatly behind a small pot of geraniums.

"Oh! Silly, silly me!" she murmured, and swooped down to pick it up and hand it back before sliding round the corner of the House. Once she was no longer visible the path was wheedled and cajoled into coming a little nearer, but the moment the Queen of Wadingburn had settled herself down with her basket on her lap it gave a convulsive twitch and a wriggle and took off. As it vanished between the trees it flicked its tail in a mocking farewell.

Foyce, snarling with anger, came running after it, but she was too late. She turned on the Ancient One, her eyes narrowed in fury. "You did that on purpose!"

Edna remained steady. "I did not. The path has its own thoughts and feelings."

With a howl of frustration Foyce lifted her hand to strike the old woman, but the blow never fell. Instead, she screamed. Billy had bitten her.

Foyce flung him off – and ran. Leaping the fence, she slipped into the forest with the fleetness of her werewolf ancestors, and was lost from view. Only a flutter of leaves told those watching that she had passed that way.

* * *

279

Edna shook her head, and turned to look for Billy. It took a moment for her to find him; he was lying amongst the dead leaves, as limp and crumpled as they were.

"Poor little hero," the Ancient One murmured, and picked him up. His fur was dull and matted, and his eyes were closed. There was no sign of a heartbeat as she bent to listen, and she sighed as she carried him into the House. She found Val and Elsie waiting for her, looking worried.

"What happened?" Elsie asked.

The Ancient One didn't answer. She went swiftly to a cupboard and took out a small black bottle; Val saw what she was doing, and gasped. "Edna! There's hardly any left!"

"Billy thought he was saving me," Edna said. "He may be beyond hope, but I have to try." Carefully she let one drop fall from the bottle into the tiny bat's open mouth, but he did not stir. The old woman's face was very grim as she laid him down in his tea-towel nest. "Dear Billy," she said, and tenderly straightened his tattered wings. "Dear, brave Billy."

Elsie and Val were watching, and each in turn stroked his fur before Edna covered him with a fold of the tea towel. "Sleep the long sleep, little friend," she said. "It will come to us all, but for you it was too soon."

"Much too soon," Val said as she wiped her eyes.

Elsie pulled her handkerchief out of her pocket, and blew her nose. "I suppose it was Foyce's doing?"

"Yes. And now, get ready." The Ancient One straightened her shoulders. "The Web has stopped for the first time in hundreds of years, and we are going out. As soon as the path gets back, we'll be off to Gorebreath." She folded her arms. "I think we might be needed…"

Chapter Twenty

Tertius was sitting on the front steps of Niven's Knowe Palace, his head in his hands. The carriage was waiting to take him and Princess Fedora to the Centenary Celebrations, but Fedora was trying on yet another dress. She had already changed her mind six times. Tertius had promised Marcus that he would arrive early; he was now beginning to wonder if he would even arrive in time to take part in the tournament. Hauling himself to his feet, he wandered back inside the palace to see how his princess was getting on.

He found her standing in a frilly petticoat, in the midst of a heap of discarded dresses. She was not looking happy.

"Sweetest one!" he cooed. "Are you nearly ready?"

"Terty!" Fedora's tone was not encouraging. "Don't NAG! You don't want me looking like a fright, do you?"

"You always look beautiful to me, my popsy poodle," Tertius told her.

This was the wrong answer. "You mean everyone else thinks I'm hideous?"

"Nobody could ever think that, my precious. Erm … what about your new dress? The one we bought together?"

His popsy poodle pouted. "Pale blue makes me look exactly like Mother. I can't think why you made me choose it." She turned her back on him, and selected yet another dress from the rack.

Tertius, making the sensible decision that she was best left alone, wandered back to his seat on the front steps. An hour later he was asleep, only to be woken by a furious Fedora. "Terty! Wake up! Whatever do you think you're doing? We mustn't be late."

Rubbing his eyes, Tertius gazed at the vision in pale blue standing beside him. "You look absolutely glorious, my petal."

"I don't," Fedora snapped. "I look like Mother. You should have made me choose the pink one. You're hopeless, Terty. Come on – let's go."

Tertius, who had never once succeeded in changing Fedora's mind, and who had had nothing to do with the choosing of the despised blue dress, made no reply.

 283

Instead, he held open the carriage door and helped her inside. He was not thanked for his pains. Fedora settled herself comfortably amongst the cushions, leaving her young husband to perch on the extreme outside edge of the seat. "Do be careful of my skirt, Terty," she said sharply as he attempted to make a little more room for himself. "I suppose you've remembered to pack your armour?"

"It went on the cart to Gorebreath along with the stage, sweetest." Tertius eased his gold watch out of his waistcoat pocket, and gave it a furtive glance. He was alarmed by how late it was; he would have very little time to get ready. "It'll be there waiting for me."

Fedora snorted. "I still don't see why the tournament had to move to Gorebreath. Sometimes I think King Frank behaves as if he rules all the Five Kingdoms. It's not fair."

"If you say so, my sweetest darling," Tertius soothed, although his own feelings about King Frank were very different. Both he and his father, King Horace, had been secretly delighted with their fellow king's decision to mastermind the celebrations. It had saved them a lot of time and effort; King Horace was now able to spend the day dozing in a comfortable armchair in the Royal Arena instead of worrying about the crowds of onlookers stamping on his flower beds. Tertius, although he would never have admitted as much, had had grave doubts about his beloved's housekeeping skills. Her plan to offer the attending crowds nothing more than well-diluted orange squash and cheap biscuits was, he thought, a mistake. Queen Mildred was sure to have handed everything over to her housekeeper, who was well experienced in catering for royal events. Indeed, the nearer they came to Gorebreath the more the smell of cheery hog roasts filled the air; Tertius drew in a deep breath and smiled. Once he had got the jousting out of the way he would be able to enjoy himself. Breakfast had been tense and, as a result, brief, and he was hungry.

"Pooh!" Fedora made a face. "What's that horrible cooking smell?"

"Roast pig, my precious pudding," Tertius said. "It's traditional at the celebrations. Very tasty, actually."

Fedora shrugged. "I suppose the peasants like that kind of thing. I don't."

"You shall have whatever you wish for," Tertius told her. He had another anxious look at his watch. "Oh dear. I wonder if the coachman could drive a little faster?"

"I suppose you're going to say that it's my fault we're late," Fedora complained.

 285

"Not at all, popsy poodle pie. Although I think I did mention once or twice that we needed to leave early..."

There was an icy silence, and Fedora suddenly became fascinated by the view from the window. Tertius sighed, and looked out of the opposite window. Gaggles of men, women and children were making their way along the road; some glanced up at the coach and bowed or curtsied, and Tertius gave them a little wave.

"Look, my precious! Everyone wants to see the beautiful Princess Fedora of Niven's Knowe!"

Fedora kept her back turned, but managed a half-hearted flutter of her fingers. A small boy cheered, and she began to look more interested. When a handsome young farmer bowed and blew her a kiss she became positively gracious, and Tertius relaxed a little. Another glance at his watch, however, and he was biting his lip.

Queen Kesta would have sympathized had she known of his problems. She had a terrible headache brought on by the stress of the morning; the Princesses Nina-Rose and Marigold had squabbled all the time they were getting dressed, and even now they were glowering at each other as the carriage carried them towards Gorebreath. The queen's headache was not helped by the fact that she was travelling in convoy; the Dreghorn Royal Band was marching in front, and the Ladies' Operatic Society was trilling happily behind. The band was walloping out the Dreghorn national anthem with more enthusiasm than skill; the ladies were loudly rejoicing that little fluffy lambs were gambolling amongst the daisies. Kesta closed her eyes.

"Mother!" Marigold's voice was sharp. "Wake up! Tell Nina-Rose to stop making faces at me!"

"I WASN'T! Mother, she's making it up!"

"Hush, my darlings." Kesta rubbed her aching forehead. "Remember what a lovely time you're going to have, sitting and watching the tournament. And keep smiling ... remember, nasty frowns make nasty wrinkles."

Nina-Rose sniffed, but said no more. Marigold pouted.

"Is there anything to eat? I'm starving!"

Silently the queen handed her a box of chocolates, and a degree of harmony was restored as the convoy moved slowly onwards.

Albion, Prince of Cockenzie Rood, was also eating. Much to his horror his cousin, the Dowager Duchess, had insisted that they drove to Gorebreath in an open carriage.

"It'll ruin my hair," he wailed.

The duchess was unsympathetic. "You'll have plenty of time to give it a good brush when we get there," she told him. "Vincent's staying in the palace, so you can use his room to change and smarten yourself up. Mildred told me the two of you are wearing matching uniforms; you'll look splendid, I'm sure."

Albion, who had secretly spent the night in curlers, was not appeased. A good brush was the last thing he wanted. Seeing the expression on his cousin's face, however, he gave up. Pulling a large bag of peppermint creams out of his pocket he settled down to eat his way through them, mournfully aware that by the time he and the duchess reached Gorebreath Palace any last vestige of curl would be long gone.

Foyce had no need of curlers. She was sitting by a stream outside the border, twirling her golden ringlets round her finger. Anger and excitement had lent wings to her feet and she had made astonishing progress; no horseman, even riding at a gallop, could have made the journey so quickly. Foyce had the additional advantage of knowing a number of short cuts, learned as a young child. It had suited her father to know every hidden path and escape route possible, as many of his dealings with the inhabitants of the Less Enchanted Forest had not been quite what the recipients had expected. His daughter had scrambled, climbed and slithered her way towards the border; her clothes were muddy and torn, but she washed her hands and face in the stream with a smile. The state of her dress didn't matter. Her smile widening, she patted her bulging pocket.

"Blue," she murmured, "blue to match my eyes. But not yet…"

There was yet another traveller making his way towards Gorebreath. Jukk had been running steadily, conserving his strength for what was to come. Now he could see the edge of the Less Enchanted Forest, and his heart beat faster; the championing of his one true love was almost within his grasp … just as long as he could find a way to cross the border. At the back of his mind was the idea that he could leap across, but that would only be possible if there were no guards; sliding into his human shape to avoid immediate confrontation, Jukk walked cautiously on.

The invisible barrier protecting the kingdoms was strong. Jukk had never attempted to break through, but he knew of many who had tried and failed painfully. Now, as he came closer, he slowed his pace;

a large zombie was leaning against a tree waving its fleshless arms in the air and making strange whooping noises. A moment later it ran a short way down the path, circled a thornbush and came back to the tree, whooping all the way. On its return it noticed Jukk, and grinned at him.

"No hurtie hurtie," it explained. "Oozy find no hurtie hurtie. Hurtie hurtie all gone!" And it set off on yet another circuit.

Jukk took a deep breath. Was the zombie right? Cautiously he approached the path that led away from the forest. A deserted guard post a couple of yards further on made it clear that this was indeed the border; he took two steps, then three, then five – and was past. The zombie was right. There was no barrier.

"Love finds a way," Jukk murmured, and leaving the zombie still whooping and circling he set off down the path towards the kingdom of Gorebreath. Before long he too could smell the roasting pig, and hear cheery voices; with a grim smile he adjusted his heavy fur cloak and strode on.

Chapter Twenty-one

Bluebell had enjoyed her ride on the path. After an initial concern about falling off, she realized she was as safe as if she were in her carriage, if not safer. The path obligingly hollowed itself out so she was held in a dip; she was able to stretch out as if she were ensconced in an armchair, while watching the trees go rushing past.

On arrival at Gorebreath, however, there was a divergence of opinion. The path stopped at the edge of Gorebreath village, and no amount of persuasion, flattery or threats could make it go all the way to the palace. Sighing, the Queen of Wadingburn stepped off, and there was a flurry of dust as the path twisted round and headed home.

Still holding her basket, Bluebell set off at a brisk walk; a number of villagers were going in the same direction, and before long she was chatting happily.

"Should be a jolly sort of day," said an elderly matron. "But that King Frank, he likes things all his own way, he does. Celebrations was due to be at Niven's Knowe, but he goes and orders it all different at the very last minute. Has to be here, he says, so here it is."

Her friend nodded. "One good thing. It'll be far better grub here in Gorebreath. You've heard of that slip of a girl as married Prince Tertius? Princess Fedora? Well, she don't know bees from bicycles, she don't. Thinks of nothing but her dresses, by all accounts. Gives that prince a terrible hard time of it, too. Nag, nag, nag all day long."

Bluebell, intrigued to find the general populace was not only well informed but also very much of her own mind, enquired what was known of Prince Marcus. At once there were smiles, and much appreciative chuckling.

"A right proper prince, that one. Worth all the rest put together. We're cheering for him today, ain't we, Dorcas?"

Dorcas grinned a toothless grin. "Best of the bunch by far. Got himself a nice girl, too, although folk says as his dad can't abide her."

"Really?" Bluebell raised her eyebrows.

"You haven't heard, Missus? She's not a royal, see, and that King Frank, he won't have it. Royal must marry royal is what he says." Dorcas shook her head.

"And THAT," the elderly matron pronounced, "is what's wrong with the lot of them. Married each other until they're nothing more than a bunch of wet petticoats."

Bluebell beamed at her. "Couldn't have put it better myself." The sound of wheels made her turn. An open carriage was approaching, and Dorcas caught at her arm to pull her out of the way.

"Careful, Missus! That there's the Dowager Duchess of Cockenzie Rood, that is. Sensible kind of woman – but see that Prince Albion sitting beside her? Big bag of wind."

The Queen of Wadingburn was about to agree most heartily, but she was interrupted. Hortense had seen her, and had given her coachman orders to stop.

"Bluebell! My dear! Can we give you a lift?"

Much to the astonishment of her new companions, Bluebell stepped into the carriage.

"I don't suppose you've got room for my friends as well, have you?" she asked cheerfully. "We've been having such an interesting chat."

Hortense looked across at her nephew, who was pale

with horror at the idea of sharing his carriage with a bunch of elderly villagers. "Move up, Albion. There'll be plenty of room if you do."

But the good women of Gorebreath were not to be persuaded. They thanked both Bluebell and the duchess, but assured them they'd be happier walking, and the carriage went off without them. As it rolled away Bluebell heard one remark, "So who was she, then?"

"Didn't you hear? That there was the Queen of Wadingburn!" The elderly matron sounded as if she were in a state of shock, and Bluebell turned round to wave a cheery wave.

"See you later!" she called, but only Dorcas was sufficiently recovered to wave back.

Fifteen minutes later the carriage was bowling up the drive that led to the palace. Bluebell had spent the journey telling her friend about her visit to the Ancient Crones, and Albion, who had listened with growing agitation, was wiping his forehead with a large handkerchief.

"Excuse me," he said earnestly, "but they aren't very safe, you know. Vincent told me! He said—"

He was stopped mid-sentence by Bluebell holding up an imperious hand. "My grandson talks a lot of rubbish."

 294

Albion was about to protest, but his eye was caught by a small bat flying low overhead. With a loud scream he dived under his seat, leaving Hortense and Bluebell staring at him in astonishment. "Don't let it bite me! I don't want to die!"

Bluebell looked round to see what could possibly be threatening the life of the heir to the kingdom of Cockenzie Rood, and saw Alf swooping round in an offended circle.

"Hello, Alf!" she boomed. "Take no notice! The boy's an idiot. What news of Marcus and Gracie?"

Alf flew down to her shoulder. "All under control, Mrs Queen. All personnel free and in good condition." He put his head on one side and peered at the basket. "Got the dress?"

"Of course." Bluebell gave the basket a pat. "So where's Gracie now?"

"In hiding." Alf gave Albion a cold look. "Unc says I'm to take you there, and not to let anyone see us."

The Dowager Duchess of Cockenzie Rood had been watching and listening with interest, and she leant forward. "Quite right. Frank's on the warpath, and Mildred's in despair. I had a message from her only this morning. She says he's determined to throw Gracie out of the kingdoms, and he wants to pass a ridiculous law making it illegal to cross the border without his personal permission."

"We'll see about that," Bluebell said, a grim expression on her face. "Stop the carriage, Hortense. I've things to do!"

The duchess gave the order, and Bluebell stepped out. Somewhat to her surprise, Hortense followed her. "I'm coming too," she announced. A plaintive wail reminded her of her cousin, and she frowned. "You go on to the palace, Albion. Vincent will be there, and you can change into your uniform. Stay with Vincent, and you'll be fine."

Without waiting for a reply she took Bluebell's arm, and nodded at Alf. "Right, Mr Bat. Which way do we go?"

As the two old women walked away, Albion crawled out from under his seat. The disappearance of Alf had cheered him immeasurably; the thought of the new uniform made him feel even better. "I do hope it's got gold buttons," he murmured as the carriage rolled on its way. "Gold buttons and gold braid. And I'll look much smarter than Vincent, because he's so fat." Albion sat back with a smile, and began to look forward to the day's events.

Bluebell and Hortense, arm in arm, followed Alf as

 296

he led them towards the back of the palace.

"We'll have a chat with Gracie," Bluebell decided, "and then we'll go and see what else is going on. Alf, where's Marcus?"

Alf looped the loop, giggling as he flew. "Up to his eyes in soap suds," he reported. "Made his escape via a chimney pot, and now he's trying to scrape the soot off. Blacker than me and Unc, he was; sent the kitchen maid into a fit of hysterics when he crept in through the kitchen. Thought she'd seen a boggart and wouldn't come out from under the table. Still, it did Mr Prince a favour. You could have marched an army through the kitchen and they'd never have noticed."

"Excellent!" Bluebell beamed. A moment later her smile vanished as she noticed where they were heading. "Goodness me! Isn't this the dungeon? I thought you said Gracie was safe, young Alf!"

Gracie, who had just finished tucking Gubble up for a sleep in Mr Briggs' battered old armchair, heard the stentorian tones of the approaching queen and hurried to greet her. A moment later she was being examined for injury, despite her protestations that she was fine.

"Gubble's not very well, though," she said. "He tried to smash his way through the walls of the dungeon, and he hurt his head – and then he and a pile of chairs collapsed, and his head fell off. That doesn't usually bother him, but he's definitely not himself. I've made him lie down and rest."

Hortense was taken aback by this information, but Bluebell was used to Gubble. "Poor old thing," she said sympathetically. "Best leave him where he is, and hope he feels better soon. Now, I've got your dress here!"

"Wait until Mr Prince sees you!" Alf fluttered over Gracie's head. "His heart'll go boom! Boom! Boom!"

"The blue silk dress?" Gracie's eyes shone. "I didn't ever think it would be finished on time."

"I helped to make it," the queen said, with enormous pride. She opened the basket with a flourish. "Just look at this – what? WHAT? Where is it?"

Gracie, peering into the empty basket, swallowed hard. *Don't cry*, she told herself. *It's only a dress. Don't cry.*

Bluebell sank down on the stone bench. "How could that have happened? I put it in the basket myself! Oh, my dear child! What have I done?"

The queen's obvious distress made it easier for Gracie to be brave. "It's all right," she said, and managed a smile. "Marcus never notices what I'm wearing. He won't mind, and he's the one that matters."

"Could it have fallen out on the way?" Hortense asked.

"Not a chance," Bluebell told her.

A thought came to Gracie. "Foyce didn't go any-where near the basket, did she?"

"Foyce?" Bluebell looked puzzled, and then appalled. "Of course! She knocked it out of my hands ... but how could she have taken the dress? She handed the basket straight back."

"She managed to take Auntie Elsie's scissors from right under her nose," Gracie said. "And lots of other things went mysteriously missing."

"Well, I never." The queen shook her head. "You could almost admire her. She's quick as a whip. I was quite nervous when I thought she was going to travel on the path with me."

Gracie's eyes grew wide. "Travel with you? But ... but how could she?"

Bluebell sighed. "I'm afraid she forced her way out of the House. But no need to worry. The path wouldn't take her. She's running about in the forest, I expect."

Hortense was watching Gracie's face. "But you *are* worried, aren't you?" she said.

"Yes." Gracie's stomach was doing somersaults, and an icy hand was squeezing her heart. Foyce was free. Foyce had stolen her dress. Foyce wanted revenge...

"She's coming after me," she said. "She's coming here to the tournament."

 300

"But my dear!" Bluebell was astonished. "She's miles away! She'd never be able to get here in time!"

Gracie shook her head. "She can run like the wind. Her mother was a werewolf."

"Even so." The queen was still dubious. "I don't think you need concern yourself. Look at all the military!"

"Military smilitary!" It was Marlon. Alf, appalled by what he had heard, had flown to report the news. "Stay cool, kid. Uncle Marlon's here! Alf? You gotta locate the dame, and you gotta locate her NOW! Call up emergency support. Red alert, tell them."

Alf waved a wing in salute, and shot out of the room. Marlon hovered above Gracie's shoulder. "Trust the Batsters. I'll be up above, kiddo, checking on you and that prince of yours. Keep smiling!"

"Goodness," Bluebell said as the bat vanished from view. "If Marlon thinks it's an emergency, it must be. What can we do to help? Hortense and I may be old, but we're not past it."

"Thank you," Gracie said. "You're very kind. Maybe you could pretend everything's fine for the moment. We don't want anyone to panic." She paused to think. "I'd better have a look round."

"Is that wise?" Bluebell asked. "Isn't Marcus expecting you to take your place on the stage?"

 301

Gracie pulled at the end of one of her plaits. "I can't just wait here. Not if Foyce is likely to appear. She's capable of persuading everyone that she's the sweetest girl in the kingdom – she could end up anywhere!"

The duchess frowned. "What if King Frank sees you, my dear?"

"I've been thinking about that." With a grin, Gracie unhooked Mr Briggs' all-enveloping and distinctly weather-worn cape from the back of the door, and put it on. She added a battered wide-brimmed hat from a dusty corner, and Bluebell gave a hoot of laughter. "Excellent! Most disreputable. Aha! I've had an idea!" She peered into her bag, and brought out a small jar. "Never use the stuff myself, but a gal's supposed to keep it handy. Come closer, child. Let's turn you into a healthy country lad."

When Bluebell had reddened Gracie's cheeks to her satisfaction, Hortense produced a small mirror.

"Wow!" Gracie said as she inspected herself. "I don't think even Marcus will recognize me looking like this."

"Any sign of trouble, come straight to us," Bluebell instructed. "We'll be in the Royal Enclosure. You can't miss it."

Chapter Twenty-two

To begin with Jukk attracted a certain amount of nervous attention as he strode on towards the palace of Gorebreath, but as the crowds grew there were far more exciting things to look at than a grim-faced young man dressed in rough grey fur. There were stalls selling everything from penny whistles to peppermint rock, and jugglers wearing suits of red and yellow tossed multicoloured balls high in the air. As the crowd got closer to the tournament they found rows of stripy tents offering heaped plates of roast pig and boiled cabbage; the ground itself was circled with wooden benches, and already families were staking their claim to the seats with the best view. At one end a large banner emblazoned with the arms of Gorebreath was draped above a stage; on the stage were five chairs, and there was much speculation as to the possible occupants.

"Five chairs for the Five Kingdoms," explained a mother to her string of small children. "That's what they be. Gorebreath, Dreghorn, Niven's Knowe, Cockenzie Rood and Wadingburn. You wait and see, my pets."

The pets weren't listening. They had discovered a pile of armour at the side of the stage, and were fighting amongst themselves for the chance to try on a helmet. Seeing what they were up to, two stewards hurried forward.

"Property of the princes," one explained. "You'll see them later, after the marching. Going to be riding at each other with long poles! Got to try and knock each other off their horses, see."

Wide-eyed, the pets took in this exciting information. "Will they be deaded, Mister?"

"No, no. They won't hurt each other. It's all in fun."

Disappointed by this news, the pets made their way to their seats, and the stewards tidied the armour into a small tent behind the stage. They were unaware of a pair of keen eyes watching them; Jukk had noted their every move. His sharp ears had also heard the conversation; now, making his way with some difficulty through the gathering crowds, he made sure he was within a stone's throw of the tent. Three ponies were tethered to an overgrown holly bush on the other side;

as Jukk approached they threw up their heads and whinnied anxiously.

"Hey up, lads!" A steward tried to calm them, but they refused to be soothed. The nearer Jukk came, the more they skittered from side to side, until the biggest pony pulled so hard that a branch snapped and they were free. At once two of the three set off at a gallop in the opposite direction, scattering men, women and children as they went. Only one stayed where he was, and he was sweating and shaking his head.

The two stewards looked at each other.

"What do we do now, Mick?" asked the younger one. "King Frank'll be proper mad if there ain't no ponies."

Mick scratched his head. "We've still got one."

"Fat lot of use, that is. How can the princes charge each other if they ain't got one each?"

There was no answer to this, and both stewards looked gloomily at the broken rope.

"That's Prince Marcus's pony, that is – the one as didn't run away. Well trained. Shame the others weren't the same."

There was a long pause. Jukk, on the other side of the tent, allowed himself a grim smile before slipping quietly under the canvas.

"Should we go and look for them?" the younger

steward wanted to know. Mick shrugged.

"Look for them? Nah. Never find them now. Wonder what spooked them?"

"Probably them kids. Or the crowds. And that pig smells real strong!" There was a question in the lad's voice, and the older steward looked more cheerful.

"Excuse me! Where's my pony?" Prince Arioso of Gorebreath had arrived, resplendent in red velvet but very pale. Marcus was close behind him, well washed, but unmistakably sooty when it came to his clothes. He had not been able to get back into his room; the blue velvet outfit chosen with loving care by his mother was lying on a chair behind the locked door of his bedroom. Queen Mildred had assumed King Frank would want to speak severely to Marcus before setting him free; the king had taken it for granted that the queen would release him. Fortunately for Marcus, neither had consulted the other.

"Glee's still here," he said, with some pride. "Good boy, Glee!" He looked more carefully at the pony, and whistled. "He's all of a lather! What's been going on?"

Mick coughed. "Harrumph. We don't exactly know, sir. Something set them all of a dither, and next thing they was off! Off and away, and no stopping them, neither, as the lad here will bear witness."

The lad nodded. "Spooked, sir. That's what it was."

"He still is." Marcus stroked the pony's neck. "Poor old Glee." He glanced at his brother. "This isn't good, bro. We'd better think of a plan, quick smart. This is meant to be the highlight of the day, but we need at least two ponies ... and I haven't had time to collect Gracie yet. AND Tertius isn't here, and he promised he'd be early. I bet Fedora's stroking a kitten or something, and he'll be late. Father's going to have a total fit!"

His twin, never at his best in an emergency, adjusted his lace collar. "Erm ... couldn't we just run at each other? Or something like that?"

Marcus didn't bother to reply. His eye had been caught by a beer tent. Standing behind it was the brewer's dray, and harnessed to the dray were two enormous carthorses. "Wait here," he ordered. "I'm going to see if I can borrow those."

Arioso went green. "I can't ride one of those! They're ... they're as big as elephants!"

"But you're only going to ride round the arena, aren't you?" Marcus tried not to sound as irritated as he felt. "Surely you can cope with that."

"Oh yes." His brother managed a faint smile. "But what about Terty?"

Marcus shrugged. "He can ride Glee if he prefers."

A few moments later he was in earnest conversation with the brewer; he came back frowning. "Called me a grubby urchin," he reported. "Come on, bro – you look much more the thing. You come and ask him!"

This was more successful, and the two dray horses were led back to be tied to a corner of the stage. They too showed a certain unwillingness, but, being placid beasts by nature, allowed themselves to be coaxed with a handful of oats provided by the brewer.

"There," Marcus said triumphantly. "They're pretty impressive, aren't they? Now, are you OK to stay here while I fetch Gracie? The bands and the army are going to march around a bit, and then it'll be our turn. When Terty shows up tell him to hurry up and get his armour on – and you'd better start getting yours on, too. You're meant to be on first, remember."

As if to echo Marcus's words, two heralds stepped out into the arena, and the first blew his trumpet for silence. When the noise of the crowd had subsided, the second cleared his throat and looked at King Frank. The king gave a regal nod.

"Welcome to the Centenary Celebration Tournament!" The herald paused, waiting for applause, but as none came he went hastily on. "The Dreghorn Royal Band will begin the proceedings, followed by the delightful

 308

Ladies' Operatic Society. The Gorebreath Army will be next, and then the event you've all been waiting for – the jousting! Prince Arioso, heir of Gorebreath, will ride first against Prince Tertius of Niven's Knowe, and the victor will then challenge Prince Arioso's brother, Marcus of Gorebreath. Let the celebrations begin!" And with a final blast of the trumpet, both heralds retired.

"Here we go," Marcus said cheerfully. Then, seeing his brother's strained expression, he added, "Don't worry, bro. It'll all be fine."

Arry nodded, and sat down on the edge of the stage to pull off his boots. Behind him, on silent feet, Jukk moved out of the tent and stepped into the shadow of the holly bush.

"Mere boys," he growled. "There is no challenge here ... but Jukk is a fair fighter. I will give Prince Arioso his chance before I kill my rival and set my beloved free from her chains."

Marcus was whistling cheerfully as he hurried towards Mr Briggs' guardroom, but his tune died on his lips as he swung through the door. Gubble was asleep in Mr Briggs' armchair, snoring loudly, but there was no sign of Gracie. After a moment of hesitation, the prince shook Gubble's arm.

"Gubble – Gubble, it's me. Marcus. Where's Gracie?"

The troll stirred, but did not wake. Harder shaking had no effect, and no amount of shouting worked either. Frustrated and worried, Marcus was forced to leave Gubble asleep and head back through the crowds.

"If anything's happened to her, I'll … I don't what I'll do," he muttered as he wormed his way in between clusters of chattering men and women and knots of over-excited children. "I'll have to go and live in a cave somewhere. Nothing'll be any fun any more." A moment later the thought occurred to him that Gracie was probably on her way to take her place on the stage, and Marcus began to whistle again.

He found Arioso sitting outside the tent, encased in shining armour with his helmet by his side. There was no sign of Gracie, and Marcus felt a stab of concern. Where could she be? Hoping against hope that she would arrive before the tournament began, he looked round for Tertius. "Where's Terty? Is he in the tent?"

"He's not here yet," Arry said. "And nor is Fedora. Nor Nina-Rose."

Marcus groaned, and began strapping himself into a suit of silver, muttering as he did so. "What IS Terty doing? It's all going wrong. It's going to be a disaster… Should I have gone to look for Gracie? She can't be

back in the dungeon, 'cos they'd have locked Gubble up as well … and she won't be waiting to make a grand entrance, because she'd never do anything like that… Oh, BLAST this stupid tournament!"

The sound of pipes and drums made Marcus rush to buckle his breastplate. The Dreghorn Royal Band was approaching, still playing their national anthem.

King Frank, settling himself in the Royal Enclosure, frowned.

"Bad form," he whispered to Queen Mildred. "Very bad form!"

Mildred had no time to reply. Queen Kesta had come hurrying to take her place beside her, clutching her smelling salts and looking pale.

"Aren't they awful?" she said. "I'm so sorry. They can't play any other tune except "John Brown's Body", and that hardly seemed appropriate. Do excuse them!"

King Frank, mollified, smiled graciously. "I'm sure they're doing their best."

Kesta sighed. "If only their best was a little better. And I'm afraid the Ladies' Operatic Society is even worse."

Mildred patted her friend's knee. "Don't worry, dear. You've got to suffer the Gorebreath Army demonstrating their marching skills." She turned to her husband. "Are any of the other kingdoms sending singers? Or dancers?"

"No." King Frank stroked his chin. "Bit of a poor show. Cockenzie Rood seem to think it's enough to have Tertius riding in the tournament, and Bluebell and Hortense have nothing arranged at all."

"Albion and Vincent are going to be leading the procession, Frank," Mildred pointed out.

The king snorted. "And who had to provide them with a uniform? Me! You'd have thought they could have managed that, at least."

The two women exchanged glances, but said nothing. The sound of the pipes and drums was deafening, and any further conversation was impossible.

At the other end of the arena Marigold was climbing the steps to the stage.

"I'm here first," she told Marcus and Arioso with a gleeful smile. "That means I can sit where I like!" And she stomped her way to the centre of the stage.

Marcus looked at his brother. "Where's Nina-Rose?"

"I'm here," said a peevish voice. "Arry! I'm here!"

Arioso got to his feet as fast as a suit of silver armour would allow. "Darling Nina-Rose! You've got here at last!"

Nina-Rose pouted. "I rather hoped you'd say you were pleased to see me."

"Oh, I'm very pleased!" Arry assured her, but he was too late. Nina-Rose tossed her head, and turned her back on him.

"Hello, Marcus! I hear your little Gracie has been put in a dungeon. Such a shame that she won't be able to be here, but I'm sure she'll be let out sometime soon."

Marcus glowered at her. "Actually," he said coldly, "she will be here."

Arry looked at him in surprise. "Will she? Oh, good! Did Father change his mind?"

"I rescued her," Marcus said. "Goodness! What on earth are those enormous women singing about? And what are we going to do about Terty? He's going to ruin everything if he isn't here soon!"

Tertius was not far away, but it was impossible for the coach to move at more than a snail's pace. The crowds were densely packed, and the coachman's shouts and entreaties had little effect.

"Poppet – I really think we'd do better if we got out of the coach and walked," Tertius said.

"Walk?" Princess Fedora was as horrified as if her young husband had suggested she dance naked on the roof. "I'm a princess, Terty! A future queen! I can't possibly be expected to walk!"

"But we'll never get there on time if we don't," Tertius protested.

Fedora gave him a look that sent chills running down his spine. "Darling Terty werty doodle woodle! For the last time, I am NOT going to walk! Don't be so – so unroyal! Think who you are! Think who I am! We're the most important people there. They won't start the tournament without us. Now stop fussing, or I won't smile at you when you're galloping up and down and knocking Arry off his horse."

Tertius gulped. "I'm sure you're right, my pet. You always are. But Marcus will be worrying, and I've got to get into my armour and that takes ages – so if you'll excuse me, I'll see you there." And with a last apologetic wriggle he opened the coach door and jumped out, leaving an apoplectic Fedora staring after him.

Chapter Twenty-three

The Dreghorn Royal Band and the Ladies' Operatic Society were long gone by the time Tertius, flushed and panting, arrived at the tent. The stalwart members of Gorebreath Army were marching up and down to a somewhat erratic drumbeat, and the two royal heralds were already polishing their trumpets in preparation for the much-anticipated jousting competition.

"Hurry up!" Marcus said. "Your armour's in there! We're on next ... you've got about two minutes!"

Tertius was too out of breath to answer. He rushed into the tent just as the army drummer began his famous drum roll for the finale. The drum was not loud, but it was loud enough to conceal a muffled exclamation, and the thud of a falling body.

Outside, Marcus was helping his brother fasten his helmet, resplendent with blue feathers.

"I can't see a thing!" Arry complained. "And I can't hear properly either! And I'll NEVER be able to ride one of those elephantine brutes!"

Marcus gave him a consoling slap on the shoulder. "Tell you what, bro – you can ride Glee. Actually, that'll be extra clever, as then Father will be sure you're me. You did tell him you were wearing the helmet with the red feathers, didn't you?"

Arioso started to nod, but changed his mind. The helmet was so heavy he had a nasty suspicion that he might fall over. "Yes," he said. "I told him twice. And Vincent and Albion too."

"Good. So here's the plan. We process round the arena, and everyone will be watching, thinking you're me and I'm you. Father's going to announce that the first bout is between you and Terty, and I'll let Terty knock me off my horse so he wins. Father'll be disappointed, but we can't help that because the winner has to fight me, and if Terty doesn't win I'll have to fight you."

There was a wail from inside the blue-plumed helmet.

"Don't worry. There's no way I'll let Terty lose. Then I'll dash back – well, as fast as I can in this tin can – and we both rush into the tent and swap helmets … and then I come out as me and this time I get to knock Terty flat on his face."

The blue-plumed helmet made a faint noise of agreement.

"Good," Marcus said. "Now, I'll put on my helmet and we'll get you up on Glee." Turning to the tent wall he called out, "Terty? Are you ready? You're going to have to ride a carthorse. You don't mind, do you?"

The reply was gruff, but in the affirmative, and Marcus grinned at Arioso. "Guess he's got his helmet on. Come on, bro."

Prince Albion and Prince Vincent, dressed in identical uniforms, were standing ready to lead Marcus, Arioso and Tertius in procession round the arena. Each considered himself superior to the other, and both were wishing their buttons were gold instead of silver, but on the whole they were satisfied with their appearance. Vincent was inclined to puff his chest out a little further than Albion; after all, he had a princess dressed in tight purple satin waving madly at him from the stage, and all Albion had to support him was an empty chair.

"Never mind, Albie," he said. "I'm sure you'll find true love one day."

Albion wasn't listening. He was staring at the other side of the arena, where a knight in shining armour

 318

was being assisted onto a pony. Beside him another knight was sitting proudly on his much larger steed.

"That's ever so odd," he remarked. "That's Marcus and his pony, but it looks as if he can't get on! But Arry – I know it's Arry, 'cos he's got a red tuft on his hemet – he looks absolutely OK and he usually wobbles about like anything!"

Vincent followed the direction of Albion's pointing finger. "Crikey! What's he riding? It looks like a hairy elephant!"

"Here comes Tertius," Albion reported. "He's got a hairy elephant as well. This should be funny – oh! Oh my goodness!"

Eyes on stalks, the two princes watched the tall figure as it took a firm hold of the bridle. The brewer's horse was sidling and snorting and showing the whites of its eyes, but a stinging slap with the reins and something hissed in its ear made it stand very still.

"What's he doing?" Albion asked. "He's made it go all quiet! You said Tertius wasn't any good at riding."

"He isn't," Vincent said.

"Well, he's just got on that hairy monster's back with no trouble at all."

Vincent and Albion were not the only observers to note Tertius's sudden skill with a horse. Bluebell was sitting very upright, peering through her lorgnette, a puzzled frown on her face.

"Hortense! There's something very odd about that knight! Do you know what? I don't believe it's Tertius!"

The duchess smiled. "Nonsense, Bluebell. Who else could it be? The boys have been planning this for ages."

Bluebell shook her head. "Keep watching. I'm beginning to feel distinctly suspicious."

Gracie, hidden in the middle of a group of pie salesmen, was also suspicious. There was no sign of Foyce, and she had decided to watch from the edge of the crowd until it was Marcus's turn. Then, she told herself, she would take her place on the stage as she had promised, regardless of what she looked like. Now she rubbed her eyes, and edged a little nearer. An unease was creeping over her, a sense that something was very wrong. She shivered.

"No pushing forward, lad," said a pieman. "You'll see well enough from where you are."

"Sorry," Gracie murmured, and stepped back. High above, Alf was circling; the huge numbers of closely packed spectators were making his task of observer almost impossible, and he was beginning to grow anxious about his charge's safety. A moment later

Marlon came swooping towards him.

"Kid! Where's our Gracie? The dame's on her way – and she's travelling fast!"

Alf gulped. "Down there … somewhere…"

"Find her," Marlon snapped, and was gone.

TANTARRAAA! TANTARRAAA!

The trumpets sounded. Albion and Vincent seized their moment of glory. Chests expanded, they strutted out, waving with regal condescension to the cheering crowds crammed on the surrounding benches. As they reached the far side the three riders wheeled in behind them, and they completed a circuit of the arena. If King Frank had not stepped forward, hand held high, Albion and Vincent would have happily continued; they retired with reluctance, waving as they went.

"Ladies, gentlemen, boys and girls!" The king's voice rang out. "I am happy to announce the grand finale of the Centenary Celebrations! My noble eldest son, Prince Arioso, heir to the throne of Gorebreath, is here to defend the honour of our kingdom against Prince Tertius of Niven's Knowe. Prince Arioso is wearing the helmet with plumes of red. Prince Tertius has plumes of purple."

There was loud and enthusiastic cheering from the crowd. Marcus, encased in silver armour, winced at the all-too-obvious favouritism. On the stage Nina-Rose and Fedora, deciding that now was not the moment to hold a grudge, stood up and fluttered their silk handkerchiefs; red for Nina-Rose, and purple for Fedora. Marigold, who had been cheering loudly for Prince Vincent, sat down and folded her arms.

"The winner," the king continued, "will have a second chance to show his skill and finesse with the lance by riding against my second son, Prince Marcus. Marcus, please leave the field."

Marcus, squinting through his visor, saw Arioso was not moving. Leaning down from his horse he whispered, "That's you, dummy!"

With a jolt, Arry realized what he was meant to do. Hanging on to Glee's mane for safety, he trotted off the field. Watching him, Gracie's stomach filled with butterflies. "That's Arry. So Marcus is riding under Arry's colours ... but who is he riding against?"

The knight wearing the colours of Niven's Knowe was now in position at one end of the arena. He was handed a lance by one of the heralds, and he took it with casual ease. His horse was covered in a nervous lather and restlessly pawing the ground, but the rider showed no sign of emotion. Marcus, facing him from thirty metres away, was also handed a lance.

He raised it in greeting, but there was no response.

"That's not Terty!" Marcus found his hands were shaking. "THAT'S NOT TERTY!"

He had no time to consider further. Before any signal had been given, his opponent had kicked his horse into a wild gallop. The ground shook as the huge animal thundered towards the prince, and the entire crowd gasped and cheered; this was infinitely more exciting than they had expected. All Marcus could do was haul on the reins and get himself out of the way of the oncoming charge.

The purple-plumed knight pulled up with a savage yank on the bridle, and turned to face Marcus for the second time.

"Coward!" he taunted. "Coward!"

Marcus, taking a firmer grip on his lance, hardly heard him. He was desperately trying to remember the Ancient One's descriptions of tournaments, and how they were won. "There's no way that's Terty," he told himself. "But I have to beat him! If he rides like that at Arry he'll kill him. If I can get him on the ground, I might just have a chance—"

The knight was getting ready for a second charge. Marcus took a deep breath. "Come on, boy! Let's go for it!"

Clods of mud flew in the air as the two giant horses careered across the grass, their riders crouched over their necks, lances at the ready. The crowd drew back, and several mothers hastily removed their children from the front rows. The massive hooves tore up the ground, and Foyce, pausing for breath half a mile away, could feel a trembling beneath her feet.

"So it's begun," she thought, her eyes gleaming. "May the little worm suffer … may her heart be twisted and torn, and her eyes blinded by the terrors she will see!" She straightened the blue silk dress, pulled her fingers through her curls, and ran on.

The collision sent sparks flying in every direction. There was little skill in Marcus's attack, but he threw himself at his foe with all the force he could muster, and Jukk was taken by surprise. The sound of armour crashing against armour rang out like the sound of bells falling from a belfry, and the three princesses on the stage screamed and clutched at each other. King Frank jumped to his feet.

"What? What's this? What are they doing?"

Queen Mildred was holding a handkerchief to her mouth. "Arry! Darling Arry! Dead! I'm sure he's dead!"

Both riders were on the ground, and for a moment

both lay still, stunned by the fall from the giant horses. Marcus was the first to recover; heaving himself to his feet he looked down at his opponent.

"Who are you?" he asked. "Where's Tertius?"

Jukk only growled in reply, and rolled himself over so he could snatch up his broken lance. With all his strength he hurled it at the prince; Marcus attempted to dodge out of the way, but the heavy armour slowed him and the lance caught him a glancing blow. Next moment he saw Jukk rise up in front of him, and a mailed fist swung at his head.

Staggering backwards, Marcus managed to duck, but he could see the wild eyes glaring at him and knew that he was in terrible danger. With a massive effort he sidestepped the next punch and caught at Jukk's arm to try and unbalance him, but he was tossed to one side as if he weighed nothing.

"Arry! Arry!" Nina-Rose's scream was piercing, and Jukk glanced in her direction just long enough to allow Marcus to scoop up his lance. He used it to deflect the furious attack that followed until, with a sharp crack, the lance broke in two. Immediately Jukk seized one of the halves and began to rain blows on Marcus's head and shoulders; Marcus did his best to protect himself, but felt himself weakening. He tried twisting and turning, but Jukk was taller and stronger, and Marcus was finding it harder and harder to see as sweat dripped into his eyes and blurred his already limited vision. With a gasp of pain and frustration he tore off his helmet; the crowd, convinced this was a fight staged entirely for their entertainment, roared approval.

King Frank leant forward to see more clearly, and a pale Queen Mildred touched his hand. "That's not Arry, Frank! It's Marcus!"

Someone heard her, and called out, "Marcus! It's Prince Marcus! Go for it, Marcus!"

"I'm for Niven's Knowe!" shouted a second voice. "Whack him, Tertius! Knock him down!"

At once the crowd took sides, until everyone was hooting and clapping and yelling at the tops of their voices. "Marcus! Tertius! Tertius! Marcus!"

Jukk's eyes narrowed. Up until this moment he had felt a grudging respect for his opponent, who was fighting to the best of his ability, and fighting fair … but now the crowd were telling him this was not Prince Arioso. He was facing Marcus, his mortal enemy and rival. He gave a deep menacing growl, and pulled off his own helmet. The crowd fell suddenly silent. Who was this fierce young man attacking their prince with such mad determination?

Chapter Twenty-four

Gracie had been watching every move, her heart in her mouth. Now, elbowing and pushing her way between the indignant piemakers, she forced her way through to the arena. Once clear, she took a deep breath and ran towards the combatants, who were now locked together and swaying to and fro. Jukk had his right arm pressed against Marcus's throat; Marcus was only just managing to resist. A whirling darkness was threatening to engulf him, and his breathing was heavy and laboured.

"Who ... are ... you?" he gasped as he slumped to the ground.

"I am Foyce's avenger," Jukk snarled. "I come to wreak revenge on those who imprisoned her, and to claim her for my own!" He raised the broken lance above his head—

"NO!" Gracie threw off her hat, and spread her arms wide. "NO!"

Startled, Jukk turned.

"It's me you should be fighting," Gracie said. Her heart was beating so wildly she was trembling from head to foot, but she stood her ground. "It's me that Foyce hates."

"Gracie!" Marcus coughed breath back into his lungs. "Gracie! Get away!"

Gracie ignored him. She stayed where she was, looking straight at Jukk. "It's true that Foyce was kept prisoner ... but Marcus had nothing to do with it."

The tall man looked down into Gracie's clear blue eyes. "I could kill you with one blow," he said hoarsely.

"Yes. And Foyce would be happy." Gracie let Mr Briggs' cape slide off her shoulders, and stood very still. "I'm ready."

Jukk glowered at her. "My enemy wants my own true love. He wants her for his own, but she is mine! I fight Prince Marcus for her freedom!"

"You ... you're fighting me for Foyce?" Marcus, even though his throat was aching and his body was racked with pain, began to laugh until the laughter turned into agonized coughing.

 329

Gracie saw Jukk's face darken, and took a step forward. "Marcus loves me," she said, her eyes never leaving Jukk's face. "And I love him. Whoever told you he loved Foyce was lying."

"It's true." Marcus's voice was a feeble croak. "I love Gracie. Always have. Didn't think she knew, though…"

Marlon and Alf, hovering overhead, held their breath.

The werewolf blinked. Gracie, clasping her hands tightly together so that no one could see how much she was shaking, was willing him with every fibre of her being to choose good over evil, and the intensity of her blue-eyed gaze made it impossible for him to look away. Images flashed into his mind: Foyce at her window, beautiful and sad; Foyce begging him to save her; Foyce whispering that Marcus was the one who held her prisoner, the one who would hold her prisoner until she promised to be his bride…

The memory of Foyce's song floated into Jukk's consciousness, but it no longer sounded sweet. The honeyed words echoed sourly. With a shock he realized that he believed Gracie. He shook his head to clear away the last of the false sugared threads that Foyce had spun in order to ensnare him.

"Kill him!" A cry rang out. "Kill him! Kill him! KILL HIM!" Foyce was running across the grass.

 330

"There he is! That's the monster that captured me and tortured me and kept me in captivity! KILL HIM!"

Jukk drew himself to his full height. "I am Jukk," he said. "And in all my years as leader of the werewolves I have always known what was right, and what was wrong ... but now I am at a loss." He bent his head to Gracie. "I believe you are that rarest of beings, a Trueheart. Tell me. What should I do?"

Gracie smiled her sunniest smile and Marcus, still lying on the ground, felt an unreasonable stab of jealousy as she put out her hand to touch Jukk's arm. "Leader of werewolves, go back to your people. Go in peace."

"NOOOO!" Foyce threw back her head and howled, a long howl of fury. "Kill him! She must suffer! He must be killed!" She rushed at Jukk, and tried to pull the broken lance from his hands, but his grip was too strong. She flailed at him with her fists, screeching that he had broken his promise, that he had sworn to her on his life, that he had promised to be her slave ... but the words grew more and more garbled, until all that could be heard was whimpering and howling. The crowd, open-mouthed, saw her drop to all fours ... and her eyes were yellow, and her mouth full of sharp teeth, and her tongue long and wet and red ... and she sprang at Gracie's throat.

Jukk's arm swung out and she went flying, only to leap again, and again until…

"Bad wolfie," said a voice, and Foyce was held fast.

A ripple of laughter ran round the spectators. Gubble was holding Foyce by the tail, a skinny, scabby wolf with agonized eyes who snapped and scrabbled to get free. With a loud grunt he picked her up and carried her away.

The blue silk dress lay abandoned on the grass.

Gracie looked at Jukk. "I'm sorry," she said.

Jukk shrugged. "She was evil. I owe you a life, Trueheart, and more. I would have slain your prince in the name of a false love, had you not prevented me. And —" he pointed towards the Royal Enclosure – "and it would not be forgotten. I would have put my people in danger. We would have been hunted for ever and ever."

Marcus, who had struggled to his feet, put a proprietary arm round Gracie's shoulders. "She's amazing, isn't she?"

"She is a Trueheart," Jukk said. He paused, then added, "You fight well, Prince. If you have need of me and mine, we are at your service." He bowed deeply and then, in a voice that resonated from one end of the arena to the other, called out, "I salute the winner! Marcus, Prince of Gorebreath!"

A moment later he was gone.

The crowd erupted; the cheering echoed to the very edges of the Five Kingdoms. Oozy the zombie, still running round his tree, stopped to listen and grin a toothless grin.

"Much cheery cheery!" he said. "Oozy go see!"

The Ancient Crones, making their descent towards Gorebreath Palace, smiled at each other.

"I don't think we need worry any more," Elsie remarked as the path landed with a bump. "It all sounds very jolly."

The Ancient One was not so certain. "Let's find out for ourselves, shall we?"

Val was looking at the arm-waving, hat-throwing, totally ecstatic audience in consternation. "But we'll never get to see what's going on! Look at all those people in front of us! Packed together like sardines!"

"I think we will, dear," was all the Ancient One said, and she was right. As the three old women approached, men, women and children moved to one side to let them through without so much as a glance. Elsie raised her eyebrows, but made no comment.

She had known the Ancient One for over a hundred years, and nothing surprised her.

Val nudged her. "Useful!" she whispered, and Elsie nodded.

The crowd continued to applaud the best entertainment they had ever seen.

"Gor love us … how did they do that switching trick? That girl looked 'zactly like she turned into a wolf!"

"Nah. It was all trickery. Clever, though, I'll give you that. Very clever!"

"That was some fight, missus, weren't it? Looked almost real!"

"Must have been practising for weeks, those lads."

"And to finish it up with a fat green troll carting off the wolf … only goes to show, they aren't all bad, those trolls."

"Made me laugh like a drain, that did!"

"Strange it wasn't Prince Tertius riding t'other big horse, though."

"He took a funny turn, my wife says. She saw him staggering out of that little tent. White as a fish, she said, and holding his head, but still gave her a wave."

"Ah. Nothing like royalty for giving a wave when it's needed."

As the three Ancient Crones reached the front of the crowd, King Frank marched out into the middle of the arena. The crowds gave him an extra loud cheer, but his expression was grim. When Bluebell and Hortense came to join him, his frown increased.

"Just what I expected!" he said. "A ridiculously overdramatic fight, and Gracie Gillypot prancing about in the middle of the arena as if she was part of it! And then that silly girl running in and shouting about killing Marcus. A totally appalling exhibition. I'm angry, Bluebell. Very, VERY angry. And as for allowing that troll to make an appearance ... all I can say is, I'm speechless. I'll be having words with Marcus, and that's for sure. That young man has gone too far this time. Didn't even allow his brother to take part! The very idea! Jealous of Arioso, that's what he is! Always has been, always will be. No, no. He's gone much too far!"

Bluebell heard him out in silence. When he finally stopped to draw breath, she said, "But Frank! Can't you hear the crowd? Stop thinking about yourself for once, and listen!"

The king stared. "What? What do you mean?"

The queen sighed. "Just LISTEN!"

Before the king could do as he was told, King Horace of Niven's Knowe came bustling up, closely followed by Queen Kesta and Queen Mildred.

"I say, Frank old chap! What a triumph! What a show! Never seen anything like it — and all arranged by your young Marcus, Tertius tells me! Shame poor Terty couldn't take part. He walked into a tent pole and knocked himself out, silly lad, but what does your boy do? Finds a replacement, cool as you like, and puts on the best show the Five Kingdoms has ever seen!"

Bluebell, a cunning glint in her eye, nodded. "And did Tertius tell you that his replacement came from the Less Enchanted Forest? A werewolf, I believe. Looked most realistically fierce, don't you think?"

"A WHAT?" The King of Gorebreath was turning purple, and Queen Mildred gave him an anxious glance.

The Dowager Duchess of Cockenzie Rood, prodded by Bluebell, hurried forward. "SO clever of you, Frank. We're all wildly jealous, of course—"

"Indeed we are." Queen Kesta shook her head. "Do you know, I really believed that wild young man was about to finish Marcus off! Poor Fedora and Nina-Rose nearly fainted — but then that funny little troll came on and made us all laugh. SO much more fun than that terrible marching about."

King Frank looked from one beaming royal face to another. "Ah," he said feebly, and then, "But I'm still going to have to have a serious word with young Marcus—"

"A very fine young man, and a credit to Your Majesty." The voice was old and cracked, but it had such authority that the king jumped. He swung round, and saw three extraordinary-looking old women standing in a row behind him. He had no chance to ask who they were, and where they had come from; both Marcus and Gracie had come running forward, Gracie to hug each of them in turn, and Marcus to shake their hands with a warmth and enthusiasm his father had never seen before.

"Mother – and, er, Father," Marcus said, "allow me to introduce three very dear friends. The Ancient Crones – Edna, Elsie and Val."

It was not often that King Frank of Gorebreath was at a loss for words, but this introduction took his breath away. It was Queen Mildred who stepped out to welcome the crones to the Centenary Celebrations, and Bluebell who embraced all three in the most affectionate manner.

Gracie, alight with excitement, turned to Marcus's mother. "Your Majesty! These are my adopted aunties! They took me in when I was—" Her face changed, and she suddenly paled. "The Web! Who's looking after the Web?"

The Ancient One shook her head. "No one. For the moment, the Web lies still. Tonight, when the full moon rises, we can begin weaving again, but –" she turned and looked at King Frank, Queen Kesta, King Horace and the Dowager Duchess – "but only if the rulers of the Five Kingdoms wish it."

King Frank began to bristle. "Web? What web?"

"Protection of the kingdoms, Frank," Bluebell explained. "If you ask me, which I know you won't, but I'm going to give you my opinion anyway so you may as well stop huffing and puffing and listen, we should ask the young. They're the future, not us." She turned to Marcus. "What do you think?"

Marcus drew Gracie a little closer. "I think we should learn to live with the world outside, and not just shut it out and pretend it isn't there."

Bluebell nodded. "Well said."

"But Marcus isn't going to be a king!" Princess Fedora, aware that something interesting was going on, had come hurrying down from her seat on the stage. Tertius, still pale and with a growing purple bruise on his forehead, was close behind her, and so was Nina-Rose. Marigold, seeing no evidence of cake or chocolate, remained where she was. A well-packed picnic basket hidden behind her chair was calling for her attention.

"You shouldn't ask him," Fedora went on. "It's me and Terty who are important! And I say we shouldn't ever, ever, EVER have anything to do with what's on the other side of the border, and Terty agrees with me, don't you, Terty pops?"

"No." Tertius was gazing at Gracie with undisguised admiration. "I'm sorry, Fedora, but I don't agree. Actually. Not at all. Weren't you watching? Gracie did the bravest thing I've ever seen, and she comes from outside the border … and if there are people like Gracie out there we shouldn't shut them out."

"But Terty − Terty werty poppitty poodle!" Fedora's voice was shrill. "That was all pretend! They weren't really fighting! It was a silly make-believe fight, and Gracie just came running on because—"

"Because she's brave." Tertius put up his hand and rubbed his bruise. "And it didn't look like pretending to me. I agree with Marcus."

"So do I." Arioso had come to join the Royals,

 341

Albion and Vincent swaggering beside him. He saw his father's face, and blushed scarlet. "I'm sorry, Father, but it's true. I don't know how that man came to be here, but he could have killed Marcus – only he didn't. He listened to Gracie. He wasn't a monster, or a wild animal. And –" he gave Nina-Rose a sideways look – "Marcus is right: Gracie's wonderful."

King Horace was puzzled. "Just a minute! Are you lads saying it wasn't a put-up show? You didn't plan it?"

Marcus and Arry exchanged glances. "We did and we didn't," Marcus said, and was saved from further explanation by Bluebell.

"The best entertainment always leaves one wondering how much was pretence, and how much reality. The mystery's part of the fun." She held up a hand. "Just listen to that crowd! They certainly think so!"

The cheers around them were continuing unabated; many were shouting, "Speech! Speech! Speech from our Marcus!"

Nina-Rose sniffed. "Really! Why on earth should Marcus give a speech? I just don't understand the peasants."

Arioso, heir to the throne of Gorebreath, took a deep breath. "I'll tell you something Gracie taught me, Nina-Rose. Those are people, just like us. And just because we have crowns and thrones doesn't make us any better ... in fact, it probably makes us worse."

"What?" Nina-Rose stared at her fiancé. "Arry, I don't want to marry you any more! You're ... you're MAD!" And she flounced away to join the picnic party on the stage, where Marigold, Vincent and Albion were enjoying themselves hugely.

"But what about the kingdoms?" King Frank's brow was furrowed as he tried to make sense of all that was happening. "I don't understand!"

"May I make a suggestion?" It was the Ancient One. "Changes take time, and so they should." She paused. "I've been giving the situation a lot of thought. And I've come to the conclusion that perhaps we are as much to blame as you; we've always kept ourselves apart, and never shared our secrets. But now – thanks to Gracie and Marcus – we are friends, so we can work together, as used to happen many years ago."

King Horace, who had been listening intently, leant forward. "Many years ago? How was that, dear lady?"

Edna smiled at him. "Your grandfather was a good friend of mine."

The old king's eyes shone. "Never! You couldn't ... could you? Could you be Edna? The holder of the power of good against evil? I remember hearing stories. When I was a little boy…" His voice faded away, and a dreamy look came over his face.

"Yes – well – that's all very charming, but it doesn't help us now." King Frank began to tap his foot. "I'm sure you mean well, madam, but I believe our guards can protect us just as well as you can, if not better—"

"Wooooooooooooooeeeeeeeooooooo," wailed a voice. "Wooooooooooooooeeeeoooooooooo…"

All eyes turned to see where the noise was coming from.

"Wooooooooooooooeeeeeeoooooo! Oozy's lost lost lost! Oozy can't find his way home…"

The zombie, rags flapping and bone gleaming white in the late sunshine, came shuffling towards them. The watching crowd, who by this time would have believed an invasion of ravening tigers was all part of the show, redoubled their cheers.

"Oh – POOR Oozy." Gracie ran to rescue the miserable zombie. "It's all right. Don't be frightened – we'll show you which way to go." She looked over her shoulder at Marcus. "He used to come knocking on the door when I lived in Fracture. He's quite harmless, but he does get a bit muddled when it's full moon."

Edna, Elsie and Val nodded, and Edna took a pale

King Frank by the arm. "Dear sir," she said, "that zombie is a classic example of someone who needs the border for his own protection … at least, until we all get to know one another. He's never seen a crowd of humans before, you see, and he's scared. Just like you're seeing a zombie for the first time, and you're suffering from shock. Why don't you go home and have a cup of sweet tea, and we'll meet again after you've had a chance to consider things? I know you'll make a wise decision."

She gave the king's arm a reassuring squeeze. "Nothing like tea and cake to make you feel better. And now I must be getting home to my own tea and cake, and to prepare the Web so it's ready to be woven once more … and the path will be getting impatient." She snapped her fingers, and to the intense delight of all watching the path came looping down into the arena. Realizing it had an audience, it began to twist and turn itself into figures of eight; it wasn't until Gubble came stomping back that it finally subsided. Alf and Marlon, who had been ducking and diving to avoid its wilder whirls and swirls, breathed a sigh of relief.

"Bad path," Gubble said, and sat down heavily on the end. Edna, Elsie and Val processed towards it, and settled themselves comfortably.

Marcus looked at Gracie. "Shall we go with them?"

He grinned. "Sorry, Gracie – but you're stuck with me now. You told that werewolf you loved me, so it must be true."

Gracie gave him her sunniest smile. "It is."

"So that's all right, then." Marcus swept her into his arms and kissed her. "Right! Let's go!"

"Just a minute!" King Frank began, but then stopped, and looked at Queen Mildred and Arioso. "What do you think about all this, Mildred? Arry?"

"I think it's simply splendid," Arry said. "They'll be back to visit us, you know." He looked wistfully at Marcus and Gracie's glowing faces. "And maybe I can go and visit them. Would that be all right, bro?"

"Come whenever you like," Marcus told him. "Terty – you come too!"

There was a small explosion as Fedora covered up a horrified exclamation with a cough. "No! I mean … ahem. Maybe we could go by coach, Terty darling."

"Great. So that's settled." Marcus gave a decisive nod, and went to sit beside Gubble.

Gracie, hand in hand with Oozy, gave Bluebell a hug. "See you very soon," she said, "and thank you so very much for everything."

"It's us who should thank you, dear," Bluebell told her. "Isn't that right, Frank?"

This was almost too much for the king, but he swallowed hard and did his best. "Quite. Absolutely. Indeed."

Suppressing a desire to giggle, Gracie curtsied. "Excuse me, Your Majesties … there's just one thing I'd like to mention. Mr Briggs is locked up in your dungeon, but he tried VERY hard to keep me and Gubble locked in. I think he should have a medal. Would that be possible?"

"I'm sure it can be done." Queen Mildred, trying to avoid looking too closely at Oozy, blew Gracie a kiss. "But we must be off. Tea, Frank – tea! Horace? Bluebell? Hortense? Will you join us?"

Gracie smiled, and led Oozy towards the path. After sitting him down, she leant forward to whisper in Gubble's ear. "What happened to Foyce?"

Gubble shrugged. "Wolfies ran away." He waved a hand. "Right away. Woods."

"Wolfies?" Gracie asked in surprise. "Did Jukk wait for her after all?"

"Lady wolfie was waiting," Gubble said. "Old lady who was old wolfie." He wrapped his arms round his stout green body. "Hugging! Old wolfie howled happy howls! Bad wolfie didn't like … but bad wolfie and old wolfie, they ran away together. Old wolfie said…"

347

He rubbed his flat green face while he struggled to remember. "Old wolfie said, 'Never too late to change.'"

"That's good." Gracie leant back against Marcus's knees. "I hope they can be happy. I wonder if she'll turn back into a girl?"

The Ancient One heard her. "No chance," she said crisply. "She'll be much less trouble the way she is. My dears – we really ought to go!"

As the path lifted up from the ground, there was a collective "Ooooh!" and "Aaaaah!" of satisfaction.

"That's the way to finish a celebration. Never seen nothing like that before!"

"The Royals did us proud today, and that's for sure."

"Shame there weren't no speeches, though."

"SPEECHES? Rubbish! You know what that king's like once he gets going. Doesn't know when to stop, and I need to get home for my dinner."

"Been a good day, though."

"Best ever, I'd say…"

Gracie, walking into the House of the Ancient Crones arm in arm with Marcus, also thought the day had ended well. She was humming as they went into the kitchen, and she gave a little skip of happiness as she looked round. "It's so lovely to be back. Is Billy here? How's he doing?"

The silence that followed was long and ominous. Gracie looked from one face to another; each crone sighed, and shook her head.

"I'm so sorry, dear," Edna said at last. "We didn't tell you…" She walked towards the drawer and drew back the tea towel to reveal the tiny body.

Gracie gave a cry. "Billy! Oh, Billy!"

There was a flutter … the slightest of movements.

"Hello, Miss Gracie." Billy's voice was faint, but clear. "Hello, Mr Prince. Welcome home!"

Marlon, hanging from the curtain rail, chuckled. "Can't keep a good bat down."

"That's right!" Alf squeaked. "Batster Super Spotters rule OK!"

Gubble folded his arms. "Ug! Batties OK. Gubble OK. All OK."

With a splutter of ink, a flash of purple, the pen arrived. Whizzing round Gracie and Marcus, it headed for the wall and proceeded to draw a succession of hearts, each one bigger than the one before.

"Oh NO!" Gracie said, and made a grab at the pen – but she was too late.

It had started writing, and as they watched it wrote:

And they all lived happily ever after...

Elsie took off her wig, shook off the droplets of purple ink, and put it back on again. "Isn't that nice? Just what we all like to hear."

"Don't encourage it," Val said, looking in dismay at the ink running down the walls, but the pen was already off again.

Once upon a time there were Five Kingdoms, and the kingdoms had a king called Marcus and a queen called Gracie...

"Really?" Marcus was open-mouthed. "Can it tell the future?"

"Time enough for the future when the future comes," said the Ancient One, but her eye was twinkling, and her smile very warm. "Now, who wants tea?"